LOOKING PAST

D1324165

Katharine E. Smith

HEDDON PUBLISHING

Third edition published in 2017 by Heddon Publishing.

ISBN 978-0-9932101-3-6

Cover design by Catherine Clarke

Book design and layout by Heddon Publishing.

www.heddonpublishing.com
www.facebook.com/heddonpublishing
@PublishHeddon

Katharine E. Smith runs Heddon Publishing - an independent publishing house. She also works as a freelance proofreader, editor and copywriter.

She has a degree in Philosophy and a love for the written word. She works with authors all over the world and considers herself extremely privileged to do so.

A Yorkshire-woman by birth, Katharine now lives in Shropshire with her husband and their two children.

Other books by Katharine E. Smith

Writing the Town Read
ISBN 978-0-9932101-2-9

On July 7th 2005, terrorists attack the city's transport network, striking Underground trains and a bus during the morning rush hour. In Cornwall, journalist Jamie Calder loses contact with her boyfriend Dave, in London that day for business.

Writing the Town Read is full of intrigue, angst, excitement and humour. The evocative descriptions and convincing narrative voice instantly draw readers into Jamie's life as they experience her disappointments, emotions and triumphs alongside her.

Amongst Friends
ISBN 978-0993487040

A group of three friends meet for the first time at primary school, aged four. Despite their differing backgrounds, they quickly form a strong bond, which sees them through secondary school and into the wide world beyond. Life becomes complicated when love gets in the way.

Amongst Friends turns traditional story-telling on its head, beginning with the dramatic end to the friends' story and tracing step-by-step through the twists and turns of fate and fortune.

For my friend Gennie

LOOKING PAST

PROLOGUE

To say that the pain was a surprise is to put it mildly.

Of course I had expected pain but not having been through anything like it before, I'd had no idea really.

It was probably a good thing, I thought, eyes squeezed shut and mouth clamping firmly around the mouthpiece for the gas and air.

Hazel gently eased away my white-knuckled hand.

"That's enough now, just take a break," she advised, "You're all gas and no air."

She chuckled softly and I just knew that she would be looking to the midwife for approval for her witticism.

I kept my eyes closed. It seemed the best way. I had to get through this and I had to draw on my inner strength. I also had to try to ignore that it was Hazel there with me, at this most personal, testing, and let's face it, undignified, time.

Not my fiancé, no – the father of this child was not there to share this experience with me. I felt this was wrong and mostly because I thought he was missing out on something he could never get back. For despite the intense, immense pain, I still knew what this was all about. I was still glad it was happening because I knew it meant that our child was on its way and that soon, I would be able to hold our baby.

The strange little kicking and wriggling thing which I had felt grow inside me, and which had changed me both inside and out, was about to make its entrance into the world and its father was nowhere to be seen.

I tensed up as another contraction kicked in. I grabbed the gas and air back from Hazel and let out about the only real noise I think I made during the whole labour.

"Mum!" I cried, "Mum!"

I rammed the mouthpiece back in and sucked greedily, desperately. Dimly aware of Hazel's voice.

"Oh, she called me Mum," she gushed, and again I knew she would have that look on her face.

Only it wasn't that. I wasn't calling Hazel 'Mum'. I was calling for the person I most wanted to be there with me, but who I knew I could never see again.

PART ONE

Chapter One

How does an eleven-year-old girl deal with the death of her mother?

I can't answer for every eleven-year-old girl who has been in that position but for me, I withdrew, from pretty much everything and everyone, except, for some reason, from my schoolwork.

My friends had become awkward with me anyway, not knowing what to say and worrying that they would say something stupid or 'wrong'. I could sense this and I didn't have the strength to put them right, tell them that I just needed them to be there. What they said didn't really matter. It couldn't change anything. They wanted the old Sarah back, though – jokey and always looking to have some fun. It's not that they didn't understand why I had changed. It's just that, I think understandably considering our age, they didn't know how to handle this sudden and unexpected alteration to my circumstances, and probably my personality too.

I vividly remember hours spent sitting on the windowsill of my bedroom, staring at the cherry blossom falling from the tree whose branches were so close they would tap on the glass panes when it was windy.

My grandparents came round more often, but I didn't feel I could talk to them. Mum's parents were grieving themselves, for their own dear daughter. Grandma would hug me tightly but I couldn't stand it really. Maybe she was just a bit too much like Mum but at the same time she wasn't her. I would tolerate the hugs because I knew it would hurt Grandma far too much if I didn't, but inside I felt almost panicked. I don't know if Grandad S experienced a similar sensation when he looked at me, as I knew I looked a lot like Mum had when she was my age. Maybe he was looking at me but saw only the daughter he had lost. Despite his smiles and calmness, I knew that his heart was broken.

My dad's parents were undemonstrative people, which didn't mean that they didn't care. However, they didn't seem to know how to show this in any other way than practical. Granny would keep the house clean and make healthy and hearty dinners which I couldn't eat.

Grandad M would ask me questions about school, seeming not to notice my replies only ever involved subjects, not people.

Mum's sister Elizabeth lives in America so we only saw her for a short while. On reflection I think that this was a shame as she may have been the very person we all needed to pull us together. She is so like Mum; positive, wanting to sort things out, that I think she may have been the one to look beyond herself and her own feelings, and see how we could begin to have a life again.

Then there was Dad.

My poor dad. How could I put into words how he felt when his wife, just out-of-the-blue, dropped down dead?

All the photos I had ever seen of Mum and Dad together were beautiful. I am not calling my parents devastatingly attractive people. Film-star good looks and model figures do not run in my family. There was beauty in those pictures though, in how happy my parents looked when they were together. In the glances caught between them, and the balance that was somehow conveyed even in faded old photos from their dating days. The comfort and contentedness they shared should not be underestimated and to my mind is a thing of beauty.

How many clichés is it possible to use when I talk about the effect Mum's death had on Dad? His world fell apart, or crumbled, or was turned upside down. Clichés they may be but true nevertheless. I guess clichés must come from truth. Don't get me started on the clichés people doled out to us in an effort to comfort. Not their fault, they were just trying to help – but they didn't.

But back to Dad. I hated it. Seeing what was happening to him. Feeling unable to do anything about it and eventually unable to connect with him. I hate to think about it, what happened to us when Mum died. We had always had such fun together, Dad and I. He was funny, and light-hearted, and always wanting to do things. Days at the park, the zoo, the seaside. Bike rides in the summer, sledge rides in the winter. He taught me to play football and cricket so I was a match for most of the boys in my year.

For a time, just after Mum died, this all stopped. I don't think I even noticed then. I don't know what we did in those days, or weeks, after she had gone.

Eventually, after the funeral, we had to go back to our work/school routine. What about our 'free time' though? I really can't remember. Did we have a succession of visitors for a while? I seem to remember this – aside from family, there were Mum's friends, Dad's friends, my grandparents' friends. All meaning well, all in their grown up way realising they should not neglect us at this time (unlike my own friends) but still few of whom seemed to know how to talk to us or what to say.

I felt close to Dad during some of these visits; could imagine him cringing inside, as I was, at the pitying expressions, and those clichés. *Time is a great healer. It will get easier.* I knew what Dad was like, how down-to-earth and practical he was. These words would mean little to him, and just serve to make him feel awkward. He did his best though and always graciously thanked people for making the effort to see us.

As time drew on, the visits dried up and the house was ours again. Mine and Dad's. Only there was a large empty space in it. We could reorganise the furniture and even buy replacements (we did), redecorate (that too), keep the radio and/or TV on at all times that the house was occupied and yet this glaringly obvious silent space was always there. We were a body with a missing limb. A rudderless boat. A bike with no wheels. Whatever words you might choose, there was no escaping the fact that we were no longer whole. My ever-practical father did not have the skills or the tools to fix this problem.

We rarely talked about 'it', Dad and I, though we sometimes talked about her. We could remember her, and remind each other of times that we had enjoyed together or even simple things such as how she cooked a certain dish and what times of the year she had cut back the buddleia. Somehow though, we could not acknowledge to each other that we had to deal with this new situation, without her. She had held that role in our family – the emotional, open, 'let's talk about it' role, so it was almost ironic that it was she who was gone. Leaving two quiet, shocked people in her wake.

I could bore you with details of Christmases, birthdays, anniversaries. You don't need to know but can probably imagine. The detail which is important about the birthdays, though, is my getting older. Becoming a teenager. Crucially, hitting puberty.

I had never thought of this when Mum died and I don't know if Dad had. Suddenly I was 'becoming a woman' and I had nobody to talk to who had been through it before. I think that Elizabeth had made some attempts to get me to talk to her, but I couldn't, not over the phone. I needed somebody real, tangible, and just *there*.

If I had talked to Dad about it I am sure he would have done his best, but I was thirteen years old and mightily embarrassed when my periods started. A dragging, aching pain the likes of which I had never experienced before, followed by bleeding, the shock of which no sex education classes could really, truly have prepared me for. I mean, I knew they were coming at some point, I knew that there would seem to be a lot of blood 'but really it's about a thimble full' (really?).

Although Elizabeth had left me some tampons and towels, I had to ask Dad for some money to get more. When he asked what for, I went so red that he just gave it to me, and looked concerned. Maybe even sympathetic. Had he guessed? I think now that he probably had. By nature he tended to be a great respecter of privacy and I think this is where things went slightly awry for us. Though I was painfully embarrassed by the onset of my bleeding, and Dad would have had to drag the details out of me, on this occasion I think that he should have done. It was not a time for privacy but for openness and understanding. Anyway, between us, we managed never to talk about this either. I will say this for us; we were bloody brilliant at not talking about stuff.

Our years passed quietly, routinely, and I suppose peacefully. I managed to integrate with my friends again and gradually I began to redevelop my sense of fun. So they were right; time is a great healer, it does get easier, but having said that, they never saw those moments when I would throw myself onto my bed and sob, wrecked by the grief and the missing her, and the needing a mother. Needing my mum. These were my moments and nobody else needed to be aware of them.

I am sure Dad had them too. We kept them neatly enclosed in our respective private spaces, the evidence confined to tear-dampened duvets and pillows and the knowledge locked away in our minds.

Over these years, I lost three of my grandparents, too. There was only Grandma left from that generation. How did she feel; one daughter overseas, and her husband and other daughter both dead?

Dad seemed to accept the loss of his parents tiredly. He already knew life was sad. He was still grieving for his wife.

I left Dad to go to university. He dropped me off at my Halls of Residence, all bright smiles and cheerfulness, and pressed a £50 note into my hand after he had helped me unload my stuff. This gesture choked me for some reason, but I was keen for him to leave me, because I knew that I had to just get on with it.

I felt so sad though, watching him walk back to the car. I wondered how he would get on with the house all his own. I wished so hard that we were better at speaking about things and that I could tell him how much I loved him, and I thought about running after him but then there was a knock at my door and one of my fellow residents was there, excitedly introducing herself. When I looked back through the window, Dad had gone.

Chapter Two

University was fun. Probably too much fun, at least during that first term.

Chloe, the girl who had come knocking at my door when I was watching Dad leave, had an older brother who had just graduated from the same university and who had stayed in the city to work.

Jim provided us with a ready-made social life, with older friends, and a bit of relief from the non-stop ridiculous partying of our fellow Halls-dwellers. We had soon found that some of the people we shared kitchens and bathrooms with seemed to have split personalities. Or more realistically, they couldn't handle their drink. And there was a lot of drinking going on.

Eighteen is a fairly young age to leave home, and then to be allowed to live with a bunch of other eighteen-year-olds. All of whom have more free hours than the average person, some dispensable income, and little to dispense it on except booze.

There were 27 of us in our block, split nine to a floor. I just thanked my lucky stars that I had refused to share a room. It would have been completely luck of the draw, and I could see from some of the pairings that certain fellow students had fallen short on luck. My friend Mandy had a completely crazy room-mate called Emma who was studying some form of software development.

By day, Emma wore pink jogging suits and scraped her hair back into a way-too-tight ponytail, and by night she transformed herself into some sort of goth assemblage, and seduced the small pale boys who were on her course.

Chloe and I were paying slightly more for the privilege of our own space than those who shared a room but I would have gladly paid twice as much.

We did socialise with our fellow residents a fair bit but their taste tended more towards karaoke and cheesy nightclubs whereas Chloe and I were happy to go to what we considered some serious clubs with Jim and his mates.

We liked house music, drum'n'bass, and reggae. We always had a laugh at karaoke but inwardly I was cringing as this scene was a far cry from what my friends back home and I considered cool.

You may have noticed a theme here. I had started university yet what I seem to be describing is my social life. You may be asking, what about the studying? You've got a point. Well studying did happen, but that first term it all seemed to be fairly low level and my course, Philosophy, had very few hours of actual lectures. It depended a great deal on independent study and I had chosen some module subjects I already had some knowledge of so I thought I could probably get away with slightly less than the prescribed reading.

Everybody was pretty much the same. We were free at last! Out on our own in the world – except for the wardens and cleaners at the Halls of Residence, and of course parents who were largely supportive both financially and practically. Other than that though, we really were looking after ourselves. Oh, and had I mentioned that our evening meals were prepared for us and served in a huge cafeteria which catered for the 300 or so students who lived on the same site as us?

I had a whale of a time though, I really did, until around mid-November when I caught a really bad dose of flu. The germs had been making their way steadily around the campus. The buses to university - windows steamed up with condensation against the first chill days of the winter – were uncomfortably warm and overcrowded with coughing, sneezing, nose-blowing teenagers. It was only a matter of time.

Unfortunately, I have always been susceptible to colds, flu and the like. I suffered from asthma when I was a lot younger, and although that has long since stopped bothering me, I almost always find flu or a bad cold will end up on my chest.

This is exactly what happened that year, only then I tried to ignore it. I desperately didn't want to miss out, although now I think of it, what was I going to miss out on? Fun, yes, but the nights out we had very rarely differed. Whether we were with our fellow students or Jim and his friends, we went to the same places, danced to the same music, and drank the same drinks. We returned to our rooms in high spirits unless too much alcohol had taken its toll, in the form of stupor or sickness. I could have missed a week and nothing would have changed.

Silly me, though, I just couldn't stay in. I ended up with an upper respiratory tract infection and feeling very sorry for myself. I had nobody to look after me and although my friends were sympathetic, they had lectures and social lives to worry about.

I called my dad.

"Oh love, you sound awful," he said. "Can I bring you home?"

I hadn't been home so far that term. In fact I had probably not phoned home nearly half as much as I should have done. Dad was understanding, he never put any pressure on me. Now when I heard his words it was all I could do to hold back the tears.

"Yes please," I sniffed.

"I'm on my way."

I had been too busy enjoying myself to realise how much I missed him, and home. Now, run down and worn out, I couldn't think of any place I would rather be, or any person I would rather be with.

I no longer cared about missing out. I wrote Chloe a note explaining and slipped it under her door. I would text her later but I didn't want to bring any attention to myself. I just wanted to slide away, unnoticed.

I sat in my room and waited for my dad.

Chapter Three

When I saw Dad's car pull up outside the Halls, quick as a flash I was out of my room and locking the door, praying that none of my friends were back from their lectures. I snuck down the stairs, and surprised Dad by appearing at the front door before he'd had a chance to use the intercom.

"Dad!" I said, throwing my arms around him.

"Hello love," he said, and held me tightly but I was still worried about bumping into my friends.

"Can we get to the car please, Dad? I need to sit down."

"Of course we can, love," Dad's expression was concerned. I knew I didn't look great. Greasy hair and pale complexion. I had not been eating particularly well. The vegetarian meals provided by the Halls canteen were not fantastic and I sometimes skipped them, letting late night snacks of sandwiches and crisps take their place. Fruit and veg, bought with the best of intentions, would slowly shrivel, skins wrinkled and grey. Neglected.

No wonder I was feeling this way. My poor diet, coupled with late nights and the less than relaxing (though undeniably fun) life in Halls of Residence had taken their toll, preparing my body to be totally flummoxed by this chest infection.

I was almost overwhelmed with a feeling of relief when I got into the passenger seat of Dad's car. Why hadn't I gone home for a visit before now? I knew I had been swept up in the newness of my university life, my friends and freedoms. Dad would understand. There was very little he wouldn't understand, or at the very least accept. He is a very laidback person.

"Alright?" he asked as he started the engine.

"I am now," I smiled at him, and before we had even left the driveway I had started to doze off. I slept fitfully for the hour-long journey home and awoke as we pulled into the driveway. Dad carried my bags in through the back door and I followed, breathing in the familiar smell of our home.

"Just sit down, love," he said, "I'll get you a drink. And something to eat if you like?"

I shook my head. "Just a cup of tea please, Dad, and then maybe I need to get some more sleep."

"Of course, of course. Just let me know if you need anything, though. I'm not going into work tomorrow, or the next day if you still need me."

"I always do. Need you, I mean."

I could see he was pleased as he walked off to the kitchen. It hadn't taken much for me to tell him that, so I resolved then and there that I would tell him what he meant to me more often.

As it happened, Dad didn't return to work until after I had gone back to university.

The first couple of days, I really was weak with my illness. The coughing fits during the night weren't helping as I couldn't get a good night's sleep.

During the day, I lay in bed watching daytime TV or sometimes, when I was too tired to even concentrate on *Neighbours*, I would lie and gaze at the branches of the cherry blossom tree, now bare and knobbly, wizened fingers tapping agitatedly at the window in the gusty wind.

Dad took me to our usual doctor, who prescribed me more antibiotics, and these soon kicked in. As I started to recover, I almost didn't want to tell Dad I was feeling better. I realised I was really enjoying this time with him.

We'd spend the afternoons watching films, quietly but comfortably. In the evenings we would cosy up in front of the fire reading our books and bringing each other occasional cups of tea.

In the lounge was a picture of Mum, on her own, when she was about 20 or so; the age she was when she and Dad met. Next to it, a photo of the three of us, when I was about four years old.

The family photo had been up while Mum was alive but Dad had framed and displayed the photo of Mum on her own some time after she had died. I liked the fact he had done that and not hidden it away in his bedroom. To me it spoke volumes about his feelings for her. He may not have been the best at discussing emotions but he wasn't ashamed of them. I think he just didn't really know where to start with talking about them. To that point I had followed suit but one night, when I had been back home for about three days, I broke the pattern.

"Didn't you want any more children?" I asked abruptly, looking at our family portrait.

Dad didn't answer immediately.

"We did," he said cautiously, "We really did, but we weren't lucky that way. However, we had already been lucky because we had you."

I cast my eyes to the floor, shy even though it was my dad speaking, expressing natural sentiments about his only child. I suppose there was the faint allusion to sex which I felt slightly uncomfortable with as well.

"Sarah," he said, after a moment or two of silence, "You know how your mum died?"

"Yes," I said.

Mum had collapsed suddenly one day. She had gone to the bathroom while Dad and I were playing a game of Downfall. After quite some time, Dad called up to her but there was no response.

He had to break down the door, having told me to stay downstairs; it was obvious something wasn't right, and there he found her. Not a particularly dignified way to go but death levels the playing field somewhat and you realise that nothing like that is of any importance. She could have been sitting on the toilet or sitting on a throne. Either way, she had died. She had died without warning.

A post mortem, however, revealed that her body had been preparing for this sudden demise for some time. She had three types of cancer, including bowel cancer, which it seemed had been the actual cause of her death.

"And you know it was a shock to us all."

"Yes," I said again.

"Well, I've never told you this before, and I don't know why not, but actually I don't know if your mum really was completely unaware of her illness."

"What do you mean?" I asked, shocked.

"We had lots of tests you see, your mum and I, when we couldn't conceive. We started trying when you were about three – about the time that picture was taken," Dad gestured to the photograph, "and we were really very patient. But after two years or so we went to see the doctor, together."

I didn't speak, just met Dad's eyes, hoping to convey to him that I wanted to hear more.

"So we had tests, both of us, and from my point of view everything seemed to be OK. However, your mum's tests were inconclusive and she had to have more. I asked her if she wanted me to come with her but you know what she was like," I do, I think, I was old enough when she died to have gained a good knowledge of Mum's character. Down-to-earth and calm. She never liked to make a fuss. I could imagine her telling Dad to just get to work and that she'd be fine on her own.

"Well she never said much else about her tests." Dad looked sad. "I did realise that it couldn't have been great news, as she sat me down one evening and said that she thought we should stop trying for a brother or sister for you. I put it down to 'women's troubles'. As you know, I'm not exactly great in the area, sorry. We carried on as before. We were really very happy and so grateful to have you. Your aunt Elizabeth couldn't have children at all, as you know, so Georgina was well aware of how lucky we were."

I blushed then. I don't know why. I thought of Mum as 'Georgina'. As the woman Dad had known rather than the mother I had.

"So what was the problem? Did you ever find out?" I asked.

"Well, not really, not definitely," Dad replied, "But I found things George... your mum... had written. A journal with just the odd entry, and I asked Elizabeth about what I found. Whether she knew anything about it."

"About what?" I asked, my heart suddenly thumping fast although I was not quite sure why.

"Well as far as I can make out, your mum knew about the cancer. She certainly knew about something. Years before she died. Elizabeth has sworn to me that she didn't know details but she thought that Georgina had nearly confided in her once. From what I could piece together, those initial tests had thrown up some questionable results. Your mum must have had quite a lot of other tests I knew nothing about."

"But if she knew she was ill, why didn't she do something about it? Why didn't the doctors?"

"Well that's what puzzled me," said Dad, "but I began recalling things she'd said, conversations we'd had. To me, we were just chatting generally, discussing our opinions. I recall clearly your mum telling me what she thought of cancer treatment, of how it would reduce quality of life even if it could extend it. I remember her telling me in these exact words, 'I want to be here for Sarah and you, for as long as I can be, and be the best that I can be.' I know now, at least I am pretty sure, that she was talking about not having treatment. She would have been worried about it taking over her life, and yours, and mine."

I was aware suddenly of tears streaming down my face.

"Dad," I sobbed, "Why didn't you tell me this before?" I wasn't sure how to feel. Should I be annoyed at Mum or admire her for this resilience? What I did know was that I felt endlessly sorry for Dad, whose wife and soulmate had kept this knowledge from him, and who had carried this knowledge around with him for the past few years.

Dad squeezed my hand.

"She was a great woman, Sarah," he said. "And I completely get it. I didn't at first. I was angry. I even went to counselling."

I almost smiled at this. Dad... counselling... that would have meant talking, surely? I kept quiet though and returned his squeeze.

"Eventually I came to realise that she did it for us. Particularly you, I think. And if I had picked up on all the things she'd said to me over the years I may have been a bit better prepared for bringing up a daughter but I didn't pay attention. I feel like I rarely looked *at* her, if you know what I mean. I was too busy thinking about my work, paying the mortgage, that kind of thing. We were happy, we had you, a lovely house, and a job each; I took it all for granted and never questioned anything. It's only in retrospect that everything comes together and I wish that I'd listened more, talked more, but I didn't know that there was any reason to."

Chapter Four

The rest of my time with Dad was a revelation, to us both I think. Somehow we both threw off our inability to speak to each other; properly, I mean.

We talked about anything and everything. Dad told me all about his life when he was my age. We laughed and laughed at some photos of him trying to be a hippy. Granny and Grandad M were quite straight-laced and were disappointed to say the least when their only son decided to grow his hair and drop out of a Business Studies course to go to art college.

However, Dad has made a very successful career, initially as an art teacher at a secondary school and then as a lecturer in Fine Art at our local university. He has even had a couple of books published so my grandparents became very proud to speak, at length, of their son's achievements.

In turn, I described life at university to Dad. Being a lecturer, and apparently having been young once himself, he was no stranger to the kind of shenanigans which go on in Halls of Residence, student nightclubs and so on, up and down the country.

"Are you enjoying it though, Sarah?"

"I am... I think I am," I said, truthfully. I had been enjoying it, I thought, but this illness had given me time to stop and breathe (despite the respiratory tract infection). I really had formed a strong attachment to Chloe, and Jim. I also liked a lot of my fellow students but was I really enjoying life? It was a whirlwind, of parties and nights out, or late night drinking in our shared social area. Was I actually enjoying it?

My social life since I had turned 16 had largely involved going to a couple of local pubs in the smallish town I lived in.

The pubs were renowned for being part of the 'alternative' scene, i.e. not full of carefully groomed girls and 'lads' out on the pull, and they do not pump out terrible chart music. There were no booze-sticky dance floors in the pubs I liked, and the House on the Hill even had a jukebox with what I and my friends snobbily called 'proper music'. Rock, dance, reggae, 70s classics, drum'n'bass. We would have relaxed evenings, usually a group of about ten of us from college, sitting at our regular table and talking about nothing in particular. Yes, we would drink, but rarely to excess; certainly nothing in the realms of what I'd been experiencing at university.

"I don't know, actually, Dad. I can't work out if it's going to stay like this forever or if we will all settle down a bit."

"Well in my experience, things do settle a bit after the Christmas break," Dad said, "But only a bit. What about your course though, do you like it? Is it a good fit for you?"

"I love it. I really do. I guess it gets pushed to the back of my mind sometimes, which is pretty terrible given that it's really why I'm at uni. But it's so interesting. And there are quite a few mature students too, which makes it different from life at Halls."

"Well that's great, that's important. You'll settle, Sarah. Don't forget you're still getting over your illness. You're run down at the moment, it can make you feel a bit glum about things. Give it a couple of days and I bet you'll be feeling differently again."

"You're probably right," I said, and smiled at Dad.

I cast my mind to university though, and realised that all of my new friends there, with the exception of Chloe, still seemed like strangers. They were very nice but they didn't know me. They knew nothing of Mum dying, or my real life as I had started to think of it. University seemed like a playground; a bit of a joke. Maybe a practice run for the real world, but if that was the case I didn't think we were doing a very good job of it.

As my strength grew and the colour returned to my cheeks (according to Dad), I braved a few questions of him. There was something which had crossed my mind frequently, and more so now that I had left him for university.

"Do you think you will meet anyone else, Dad?"

He looked up sharply from the radio he had been fixing and

was now trying to screw together. I could see one of the screws had rolled off the table but I was enjoying watching him get increasingly frustrated. Now that I had posed this question though, I gestured to it with my foot. It seemed cruel to play with him any longer when I'd introduced such a serious subject.

"Wow. I, erm, I don't know, Sarah. I do think about it, of course. I mean you're grown up now, you'll be going off to do your own thing after uni. It's a strange thought, though. When you marry somebody you do it with an image of a lifetime together. I certainly did anyway. That was how I saw my life panning out – your mother part of it all the way. If anything, I thought I would almost certainly die before she did. It's often the way, isn't it? The man going first, I mean. Anyway, sorry, I digress. Well, erm, what would you think about it if I did?"

"I think it would be good for you, Dad. I mean, you're only 46. That is pretty young really. You've got a lot of life left to live."

"We hope," he interrupted.

"We hope," I agreed, and continued, "I think you deserve somebody in your life. Besides me, I mean. You've looked after me on your own for seven years now. And I do appreciate it, you know. You deserve to be happy."

I felt grown up as I said this but also very aware of Mum's image in the photo that was just visible in the periphery of my vision. I didn't want to say to him that she would want him to move on. That is another excellent cliché. *She'd want you to be happy.* Blah, blah, blah. I snuck a look at her, though, and I saw her smiling face. I knew that once again the clichés were right, as annoying as they were. She was a happy person, and generous. My happiness and Dad's had been of paramount importance to her. She genuinely would want him to be happy. I reasoned that, if that meant him meeting somebody else, then so be it.

However, I thought selfishly, not too soon. I felt like I'd only just got him back somehow.

"We'll see," was Dad's answer and I was happy with that.

When I'd been home about six days, I was almost bouncing off the walls. Other than a short trip to the shops, I'd not been out. Dad and I got up early, in the dark winter chill, and prepared a flask of soup then cooked some pasties, wrapping them in multiple layers of foil to retain their heat as well as possible.

We'd picked up the pasty habit on regular holidays to Cornwall, when Mum was still alive. We'd always stayed in a beautiful little fishing village called Portloe. A seriously idyllic place, where the white houses nestle snugly into the cliffs at the side of the bay, framing the natural harbour.

A short way along the coast is the even smaller village of Portholland. A place of few houses but an impressive sea wall and an expansive, gently sloping beach which, depending on the time of day, can take a good few minutes to walk down until you are in more than a trickle of water.

At the beginning of the day we would buy our pasties from the Post Office-cum-general store and wrap them tightly in foil. We were then free to enjoy them at our leisure, between swimming, rockpooling, kite-flying or sandcastle-building, without having to leave the beach.

Those were sunny days, happy days, watching the clouds scoot across the sky, chased by their beach-sweeping shadows. We haven't been back since Mum died.

However, the pasty habit is a hard one to shake. Dad and I discovered their suitability to days out walking. No disappointing, messy picnic sandwiches – soggy, falling apart, annoying to eat in the wind or rain. Pasties withstand all sorts of weather and their residual warmth is amazingly comforting on a cold day.

On this particular day, Dad and I planned a short scenic hike, no more than five miles, in the Dales. It would be enough to reinvigorate me, we thought, without undoing all the good work we'd put in to get me better.

I was planning to return to university two days later but I was finding that thought more and more uncomfortable. I didn't mention those feelings to Dad, though. Despite our new-found openness, I didn't want him worrying about me when I went back.

The day broke just as we were leaving the house and Dad drove us up into the vast grey-green space, with very occasional dour farmhouses and more than a few sheep scattered everywhere. We arrived at a car park near a small, lively waterfall. Hardy, woolly sheep grazed the steep sides of the valley, calling contentedly to each other. Dad and I got out of the car into a very fresh winter morning. The cold was at us immediately, nipping our fingertips and our toes as we changed into our walking boots and donned our waterproofs.

Before we set off, we sat on the tail end of the car and had a quick drink of the strong coffee we'd packed.

"See that rock up there?" Dad asked.

I looked up the steep face of the valley. A waterfall broke over the top at one point but other than that it was completely blanketed by thick shrubs and ferns, punctuated regularly by sheep, and topped by a variety of rocky outcrops.

"What, the one next to the sheep?" I asked.

Dad laughed. "Very funny, Sarah. That one!" he pointed, "The huge one at the top, right next to the waterfall."

"Oh, yeah..." I said.

"That's where I proposed to your mum," he said proudly.

"Oh."

I looked up, seeing the romance of the situation. I wondered which season it had been. Each would hold their own secrets of beauty in this place.

On a winter's day like the one we were enjoying, the sky hung with low, pale grey clouds. The day felt muted and the situation deliciously isolated, just the odd crow flapping across the sky, cawing as it went, or a scratchy scuttling in the undergrowth, barely disturbing the peace.

Summer would see a busier time and the heat of the day would have butterflies and bees busying themselves around the wild flowers which grew in abundance, unscathed by the industry and urban progress of the distant towns.

"That is quite lovely," I said, and Dad nodded. I wasn't sure what else to say. He wouldn't want me to make a fuss, and I am not the type to do so anyway. I think he just wanted to share it with me. To remember his wife with one of the only other people she meant as much to as him.

"Come on," he said, and swung the rucksack onto his back. We closed the car boot and were on our way. Trudging up the steep siding next to the waterfall, we were soon at the very rock where Dad asked Mum to marry him. We sat there for a while. I wondered what it felt like to Dad. Did he see himself back there in that moment or was it just like anywhere else now?

Sometimes places lose their magic.

"She was great, your mum," he said. "Really great. But you know that."

"I do."

"She loved you, so much. You know that too, don't you?"

I didn't speak. I couldn't answer.

How can I explain to someone who has never experienced it what it feels like to lose your mum when you are just eleven years old? Even then, more than seven years on, it hurt me afresh many times. That was one of them. I swallowed.

"I'm sorry, Sarah, I don't mean to upset you. I just need you to know that. She didn't want to leave you, I am quite sure of it. She would have doubted her actions every step of the way in hiding her illness and refusing the treatment. I just know it. Do you remember what she was like, though? So principled. So proud. I think; I have tried to make sense of what she did, and I think that she couldn't bear the thought of you seeing her lose herself. The illness was bad, severe, and I can't believe I didn't see it. I knew she kept getting ill, and I suppose it did seem to be happening more frequently, but her job put her in contact with little kids every day. I just thought she was having a particularly bad time of picking up their germs. God, I am so stupid."

"No you're not. You're not, Dad. I'm sure Mum made every effort to hide it from you. She was good with secrets, wasn't she?"

"She was," Dad allowed himself a small laugh.

"Actually, I have a confession to make. Remember when Mum broke the greenhouse window and the glass shattered all over your tomato plants and strawberries?"

"Yes..?" Dad raised an eyebrow at me.

"It wasn't Mum, it was me. I'd been messing about with a ball, and she'd told me to take it away from the greenhouse. I ignored her of course. The next thing I knew, I'd booted the ball so hard and it went straight through. I begged her not to tell you."

"Well she didn't," Dad said, "and I was so arsey with her about it for days as well!"

"There you go then. She did it for you as well you know,

Dad. I mean hiding her illness. It wouldn't have all been about me. I do remember her talking about us all making the most of our time together, and her taking you out for that surprise dinner on your birthday. Don't you think she was trying to make the most of her time with you?"

"You're right, Sarah, as usual. I do know that, I know she loved me, but I really need you to know just how much she loved you. That is more important than anything."

"Thank you Dad, I think I do know."

I tried hard to imagine Mum and Dad, there on that very rock, just a couple of years older than I was at that time; Dad trying to get up the nerve to propose and Mum oblivious, admiring the view. I stayed quiet for a few moments, hoping Dad was remembering it as it had actually happened, then suggested we move along.

We passed very few other walkers that day. It was bright but it really was cold. I tried to keep thoughts of university at bay. It felt like another world and I was happy to keep it that way. We stopped for a drink at a village pub and with the crackling fire emitting wood smoke and general good cheer, I had a sudden sense of Christmas. A childlike excitement fluttered within. If I could just keep going till then, I thought, I could come home and spend some more time with Dad. Have more times like this. And Dad had said university life would calm down a bit after that holiday. It would all be OK, I told myself. And even if it wasn't, what did it matter? I had my dad.

Chapter Five

I returned to university a very determined person. Determined to study harder, to say no to nights out that I wasn't really that bothered about, and to look after myself better.

I had also resolved to be a better daughter.

Those days at home had done me so much good, and Dad as well. His revelation about Mum had definitely cleared the lines of communication for us, but it wasn't just that. I think being away from him, and getting myself into such a state, had finally made me realise everything he meant to me. I don't think it is unusual for children to take their parents for granted but I decided on my visit home that there would be no more of that from me.

When Dad dropped me off at my Halls, I invited him in for a cup of tea. I was greeted warmly by my friends, including Chloe, who gave me a huge hug. I introduced Dad, and he sat with them all while I put the kettle on.

I watched him from the kitchen while he chatted and asked interested questions of Chloe, Fiona and Paul. He looked up and I gave him a huge smile. I realised how proud of him I was. When he left this time, I told him I loved him. Right in front of my friends. There was no way he was leaving without me saying it, though, and another of my resolutions was that I would continue to tell him that, often.

"Are you better, Sarah?" asked Chloe, after Dad had driven away and we had waved him off together. We were walking back up the steps towards our rooms.

"Yeah, I think so, sorry for just going," I said, "I just couldn't face telling anyone. Even you, sorry. I was just worn out."

"I know," Chloe said, "I've been a bit the same to be honest. I think it's a bit much. Jim told me it would be like this but I kind of didn't see it while it was happening. I haven't been out so much since you went home."

"Really?" I smiled, thinking that perhaps this was the start of a change and a more settled life.

"Yeah, really, and I think maybe some of the others have had enough of the non-stop partying too. But," she grinned, "Do you fancy a drink or two tonight?"

"Erm..."

"Just at the Arms," she said quickly. "Nothing big. Jim said he and Nick would come over and meet us if you fancy it."

"Oh OK then, I don't suppose one or two pints will hurt," I said.

Jim's mate Nick was someone I had my eye on, as Chloe well knew. He was a graduate and was working at a restaurant in the city while he tried to find a 'proper' job. He and Jim shared a flat and I really fancied him.

Chloe had told me not to even think about it, unless I just wanted to have a bit of a laugh with someone.

"He is definitely not looking to settle down," she said. "Exactly the opposite in fact!"

"Ah, I wouldn't worry about that," I'd told her, "I don't think he's so much as noticed me anyway."

It appears I was wrong about that, as Chloe told me Nick had been concerned to hear I was ill and was very interested in coming to see that I was OK. That clinched it. The Arms it was.

As I got ready that evening, I thought of Dad at home alone and my stomach tightened a little. What was he doing right then, I wondered. I pictured him eating alone, hunched over his plate and avidly working his way through the newspaper. I fought the urge to cry a little. I also realised I felt guilty about going out but I told myself not to be silly. I had promised myself that I wouldn't make myself ill again, not that I would become a nun. A few drinks in the local pub was far from a wild night out.

As soon as Chloe knocked on my door I felt better and we walked, arm in arm, down the road. Jim and Nick were already at a table and had clearly had at least a couple of pints, judging by the empty glasses and their jolly demeanour.

"Hi Sarah!" Jim said, "I'm glad you're better, Chloe said you were really ill."

"Oh, it was just a chest infection," I said, kicking myself inwardly that I blushed when I realised I'd referred to my chest. I glanced at Nick, he was smiling at me.

"Are you better now?" he asked.

"Yes, thank you. I am, much better."

"Let me get you a drink then," Jim said, "And one for you I suppose, little sis."

Chloe and Jim got on really well and made me realise what I had missed out on, being an only child. It was good to spend time around them, as they bounced off each other and made me laugh with their affectionate terms of abuse.

We sat and had a drink then the pool table became free so we moved over and had a mini pool tournament. I was pleased as I knew that I often surprised blokes with my pool skills. That night, Chloe and I won every game.

"Wow, Sarah, not bad for a girl," Nick said, grinning.

"I guess you're not," I said, emboldened by a few rum and cokes.

We smiled at each other and my stomach did a little turn. All too soon, however, it was time for Nick and Jim to get the last bus back to their flat. Chloe and I walked slowly, once more arm in arm, back to Halls.

"Well I think you're in there," she said.

"What... with Nick?" I said. I thought I had picked up the same signals but it was good to have somebody else confirm them.

"Yes," she said, "But remember what I told you about him. Don't fall for him, OK?"

"Don't be daft. Nothing's going to happen anyway."

The next day I got a text from an unknown number.

'Hi Sarah, fancy a replay of the pool match, just u and me? Nxx'

My heart flipped, or it certainly felt like it. I left it a respectable ten seconds or so before replying with an affirmative. We arranged to meet that evening, back at the Arms. I told Chloe and she was pleased but again she warned me about his reputation.

Before I left that night, I rang Dad but there was no answer. I left a message saying I was going out and I'd ring him the next day. I walked nervously to the pub, starting to worry that perhaps I'd imagined it or got the wrong Nick, or the wrong pub, or the wrong night, that kind of thing.

The doubts vanished as soon as I walked in and saw him sitting alone with a pint glass and a rum and coke, which he gestured towards as he saw me. He also stood up and kissed me, and I went all of a flutter, which is not like me at all. I was going to say I was still feeling weak from the illness but if I am really honest, I just fancied him like mad. I hadn't felt like that for a long time and this was exciting.

The pool table was occupied so we sat and chatted, discovering we liked a lot of the same music, films, and books. Nick was very well read and had studied English and Philosophy at university so we had our studies in common too. We were laughing about one of the Philosophy lecturers when all of a sudden Nick's hand was on my knee and I think minutes later we were kissing passionately. Nowadays I cannot imagine sitting in a pub; a public space, kissing someone, but there and then it seemed fairly normal. It was a student pub, by and large, so I don't suppose it was in the least bit unusual.

We did get our pool game, and I did beat him, which I was extremely pleased about. I wondered what would happen at chucking out time, and wasn't surprised with Nick's question.

"Can I come back to yours then, Sarah? I'd love to see the old Halls again."

He had lived in the next block to mine during his first year. His arms were around my waist and he was nuzzling my neck.

"Mmm... not tonight," I said, kissing him.

"Oh go on," he said, tightening his hold on me slightly.

"No!" I laughed, "I've got lectures in the morning, and you've got work."

"OK, OK," he said, "But let's get together at the weekend, shall we? Jimbob's got some free passes to a club, why don't you and Chloe come with us?"

"Yeah, that sounds good."

Sounds good? It sounded bloody amazing! I had to hide my grin with another kiss. His bus was coming up the road.

"Sure you don't want me to walk you back?" he asked but I knew that wasn't really what he was asking.

"No, it's fine thanks, that's some of my friends over there," I said, having spied Fiona with Andrew, the guy she was seeing. "I'll walk back with them."

"OK, I'd better dash then, see you Saturday!" Nick said, and he kissed me then was gone.

I had no trouble convincing Chloe to come out on the Saturday night. It just so happened that the club, Zeitgeist, was hosting a DJ she absolutely loved so she was possibly as excited as I was. We went round to Jim and Nick's first where we had a quick drink then headed into town to a bar just round the corner from Zeitgeist.

Nick was looking extra fit, I thought. He had long hair, though I had never seen it loose. He kept it neatly fastened back in a ponytail. His long eyelashes made his eyes seem soft and also leant an air of mystery to him when he was looking down. Not that I had given much thought to all of this, of course.

As soon as we were sitting down in the bar, which was fairly rowdy and clublike in itself, Nick put his hand on my leg. I almost jumped. Chloe clocked the move straight away and raised her eyebrows at me. I just grinned.

A few of Jim's and Nick's mates turned up and for a while Nick was nowhere to be seen. I was annoyed at myself for the slight anxiety I was feeling but as soon as he returned, he was at my side and holding my hand. I knew I liked him a lot but I didn't particularly want him to know that. Even though, looking back, I don't suppose I was the slightest bit subtle about it.

When it was time to head off to Zeitgeist, I walked ahead with Chloe, not just to keep Nick on his toes but to let her know that I wanted her along because I wanted to have a good night out with her. She was so excited about seeing Bob da Builda that she wasn't worried about any of that anyway. Also she knew Jim's and Nick's mates well already so she had plenty of company. This made it easy for me to slip away with Nick into one of the darker corners of the club where we talked for a while, then gave up on the talking as it was impossible to hear anything the other said anyway. It seemed to make much more sense to just spend our time kissing. A brief thought flitted through my mind that this time the previous week I had been at home with Dad, in fact probably asleep in my childhood bed. What a difference a week makes. I pushed thoughts of Dad from my mind as they immediately made me feel guilty. I don't know why; he had told me I should carry on enjoying myself when I'd discussed with him the prospect of toning down my social life. However, what would he have thought if he could have seen me then? Also, what was he doing that Saturday night? Either he would be found at the Milepost with his friend Roger or at home with a glass of wine and a good book.

When Bob da Builda came on, we went to find the others. Chloe was almost beside herself with excitement. When the set started to build up, we all made our way onto the dancefloor and must have been there for a solid 30 or 40 minutes.

Some girls joined us, friends of Nick's, and once again I was irritated to find myself slightly anxious but soon he asked if I wanted to go to the bar and get a drink to cool down. I smiled and happily went with him.

"So, are you coming home with me tonight then?" he asked, his arm snaking around my shoulders. I liked the feel of his hand on my skin.

"No, I can't tonight, sorry Nick. I promised Chloe I'd go back with her."

I'd done nothing of the sort – Chloe was extremely independent and would happily have got a cab back on her own.

"She won't mind," he pressed, "You know Chloe. Or she could come back and stay at ours too."

"Nope, sorry," I said, grinning at him and hoping I seemed more resolute than I felt. It was far too soon in my mind to be going back to his for the night, and I had also heeded Chloe's warning.

"Fair enough," he said, and we kissed a bit more but I thought I sensed a little less urgency in him. Maybe I was being paranoid but he definitely seemed slightly less interested. I was disappointed when, shortly after we had finished our drinks, he said he was going to go home. However, I wasn't going to let him know that and after all, I had come out with Chloe and I was determined to enjoy my night out with my friend. I found her and Jim on the balcony and I joined them, pushing thoughts of Nick firmly from my mind.

It was three days before I heard from him again, and I tried not to think about it. The day after Zeitgeist I slept in then headed to the library to study all afternoon. I came back to Halls and I ate the dinner provided in the canteen. A distinctly iffy puff pastry number packed with chewy mushrooms and mushy carrots (I suspected these were the previous day's leftovers), but I padded it out with lots of fresh salad.

While I was pondering over the choice of school dinner-style desserts, I was greeted by James, a bloke I knew vaguely from Chloe's English course. He had chosen one Philosophy module as well, on Fiction and the Arts, and he was in my discussion group.

"Hi Sarah, are you feeling better now?" he asked.

"I am, thank you, much better." I smiled. "Just trying to choose my pudding."

"Hmm... tough choice, stodgy lukewarm treacle pudding or dried-out ginger cake. Yep, I've been debating over it for a while as well."

We both chose the ginger cake and drowned it in custard then James came back to my table with me. We talked about our studies and life at university. I knew he'd had a gap year and he told me he'd worked for his mum, who was a Retail Director for a high street women's fashion chain.

"I bet you miss the money," I said.

"I definitely do," he grimaced, "But I don't mind missing the early mornings. Or working for Mum. Everybody knew I was her son, it was a bit embarrassing at times."

"I can imagine!" I said, "My dad's a lecturer at our local uni, I wouldn't want to be one of his students."

"Do you fancy a drink afterwards at the Arms?" he asked me. "There's a few of us going from my block. Bring Chloe too."

"I would normally," I said, "But I've got a bit of catching up to do after my time away. Thanks for asking, though."

I thought then that he looked a bit disappointed. I hoped he was just being friendly and nothing more. I really liked Nick. I was under no illusion that I was entering into a proper relationship with him. I didn't even know if he'd bother with me again after I'd turned him down twice but I've never been into seeing more than one bloke and I wanted to see where things went with him. James was nice, but Nick was exciting.

I saw James in our discussion group on the Tuesday and he was his normal self; chatty and polite, so I thought nothing more of it. On the Wednesday, Nick sent me a text and we went out for a few drinks. He didn't ask me back to his that night and I worried he'd gone off me, however I heard from him again at the weekend and he cooked me a meal at his flat as Jim and Chloe had gone home for a couple of days. I booked a taxi beforehand and I could sense he was disappointed, perhaps even a little annoyed, when I told him this at the outset. However, we had a lovely meal and got on brilliantly. We kissed a lot, on the settee, and just as I felt my resolve starting to get a little shaky, the doorbell went. The taxi.

"Sorry, sorry," I said, smiling despite my apology. I must admit that I was quite enjoying myself. I thought perhaps Nick was not used to women saying no to him.

It was soon December and Christmas was in the air. I was surprised when Nick sent me a text asking me if I wanted to go shopping with him. To this point, our relationship had been strictly night-time only. I readily agreed as I secretly have a bit of a soft spot for the romance of Christmas.

We arranged to go on a Wednesday afternoon, when there were no lectures and Nick had the day off. I went to the library in the morning but I couldn't concentrate. I kept wondering if this change in the type of date meant something. Yes, I know, pathetic. I was eighteen, OK?

I went round to his flat afterwards only to find him still getting ready. Jim let me in, and told me Nick was in the shower. He had slept in, apparently. Jim seemed to find it quite amusing that Nick and I were going shopping together.

"Don't think I've seen Nick take anyone shopping before, except his mum!"

The afternoon was wintry grey, the clouds above closing in on us, suggesting the day was already coming to a close even though it was only mid-afternoon. The year had only just started to turn cold and the novelty of the slight chill to the air was enticing.

We shopped together well. Nick helped me find a shirt and a book for my dad. I'd wanted to get Dad something extra special that year but I had no idea what. We found an old copy of *The Hobbit* in a second-hand bookshop. When I was younger, before Mum died, Dad had read the story to me and I wanted him to know that I remembered that. The edition was from 1950. It was older than Dad. It had another person's name in the front of it, J. Thompson, written in a childish script. I wondered about this person; were they male or female? Were they still alive? If so, did they think back to their copy of *The Hobbit* and wonder what had happened to it?

In turn, I helped Nick to choose a cardigan for his mum. This was so alien to me, the act of buying a gift for a mother figure, and the emotion of it must have lodged in me. When we later went to an old pub in the centre of town, and settled ourselves by the cosy open fire, I found myself with tears in my eyes. This was admittedly after a couple of drinks but I think that Christmas always made me remember Mum, who loved it so much. That, coupled with an emotionally charged afternoon, had clearly got the better of me.

"Are you crying?" asked Nick, looking full of concern.

"Oh God, I must look mental," I said, trying to laugh it off.

"Not at all, what's wrong?" he asked.

I found myself telling him about Mum, including what I had recently found out about her. I had not mentioned this newfound knowledge to anybody, so I surprised myself by opening up then as I did. I realised, though, as the words came spilling out, how good it was to talk to somebody and how unhealthy it probably was to keep things – thoughts, feelings – hidden away. Bottled up like ginger beer, ready to pop.

Nick was great and listened to me, looking almost ready to cry himself at some points. When I'd told him the whole tale, he simply said, "I can't imagine what you've been through."

I was grateful for these words as often people will say, 'I know how you feel', when in fact they can't possibly. They are just trying to be nice, I know; they don't know what to say, but believe me, those few words do not offer the comfort they are meant to.

"Sorry," I said, "That's kind of put a dampener on the afternoon."

"Don't be daft," Nick said, "I'm flattered you felt you could talk to me about it. Do you fancy some fresh air?"

I did, I realised, and we buttoned ourselves up as we walked out into the navy blue of the late afternoon, and wandered hand-in-hand towards the city docks. We walked around for a while, listening to the creaking of the boats in the harbour, and clutching our Christmas shopping bags. Once we were cold enough, we decided to go back to Nick's flat, where we opened a bottle of red wine and ordered takeaway pizza.

We watched some lame romantic comedy while we ate, and once we'd had our fill, of the food and the film, we turned to each other. I don't know where Jim was that night but we had the flat to ourselves and soon things had got fairly steamy.

"Do you want to move into my room?" Nick asked, "Just in case Jim comes back, I mean."

This time I didn't say no. I just nodded and he picked up the two glasses of wine and gestured for me to lead the way. You don't need to know any more except that this time I did stay the night and I lay awake for quite some time in Nick's arms, thinking of my mum and my dad, and how they must have lain like this for a first time, full of hope and with no knowledge of what was to come. Nobody has that knowledge of course but it made me so sad to think of what happened to those hopes.

In the morning I said a sheepish hello to Jim as I made my way towards the front door of the flat. Nick had given me a huge bear hug and persuaded me to stay in bed a little longer but I knew I had to go because I had a lecture to attend. Although I had broken my resolve on the Nick front, I was not about to let go of my other promises to myself.

"Sorry about yesterday, getting upset I mean," I'd said while I was getting dressed.

"Don't say sorry, Sarah, please. Like I said, I'm glad you felt you could talk to me. I'm not surprised you're upset. I had a great day, and night, thank you."

I smiled at him.

"I'll give you a ring later," he said. "After work. I'm on a late shift today."

All day long I felt happy. I was excited about Nick, enjoying my studies, and looking forward to seeing Dad in a couple of weeks for the Christmas break. I marvelled at how different I felt to just a month before.

When Nick didn't ring that evening as promised, I didn't think much of it. He wasn't the type to phone all the time, preferring to text, it seemed. Having said that, there was no text message either, but I wasn't worried.

However, when I had heard nothing from him the next day either, I did start to get bothered. Twice I tapped out a message to him – designed to sound light-hearted and flippant – but I deleted both before sending. I was not about to become one of those girls, I told myself.

On the third day, I had a message and I was shamefully excited to see Nick's name pop up on my screen.

'Hi Sarah, sorry no msge till now, been busy, fancy catching up next week? Nx'

That was pretty disappointing, I had to admit, but at least he still wanted to see me. I left it a while then replied.

'Yeah, sounds great, let me know what you fancy doing. I'm busy Tues. Sx'

I added the bit about being busy on Tuesday so he'd know I had other stuff going on. I don't suppose he even noticed.

A day or so later, Chloe came through my door with a slightly nervous look on her face.

"Sarah, I just need to say this, I'm sorry, Nick's been seeing someone else."

I felt my face drop, and my stomach swoop. Even though, if I was honest, I'd realised that Nick and I were going nowhere, it wasn't nice hearing it like that.

"Sorry Sarah, I know how much you like him."

"Well, yeah, I do, but don't say sorry. It's not like we were engaged or anything. And it's certainly not your fault."

"Yeah but the git could have at least let you know himself."

"He could," I said, and thought of how I'd opened up to him about Mum, "But he didn't. And you had already told me what he was like so what was I expecting, really? Don't worry, it's fine."

It wasn't fine really, obviously, but I can't say I was surprised either. Just horribly disappointed.

Never mind, I told myself, just another week till I went home to Dad. He'd sort me out. I wasn't intending to tell him about Nick but I was just looking forward to spending more time with him. Walking, drinking, eating, with my dad.

Between that day and my going home, I heard from Nick one more time.

'Sorry for being a tw@' he sent to me via a text message late one night, probably drunk.

I just ignored it. I wasn't massively angry with him, I just had nothing to say.

There was an end-of-term Christmas party at the Halls of Residence. Since I'd successfully cut down the nights out, I'd realised that others around me had started to do the same. I guess we had all started to feel the pain of it a little bit, although without outwardly acknowledging it to each other. This party, however, gave no indication of that. There were drunk teenagers snogging everywhere, a few being sick outside, and lots of silly dancing and raucous behaviour.

While Chloe was at the bar, I was tapped on the shoulder by James, the bloke from her course.

"Hi Sarah," he said, "How are you?"

"I'm fine, thanks James," I smiled, "Looking forward to Christmas."

"Me too, me too," he said. "Listen, I don't know if you'd be interested but I don't think you live that far from me and, erm, on New Year's Eve I'm having a party if you'd like to come."

"Oh right, thanks James," I said, surprised. "I don't know what I'm doing yet; probably something with my dad but give me your number and I'll let you know."

James put his number in my phone and then Chloe was back with drinks and a number of our fellow residents, who dragged us onto the dancefloor.

The next day, hangovers raging, we all said our goodbyes to each other and said "See you next year!" as though it was the funniest thing ever.

Dad came and picked me up and I practically ran over to him. I had not forgotten my resolution to let him know how much I loved him.

"Sarah, love!" he said, and hugged me.

We drove home with Christmas carols on the radio. I was quite quiet, thinking about Nick I suppose, but so happy to be in

Dad's comfortable, familiar car. I remembered just a few weeks before, travelling that same journey, feeling terrible. It seemed a lot had happened since then and, despite the Nick thing, much of it was positive. I thought I could return to uni in the New Year happier and stronger.

"So what are we going to do this Christmas then, Dad?" I asked him as we turned into our road. I felt a familiar warmth rising in me at the thought of home.

"Well, I've been meaning to talk to you about that, Sarah."

"Oh no, don't tell me you're going to have to work."

Although Dad was meant to have the same holidays as me, he sometimes did extra courses for private colleges, which often fell outside standard term times. I started to feel my hopes droop, at the thought of losing this time together which I'd thought we'd have.

"No, no, nothing like that, it's just... oh damn."

This last he muttered to himself, just as we reached our house.

"What?" I said, and saw he was looking at a strange car on our driveway. "Whose is that?"

"That," Dad said, "is what I wanted to talk to you about. I thought we'd get here before her."

"Her?" I asked, none the wiser.

"Yes, sorry Sarah, I meant to tell you about this before we got back. That's Dawn's car."

"Dawn?" I was being particularly slow.

"Yes," Dad said, "Dawn. My girlfriend."

Chapter Six

My mind worked quickly. A few clues I hadn't picked up on popped up in my memory; mysterious nights out which I'd not been interested enough to ask him about, unanswered phone calls when I'd been sure he'd have been at home alone. A lack of lamenting about the work Christmas party, which he usually hated and whinged about for weeks in the run up to.

He swung the car into the driveway and gently pulled the handbrake on before continuing.

"I work with Dawn," he said, "We've worked together for a while in fact. She did her PhD with us and stayed on to teach."

"And how long have you been seeing each other?" I asked, trying to sound grown up, trying not to let the words choke in my throat. I know I had said to him that I'd like him to meet somebody but I hadn't really thought it through. I hadn't expected anything so soon.

"Well, since about the time of your last visit," Dad said. "I felt so much better after spending all that time with you. I really think it helped me deal with some things which have been on my mind for years. And when you said what you did about me meeting somebody else. Well, I guess I thought of Dawn straight away."

"Oh, right," I said, and tried to smile. "I'm pleased for you. And now I get to meet her too!"

"Yes, I'm sorry about that, Sarah. I hadn't expected Dawn to be here now. I'd wanted you to get home before I told you so we could have a proper chat about it."

My mind working overtime, I thought I detected alarm bells. Dawn wasn't meant to be there. Dad was meant to bring his daughter back to an empty house, to their home, so they could discuss this new development in their own time. So why was Dawn here? Could she not allow him this time with his daughter?

I felt glued to my seat. I looked at our house, windows alight against the ever-darkening sky of the winter afternoon. Who was this intruder? What would she be like? What would I say to her? I realised I was scared to enter my own home.

"Come on then, love, let's get you in," said Dad, looking at me with a slightly worried expression.

I knew I had to be good for him, I had to allow him his happiness. I smiled and agreed we had better go in. I had better meet his new girlfriend.

I smiled, but I felt myself harden inside.

"Hello?" Dad called as he entered the house.

"Hello!" came a not-very-confident sounding reply. And was that an American accent? I took my shoes off in the porch, trying to delay the inevitable but then she was there, in the hallway, looking awkward but smiling at me. She hardly even acknowledged Dad at first but then she turned to him.

"I'm so sorry, I know I wasn't meant to be here but my car wouldn't start. I did try to call you. I didn't know where to go. There isn't really anywhere round here..." she gestured to the darkening outdoors.

Dawn was right. Our home was in a small Yorkshire village, with a Post Office/village stores and a pub which would not be open until the evening. Where could she possibly have gone on a cold winter's afternoon?

OK, I thought, *if she's telling the truth, that's not so bad.*

I shrugged off my coat and looked at her, realising she was younger than Dad. I guessed she was probably in her mid 30s.

"Don't worry," Dad patted her arm and then seemed to realise it had to be him who took the lead in this situation. "Sarah, this is Dawn. Dawn, Sarah."

"Hi Sarah," Dawn said, "I really am so sorry to just... be here like this. I've been trying to call Tony... your dad... but you know what he's like with his mobile."

"Ah," said Dad, patting his pocket, "I'm not sure I even took it with me."

"Dad!" I said, trying to sound light-hearted. "I bet it's in your study."

"Sorry, sorry," said Dad, "Look, come on, this is not exactly ideal, is it? Sarah, let me get you a cup of tea then I'll go and take a look at Dawn's car."

I followed him into the kitchen and looked back at Dawn standing awkwardly in the hallway.

"Do you want a cup too, Dawn?" I asked, and gestured for her to join us.

She smiled gratefully at me and I thought that actually she seemed pretty nice so far. It was a shock, that was for sure, but I had to be pleased for Dad.

Later that afternoon, after Dad had fixed Dawn's car and she had gone back to her flat in Harrogate, Dad called me downstairs to decorate the Christmas tree.

I had been unpacking my stuff in my room, and wrapping Dad's presents, trying not to think about Nick as I did so. I knew that if Nick and I had still been seeing each other – or whatever we had been doing – then I might have found it easier to be generous to Dad and Dawn. As it was, I was feeling wounded by Nick's rejection and greatly disappointed that it was not to be Dad and Sarah Against the World.

"I've been looking forward to this!" he said, popping open a bottle of Prosecco.

"Me too," I said truthfully, accepting a glass and watching his face as he filled it up. There did seem to be a lightness, a glow even, about him, which I had not seen before or which perhaps I would have been too young to appreciate if I had.

"Merry Christmas!" he clinked his glass against mine.

He'd brought the usual boxes of Christmas paraphernalia down from the attic. I don't think we had bought anything new since before Mum died. This usually made me feel sad, but comforted at the same time, somehow feeling Mum around us as we put up the tree. Now, though, I looked at the family photo of us, then at the photo of Mum, and I felt strange. I couldn't put my finger on it. Clearly it was the effect of Dawn, and her sudden presence in our lives.

Everything felt somehow out of kilter. I sipped my wine but said nothing, instead rooting out the usual cheesy Christmas CDs and sliding one into the stereo. As the familiar strains of Slade's *Merry Christmas Everybody* filled our room, I told myself to snap out of it and just enjoy myself. Dad was still Dad, I was still home, it was still Christmas.

The tree was a real one, from one of Dad's mates at a nearby farm. It was probably a bit too big for the room really but we covered it in all our tinsel, baubles and lights until it twinkled and sparkled. The open fire was crackling and the wine softening me, so that I felt slightly better.

"What shall we do for tea tonight, Dad?" I asked.

"Pizzas do for you?"

"Definitely! Will Dawn be joining us?"

I hadn't really wanted to ask this, for fear that the answer would be yes, but to my relief, Dad said that he had wanted to spend some time with me.

"Dawn completely understands," he said.

That's good of her, I thought bitchily, but chastised myself.

"However," he continued, "What would you think about her joining us on Christmas Day?"

I didn't look up, busying myself with some tangled tinsel.

"Not all day," he added hastily, "But all her family's back in Canada, and I thought it would be a shame for her to spend the day all on her own. She's really good fun, Sarah, I promise you."

"Of course," I said, more cheerfully than I felt, "No problem."

I smiled at him and he looked relieved.

So this was it; a new chapter in our lives, and I would just have to bloody well grow up and deal with it.

Christmas Day was actually very good. Dawn had been round a couple of times in between and I was getting to like her. She was, as Dad said, very good fun, and she was really lovely to talk to. I felt like she was more on my wavelength than Dad's at times, which I suppose wasn't that surprising as she was pretty much exactly halfway between us in age.

Once Dad had established that we got on quite well, he seemed to leave it at that but Dawn, luckily, was a bit more emotionally aware than Dad and knew that I would be feeling weird.

"I don't want to give you the 'I'm not trying to replace your Mum' spiel, Sarah, because that would be ridiculous. You clearly know that already. I do like your Dad though, and we're enjoying spending time together. However," she paused and looked me directly in the eye, "I really, really don't want you to feel weird about anything. My parents split up when I was in my teens and Mum had a succession of boyfriends, some of whom I met, most of whom I hated. It messed me up a bit. You are older, I know, and more grown up, but I'm not stupid. It's going to be weird for you."

Her honesty was disarming and it didn't take me long to really warm to her. So much so that I was no longer trying to persuade myself I was happy for Dad. I really was. By Christmas Day I felt at ease with her enough to gang up on Dad with her, making fun of his hippy days and his bad taste in music.

"Alright you two, flippin' 'eck, I wish I'd never introduced you!"

"Too late, Dad, too late!"

Dad absolutely loved the book I'd got him. I thought briefly of Nick but pushed the thought away. I was still hurting but the break at home and the distance were making me feel better.

Dawn had bought me some clothes, which I loved, and I felt bad that I hadn't bought her anything.

"Don't be silly," she said, "You didn't even know I existed till a few days ago. I don't expect Christmas presents. Not this year anyway."

A brief silence followed as we all took in what she'd said and the assumption that she would be around for future Christmases. However, I gave her a big hug and thanked her again. I glanced at Dad, who was grinning from ear to ear.

When it came to New Year's Eve, I was at a loss. Back at uni, I'd been imagining a night in the local with Dad. I'd caught up with my friends from school on a couple of nights out, and I somehow just didn't feel like the big night out they had planned in Leeds. Rachel and Millie had both gone to Manchester University and were a bit full of it... the Manchester scene; the clubs, the clothes, the new people they'd met. I was glad they were enjoying themselves but I felt that I'd probably heard enough of it and I really felt like a quiet night to get myself in gear for the new year. I was determined it was going to be a good one.

However, it was Dad's and Dawn's first New Year together and I wanted to let them enjoy it. Even though they insisted I should join them, I declined.

"I've been invited to a party," I surprised myself by saying, "A lad from uni who lives up near York. I'll probably go to that."

James sounded surprised and pleased when he answered my call.

"Yes, of course you're still invited! There's been a bit of a change of plan, though. Mum's not gone on her skiing trip so the party's going to be at a mate's house instead. If you like, I'll pick you up at the station. You can stay over, they've got a load of holiday lets which are being done up, so there's loads of space if you don't mind things being a bit basic. Some of the other girls from uni are coming, you can share with them."

Helen, Libby and Jenna were girls who I knew through Chloe. I wished she was able to come too but she lived miles away, in Surrey. I was really missing her so I gave her a call.

"You're going to go, then!" she said, "I thought you said no way?"

"Yeah, I did," I told her, "But I don't want to cramp Dad's style! Anyway, James seems quite nice and these holiday lets sound cool. Log cabins in the middle of some woods."

"Well watch out for werewolves," Chloe said, "And James. I think he's got the hots for you."

"No he hasn't!" I said but it got me thinking. I knew he wouldn't have invited me if he wasn't a bit interested. He seemed like a nice bloke. The complete opposite of Nick, anyway.

Chapter Seven

I surprised myself by feeling quite excited about the New Year's Eve party. I spent some time trying out which clothes I should wear and decided on the tunic Dawn had bought me for Christmas, with ripped jeans. A pair of big winter boots and the most minimal of makeup would finish the look off.

"You look great!" Dawn said when I came downstairs.

"You do," Dad beamed, looking at Dawn as he said it. I knew he was overjoyed that the two of us had hit it off. I felt a surge of love for him, and warmth for the two of them. If anybody deserved to be happy, it was my dad.

"Are you sure you're not going to need the car?" I asked.

"No, love, you're going to the back end of nowhere, you take it!"

"Thanks Dad!"

I wished them both a happy New Year's Eve, and took my bag out to the car. Suddenly I felt really nervous. I wished that Chloe was going. I knew the other girls well enough, but I hardly knew James really and I suddenly started to doubt whether I should be going at all.

"Don't be a wuss, Marchley," I muttered to myself. I decided that I would not drink anything alcoholic for the first hour or so, and that way if I was having an awful time I could get in the car and come back home. I would be intruding on Dad's and Dawn's evening of course but I could make myself scarce. It was only New Year's Eve. Not that big a deal.

"Drink, Sarah?" James was at my side within moments of my arrival. Of course I stuck firmly to my vow not to have a drink. Yeah, right. I accepted his kind offer and soon found myself with a tin mug of mulled cider in my mittened hands.

I had found his friend's place alright but, despite knowing about the holiday lets and the woods, I was still surprised at how secluded it was. There were big wrought iron gates at the entrance to the drive, which loomed suddenly on the quiet B-road and took me by surprise so that I had to make a sharp turn to avoid driving straight past. I could feel the pulsing of the bass from the PA system in the woods, guiding me along the tree-lined drive which was lit by lanterns. It gave me courage and conviction that I had come to the right place and was not about to enter some stately home uninvited, to be ravaged by guard dogs and chased away by the butler.

As I could see a clearing with lights up ahead, my nerves threatened to return but I thought of Nick and my resolve strengthened.

"Fuck you, Nick Hardcastle," I muttered, "I am going to enjoy myself."

I was annoyed that I'd even thought of him, but I determined it would be the last time that night.

I wound down my window to hear the familiar sound of the Ganja Cru's *Super Sharp Shooter* and my excitement replaced any lingering worries. Rounding a bend, I saw James' friend's house. Well it was a little more than a 'house' as the majority of us would understand the word. It was definitely more like a mansion. I counted ten upstairs windows along the front of it and gawped at the stone lions on either side of the steps which led to the front door. It was not an old house, but it had been designed to appear that way.

There were cars parked haphazardly on the sweeping gravel drive, many of them sleek and expensive-looking. I pulled up at the far end, hoping that Dad's modest saloon would go unnoticed and therefore unscathed, just in case any revellers thought of playing amusing car-related pranks.

I really appreciated the fact that James had kept an eye out for me, as I did not recognise a single person and had no idea where to go or what to do.

"Shall I take your bag?" he asked, taking it from me. "I'll show you where the other girls are; I think they're still in the cabin, and then I'll introduce you to a few people."

He seemed really confident – different somehow to the boy

I'd met at university. Perhaps he'd had a drink or two but if so, it had brought out a good side of him. He guided me off the drive, past an enormous trampoline, and down a woodchipped path which wound its way into the woods, to a large clearing. Dotted around this clearing, each in its own little patch, were the log cabins. There were fire pits by each one, all lit and crackling enticingly. James took me to the one I was to share with Jenna, Helen and Libby. He knocked on the door but there was no reply. I tentatively pushed it open but it was empty. However, there were a couple of empty wine bottles and clothes strewn on the floor, suggesting the girls had used the place to ready themselves for the party.

"Ah, I thought they were still here," said James, "Never mind, come with me!"

I was more than happy to be taken by the hand, and hoped that James would not disappear off until we had found our friends from uni. He must have known a good number of the people there from his school days so I started to worry he would find somebody more interesting and leave me to it. Luckily, it seemed he had no intention of doing so.

It was strange, that night. The party truly was one of the best I have ever been to. Rick, James' friend, clearly had some good contacts, so that the music was played by some relatively well-known DJs, using top class equipment. The whole house had been given over to the party and there was not a parent in sight.

"Where are Rick's parents?" I asked James.

"Hmm... I think they're off on a cruise or something," he said.

"I wonder what they'd say if they could see their house right now!" I laughed.

"Oh they know all about this," said James. "They're quite used to it. Rick's older sister, Melanie, used to have amazing parties. She's old and married now so it's Rick's turn."

Wow, I thought, *imagine having enough money to own this place, enough money to hold a party like this, and enough money not to worry about having a party like this.*

It was a far cry from anything I had experienced before. James seemed to feel comfortable with it and I began to feel very comfortable with him.

We wandered around the various rooms, ostensibly looking for the other girls, but talking as we went. We started out talking about uni, but soon our conversation drifted into more personal territory. He told me about his three brothers and the way he felt responsible for his mum even though he was the youngest. I found myself telling him about Mum, all the while thinking of what had happened when I'd told Nick about her.

Rick came rushing up to us excitedly, talking about the firework display he'd arranged for midnight. We listened to him, trying to make sense of his words. I suspected he was on something stronger than mere booze. Still, he was a very genial host and seemed pretty-down-to-earth considering his clearly privileged upbringing.

I was quite grateful for his interruption anyway; I wasn't really sure that the conversation James and I were having had gone the right way and I was happy to change the subject if possible. Mum's death is always there; the fact of it does not leave me on any day. Even though the rawness of it has faded, it still remains.

I didn't want to ruin what was turning out to be such a happy night by continuing down that particular route. Instead I suggested that we go outside for a while, to see where this amazing firework extravaganza was being set up. James readily agreed and we retrieved our coats from the cloakroom.

Outside, our breath puffed in crisp clouds into the night, illuminated by the lights from the house. I shivered briefly and James put his arm around me.

"Thanks for inviting me," I smiled at him, gratefully accepting another mulled cider as we stopped at the drinks table near the large bonfire which was next to the lake. Of course the house had its own lake. Obviously.

"It's my pleasure," he replied, smiling back, "I'm really glad you could come. Chloe talks about you a lot and I noticed you on our first day at the Freshers party."

"Did you really?" I asked, not wanting to mention that I had not noticed him.

"Yeah, you looked... I don't know... just really lovely."

It may have been the drink, it may have been the occasion, it may have been the effect of his words against the effects of

Nick, but I felt very emotional all of a sudden. I didn't say anything but turned my face towards the huge fire, watching the logs and branches buckle and disintegrate in the red heat.

The next thing I knew, James had gently put his hand against my face and turned me towards him, then he was kissing me. With the music pounding from the house and the fire hissing and crackling close by, my senses were on overdrive. I could hear an owl hooting from the woods as James pulled me closer, pushing his fingers into my hair and kissing me more determinedly.

I hadn't planned on this. I suppose I knew he was interested in me but I really hadn't thought I was interested in him. I had been too hung up on Nick to think about it. Suddenly what had happened with Nick seemed like a dirty secret, something I should wipe from my mind. I had been stupid to think he would treat me any differently to any other girl, but we always hope we will be the one to make somebody change their ways, don't we?

Then there had been the disappointment of finding Dad had a girlfriend. As much as I liked Dawn, if I was honest I was still finding it a bit hard that Dad and I had not had the Christmas I'd imagined for us. I had been so eager to spend time with him, time which I felt we'd missed out on up till then. I wasn't bitter, or jealous, and I was genuinely happy for him, but it didn't stop me feeling sorry for myself.

Now, here was James, with his kind words and thoughtful ways. He was a good kisser too and I let myself enjoy it.

When we pulled apart, we smiled shyly at each other and he pulled me close, hugging me. And that was that.

Eventually, we found Jenna and the others, but they were too drunk to get any sense out of. I stayed by James' side and we danced the night away with his school friends. The firework display really was something and I watched it tucked in front of James, his arms around my waist and his chin resting on my head. It felt good.

At around 4am I thought I should really get some sleep. James, perfect gentleman, walked me to the cabin where the other girls were all collapsed, and I kissed him goodnight. He wandered off up the path towards the house, where he was sleeping.

Happy New Year, I thought to myself, then I snuggled into

my sleeping bag, fully dressed, and lay on my mattress. The cabin had a wood-burning stove which was still going, just about, and it was cosy and warm.

I could hear the owl once more, it sounded very close by, and as I drifted off into a happy, if over-tired, sleep, I could smell wood smoke on my clothes and in my hair.

Chapter Eight

I remember so clearly the first time I met Hazel.

James and I had been going out with each other for about four months so it must have been April or May. James drove and, on the way, I admired the lush spring green of the hedgerows and trees coming into leaf. Fields were alive with young animals – tremulous lambs following their mothers' every move, gentle calves suckling and kicking out their legs for the sheer joy of it.

I love spring. I have always thought summer is my favourite season but actually perhaps it is spring after all; pregnant with promise, it signals new life, blue skies, sunny days and hours of daylight stretching further and further each week.

That day I was fighting my nerves. I hadn't really had a serious boyfriend before; I certainly hadn't been in a 'meet the parents' scenario. There was a large group of us back home, and we had been to school and college together so mostly I knew boys' parents anyway. If I was invited for a meal, it was definitely tea, not dinner.

Everything James had told me about his mum served only to increase my nerves. She was clearly an extremely capable, ambitious high achiever who had brought up four boys alone, from the time James was a toddler. I knew she enjoyed reading and going to the theatre. She was apparently a great shopper; only natural I suppose, given her career in Retail. She holidayed in the Caribbean most years.

James had grown up with holidays on private yachts and parties with some of the UK's top business people. Hazel had a favourite, incredibly expensive perfume brand, and had clothes designed specifically for her.

In short, Hazel and I had little in common. I only hoped that her taste in books and plays might be similar to mine so that we had something other than James to talk about.

As we drew closer to James' village, I felt my nerves set in properly. I'd told Dad about this visit and had alluded to how nervous I felt.

He merely laughed and said, "*Nil desperandum*, Sarah."

"Do you remember meeting Grandma and Grandad for the first time?" I asked.

Dad spluttered down the phone.

"Ahem, yes, I think that's a story for another time. Let's just get you through this visit, shall we?"

I pressed him but he said nothing more. In the end he wished me well and said perhaps I would like to bring James home for a visit soon as well. The thought hadn't even crossed my mind. In truth, it still felt like early days to me but apparently Hazel had 'insisted' on James bringing me home the next time he went back. I got the feeling she was a lady seldom refused.

"Nearly there," James smiled at me and squeezed my leg. "Don't worry, Mum'll love you."

He turned the car in between two large conifers and up a driveway lined with poplars. There was the house. Not quite as grand as I'd pictured, having no doubt exaggerated James' descriptions in my mind, but clearly a very nice place. It was old, double fronted, and had apparently once been a farmhouse. I saw the net curtains twitch in one of the downstairs rooms. A silver-blonde woman waving at us from the doorstep.

"Hi Mum!" shouted James.

I smiled and waved. This was it. Best foot forward, and so on.

"Hello darling, hello love, you must be Sarah," Hazel said in a voice which I hadn't been expecting. Broad West Yorkshire, it didn't quite tie with the image I had in my mind. Having said that, neither did her appearance. She was wearing jeans and a shirt. Probably very expensive jeans and a shirt, but still, it put me a little more at ease.

She ushered me out of the car and hugged me then enveloped James in an enormous squeeze which I was surprised he got out of alive. "It's so nice to meet you at last, Sarah," said Hazel, "I've heard so much about you. James couldn't talk about anything else at Christmas."

This was news to me. We weren't even seeing each other then. I was flattered though and smiled at James, who was turning a nice shade of red.

"Muuuum," he said.

"Sorry darling, didn't mean to embarrass you. Let's get you in shall we, and I'll show you where you're staying, Sarah. In the guest room."

OK, I thought, *no sharing a room, fair enough.*

"Haw haw haw," Hazel let out a huge guffaw, "Only joking, you're in with James of course!"

I smiled. She was not what I'd been expecting at all. We left our bags in the hall and went through to the enormous kitchen, where fresh coffee and bagels awaited us.

"Help yourself," Hazel said. She then sat with us and proceeded to quiz James about his course.

"I would have preferred him to do Business Studies," she said to me as though he wasn't there, "but he would insist on English Literature. I guess it doesn't matter in the long run; a degree's a degree isn't it? I hear you do Psychology."

"Philosophy," I corrected her politely.

"Yeah, I bet you can read my mind, haw haw," she continued, apparently not having heard my answer. I was used to this. People often confused the two subjects, as well as confusing Psychology with mind reading, apparently.

I just smiled politely and buttered a bagel.

"So what are you planning to do when you finish your studies?" Hazel asked me.

"I think I want to be a teacher," I said.

"Oh that's nice," came her response, though I got the distinct impression 'nice' wasn't something she was interested in.

"Following my parents' footsteps," I said, but she didn't hear me. She had already turned to James and started talking about her work.

Chapter Nine

Other than the slightly uncomfortable first visit to Hazel, my relationship with James developed gently. It felt natural and easy and I was never insecure or worried about how he felt. There may not have been such passion as I'd felt with Nick but I didn't think that was necessarily a bad thing. What we did have grew strong and sure, and I felt that I could rely on James.

After graduation, we moved in together. It was not even a question of whether or not this would happen. Before we had even really discussed the prospect, Hazel had got it all sorted.

"I've found this lovely place for the two of you, in the next village. It's a rental, of course, but you know, it's quite reasonable and it will give you a chance to find your feet and get a bit put away for buying somewhere."

I looked at James. We were visiting his mother for the weekend, the intention being that we had a bit of a break before exams began. He looked at me. We sort of smiled and shrugged at each other.

"Do you want to see it?" he asked me.

"Erm..." I was slightly taken aback, but just thought, *Why not?* I didn't particularly mind being organised in such a way. I had not yet got a job lined up whereas James had been accepted onto a graduate fast track scheme for the large department store chain Hazel used to work for.

"What a coincidence!" she had exclaimed. "I'm sure people will think I pulled a few strings but I didn't, Jamie got it all on his own merit."

Hmm, was what I thought, but I knew James was very intelligent and definitely capable. People often seemed to say that it wasn't what you knew but who you knew and why shouldn't James benefit from his connections?

For my own part, Hazel had been trying to convince me to follow suit but I already knew it wasn't for me.

"So what can you do with Psy... Phil*osophy*?" she corrected herself tentatively, still not quite sure of what I studied, two years on.

"I don't know," I replied airily. "Everything and nothing." I knew she hated these kind of answers, far too woolly and airy-fairy for her.

"I think what I'll do is have a year or so of temping and then apply for a teaching course. I just want to give myself a bit of time to make sure that is really what I want to do."

"That's a good idea," Hazel said, "Try your hand at a few things. You might find out you're really good at something." *Thanks very much*, I thought, but I just smiled at her. I knew she meant well.

"If you like," she had continued, "I could see if I could get you a job in a Retail office..?"

"Thanks Hazel, that's really kind of you but I think I'll see what else crops up first. I might well take you up on that offer at some point though."

We went to see the house Hazel had found, all together.
"I'll drive you over this afternoon if you like," Hazel had said, "And I'll wait outside while you have a look around."
"Don't be daft, Mum, you should come in too," James replied quickly, "See what you think of the place."
As it turned out, it was a lovely 'property' as Hazel termed it. A small grey stone cottage in its own well-kept garden. Two bedrooms, a big kitchen and lounge which made up the whole of downstairs and a modern bathroom.

"It's lovely!" I exclaimed, because it really was. "Good find, Hazel!"

She beamed. "So are you going to take it then?"

"I... well I think we probably need to work out some things first," I faltered, looking at James. He might have an income, but I didn't yet. He also got a company car with his new job, which he seemed to be more excited about than the job itself. However, I was carless and the nearest sizeable towns were a good 30 minutes' drive away from the village. I would need to be sure I could get about as well.

"It's a bit remote isn't it?" I suggested.

"Oh it's fine," Hazel attempted to brush my concerns aside, "You can borrow one of my cars if you need to. I can put you on the insurance, no problem."

She had three cars. A winter car, a summer car and a spare. Just like most people.

I thought of Dad. He was only about 50 minutes away from there so it would be easy to make a return visit in a day. As Dawn was living with him, I didn't think he'd mind too much if I didn't move back home. In fact that would probably be ideal for them.

"I think we should do it," James said, looking at me and then his mum, his face beaming like a little boy's.

"Wow," I said, "Can we just hang on? I mean, it's lovely, it's beautiful in fact. The village seems nice, but this is just all a bit sudden."

"Of course," said Hazel, "Take your time."

It went unsaid but I got the distinct feeling I had disappointed them both.

"But don't wait too long," she continued, "In case this place gets snapped up."

The following day we signed the contract for a six month rental and I must admit, I was excited at the prospect. I loved our bedroom, with its small cottage windows, open fireplace, and view of the fields across the road and distant sheep-strewn hills.

The garden had been well tended and was just coming into its own after the winter. There was even a cherry blossom tree, in full flower, its leafy branches spread welcomingly across the garden, petals tumbling lightly onto the lawn.

***

After the first year of university, Chloe and I had shared a flat for the remainder of our time there. I had come to love it, though it was noisy on the high street below, and the train track at the bottom of the garden carried freight trains at night, which whooshed and rattled and screeched along. I found I quite liked the noise once I had got used to it.

Jim had gone travelling when we were in the second year and I had been very careful to make sure I spent at least as much time with Chloe as I did with James. She continued to go out clubbing and I would accompany her at least once a month. James sometimes came, but often he would stay in his shared house, playing on the Nintendo with his mates. It suited me fine as I liked to be independent of him.

Our relationship had just progressed naturally. I found him so easy to be with and talk to, and he made me laugh. I was aware that my feelings for him were different to those I'd had for Nick but I felt that these feelings for James were grown up somehow, whereas how I'd been about Nick had all the hallmarks of a standard teenage crush.

Chloe liked James and had no problem with him being around at the flat a lot. Life had settled for me and I was hugely relieved to be out of Halls.

I worked harder in those two years than I had ever worked in my life, and I spoke to Dad a couple of times every week, making sure I also saw him - and often Dawn - regularly. I felt I had come a long way from that first term and was far more secure in myself and my relationships.

Shortly before graduation, Chloe and I were packing things away in our little flat. Dismantling enormous displays of photos and posters which adorned the walls of our lounge and hallway.

"I'm going to really miss you, Chlo," I said.

"God, I'm going to miss you as well," she squeezed me into a huge, all-enveloping hug.

"I can't believe that this time next month you're going to be in Thailand!"

Chloe was going to meet Jim and spend a few months travelling with him.

"And I'll probably be a full member of the WI, making jam and cakes and attending lectures on crochet..." I continued.

"I hope it doesn't come to that!" Chloe laughed. "You'll get a job, meet some new people, you'll be fine."

There was a small, envious part of me that listened to those words and found that my planned life was comparing unfavourably to Chloe's months of freedom and adventure. But I had always been someone who wanted to be settled. I knew that. Not boring; never boring, I hope, but *home* held a lot of importance for me.

Bring on your pop psychology. I was lacking a mother figure. Now my family home was really Dad's and Dawn's but in my new place, I had Hazel just down the road; she was a mother figure and a half, and a home to call my own. Perhaps I could relax at last.

"Your house looks lovely, Sarah, maybe I'll move in when I get back!"

"You are very welcome," I said, "There's a spare room just waiting for you!"

We carried on putting things into boxes, or reluctantly binning some of our memories of the time we had lived together. Fliers, tickets, that kind of thing. It was hard to do but Chloe could hardly take them to Thailand with her and I couldn't see that they would fit into the tiny cottage I was soon to move into.

Graduation day came and went. Dad, Dawn and Hazel were all present so we went out for a meal – the three of them and James and me.

Dad seemed to quite like Hazel; but then he can be hard to read and is polite and friendly to most people.

Dawn and Hazel surprised me by getting on incredibly well. They had met fleetingly on a couple of other occasions but Hazel really turned on the charm with her and they were soon chatting away, discussing ski resorts in Canada where Dawn had worked and Hazel had holidayed.

Dad left them to it and chatted with James and me about our new house and James' job.

"Have you got anything yet, Sarah?" Dad asked.

"No, nothing yet, I'll join some of the agencies as soon as we're moved in and settled," I said.

"Well look you two, I've got something for you," Dad spoke quietly, not wanting to make a fuss, and handed us a small brown envelope. Inside was a cheque for £1000.

"I'm sorry it's not much," he said, "But I hope it helps you a bit while you're starting out."

"Oh Dad, thank you!" I said.

"Thanks very much, Tony," James said.

I reached across and squeezed Dad's hand. I hadn't really been able to talk to him properly about moving in with James. It had happened so quickly that all I could do was tell him it was happening. I wanted to know his thoughts – was I making the right decision? Did he mind that we were so much closer to Hazel than him? However, I knew Dad and that he would just say that as long as I was happy, so was he. He had never been one to make judgements, and I don't suppose he was about to start.

We had a really good time that day and I felt extremely happy to have spent time together, both families, as if we were joining up and becoming a stronger unit in doing so.

I left university life with some sadness; mostly at leaving Chloe. I knew I'd had enough of studying for the time being and I quite liked the idea of a 9 – 5 job with a bit of cash to spend and a lovely home to return to at the end of the day.

Chloe went back to her parents' for three weeks and then she was off, into the air and across the seas.

James and I moved into our cottage and had a couple of weeks before he started his job so we made the most of them; unpacking, exploring the local area (although James of course knew it intimately already) and becoming a couple who lived together. We would cook meals together and share a bottle of wine at the table in our little cottage garden, watching the butterflies and bees fluttering and buzzing happily around our flowers. We went shopping together, put up curtains, and mowed the lawn.

It somehow felt like playing to me; not quite real, but that only made it all the more enjoyable.

Chapter Ten

I was surprised at how quickly I'd come to think of our little cottage as home. The first six months seemed to fly by and we renewed the rental contract for another year. I loved the location, with the soothing sounds of sheep calling to each other on the dales, and the range of countryside James and I could go walking in, with woodland and meadows to explore, a river to follow and some steep inclines to climb when we were feeling energetic.

I would go out walking sometimes on my own but James wasn't too keen on that.

"What if you got injured?" he said.

"I've got my phone," I waved it at him.

"Well what if you had no signal? Or what if you bumped into some dodgy weirdo while you were out?"

I laughed at his concerns but I didn't mind really. It was nice to know he cared, and I liked walking with him anyway. The fresh air and change of scenery did him as much good as me. His first year as a graduate trainee had already taken its toll on him. Long hours, and lots of dogged determination were needed to succeed. He might have had a good contact in Hazel, but the other graduates he was 'up against', as he put it, were just as ambitious as James, if not moreso.

In honesty, I was surprised at quite how serious he was about the job. It seemed to have brought out some attributes I had been previously unaware of. The soft-natured, quite relaxed English Literature student had grown into a harder, more focused businessman in the making. To me, he was the same as he'd always been, if a bit more tired and shorter tempered at times, but I could tell by the way that he talked about his job, he was no pushover at work.

Hazel, of course, was delighted.

"That's my boy!" she said, as James told her about some group presentation he was working on. He was paired off with Andy, who James seemed to see as his main competitor. While they were working together, I got the impression that each was trying to better the other.

James had been telling Hazel how he'd insisted that he take the lead on the presentation and that Andy had eventually backed down and agreed to this.

I was quietly flicking through a magazine while they discussed what the content should be, but I looked up when I heard Hazel say that and I caught the delighted expression on James' face. I rolled my eyes. I was well-used to his need to please his mum and it didn't really bother me. I'd rather that than somebody who treated their parents like they didn't exist.

"How's your work going, Sarah?" Hazel turned to me and I could feel the inverted commas she had inserted around the word 'work'.

As I'd planned, I had begun life after university by taking some temping jobs through an agency. The first two had been short-lived affairs, but then after about three months I had landed a job at a small communications agency, Blue Dolphin, supposedly doing admin but really doing whatever was needed. Sometimes I wrote press releases, or contacted the local press to notify them of the launch of some new scheme or other. At other times I reviewed adverts before they went into print, and sometimes I just did the filing and made the tea. It was not hard work, it was not great pay, but I liked the people – Alan, Jess and Bex, all in their 30s, who had studied together and begun the business together – I liked the hours, and being able to come home and just be at home.

I didn't have to worry about presentations or plan my strategy for success. I did what was required of me and I had an hour-long break for lunch every day, which I usually filled by aimlessly wandering around the shops or sitting on a bench eating my sandwiches and reading.

I still had it in mind that I would train to be a teacher, but Jess had approached me about taking on a longer contract with Blue Dolphin and I had found myself agreeing.

Clearly my career path was not impressing Hazel but I wasn't worried. She liked me and James living close by, and would often pop in to see me when James was working late and she was on her way home from work.

She had clearly done the competition thing and now traded on her reputation. As she believed that anybody was lucky to have her working for them (or 'with them' as she would say, she didn't believe in working *for* anybody), she followed regular working hours and got home from work in time to go out to her squash club or have some of her friends around for dinner.

James, however, did whatever hours he felt necessary to do his job to the best possible standards. I felt like he was pushing himself too hard, perhaps even in the wrong direction. I wasn't really convinced that the seemingly hard-nosed world of Retail was for him, but it was his choice. He had no problem with what I was doing, even when I was earning about half what he was, and I really appreciated that.

After a couple of years of renting the cottage, we were approached by the owners about buying it. My heart leapt. We just had to agree a price, and get a mortgage. I was aware that much of the responsibility for this would come down to James and I didn't want to put any more pressure on him. He was only 24, for goodness' sake; he needed to relax and enjoy life, not be tied to a mortgage and wrapped up in his career.

Hazel, however, came to our rescue.

"Look you two," she said, "I helped out James' brothers when they were starting out and now I want to do the same for you."

She handed us a cheque which would make a huge dent in the asking price of the house, and enable us to get a manageable mortgage. It flashed through my mind that this was not entirely altruistic – after all, by helping us buy this house she was effectively keeping us well within her reach – but I brushed that thought aside. She was, after all, enabling us to buy this house which I had quickly fallen in love with.

Chloe couldn't believe it when I told her. We were chatting on Skype one evening; she had extended her travels and was at the time working on a farm in the Australian outback.

"Oh my God, Sarah! You're so grown up!" she laughed.

"Here I am, still mucking about and living hand-to-mouth. You've got a job and a house."

"Nearly!" I laughed back, "It's not ours yet. And yes, I have got a job, but so have you. I have not yet got a career, and I do like to make that distinction."

"Well I'm coming to visit just as soon as I'm back in the UK."

"You'd better," I smiled, feeling her absence keenly just then.

"I'd better go," she said, I've got to get to work."

"Work, work, work, is that all you think about?" I grinned. "You're so boring."

"I know," she said, "Give my love to James. Tell him he's working too much and he'd better be there to say hello next time we speak."

"I will."

James and I would often go and visit Dad and Dawn at the weekends, and they always seemed incredibly happy. They both still worked at the same university and Dad was also writing a book.

They had been over to Canada together twice, and Dawn's mum had been for one long visit to the UK. I could tell Dawn missed Canada, but she seemed happy and settled. I was therefore very shocked one day when Dad turned up on my doorstep ashen-faced.

"Dad! What's wrong?" I asked, ushering him in out of the wind. He stepped inside and a few brown leaves accompanied him in, whirling onto the hallway floor.

"Hi Sarah," he said, kissing me but not looking me in the eye. He busied himself taking off his jacket and shoes and followed me into the kitchen.

"God... where to start?" he said, sitting down heavily and rubbing his eyes.

"Are you OK?" I asked, feeling an immediate panic that he might be ill.

"Yes, yes, I'm fine," he said, "It's nothing like that." He gave me a slight smile, understanding my worry without me having to tell him.

"It's not me," he continued, "it's Dawn. She's moving back to Canada."

"What?" I said, shocked. "She can't be!"

"She is," he laughed grimly.

"But what about you?" I asked.

"Oh God, it's a bloody mess. She's... do you mind me talking to you about this?"

"Of course I don't," I said emphatically, placing a mug of steaming tea in front of him.

"She wants a family, Sarah; of course she does. She's in her 30s and thinks time's running out."

"Right," I answered cautiously, a whirlpool of thoughts in my mind. "And you... don't want one?"

"I've got one!" he laughed. "You! I've got you."

Shit, I was thinking, although it had crossed my mind from time to time. I had always assumed Dawn was just not interested in being a mum. She seemed so into her work.

"Oh God, Dad," I didn't really know what to say. "Do you... could you... would you want to start another family?"

"Well I don't have to worry about it, Dawn seems to think that's just not an option. She says it wouldn't be fair on you, or me. She's seen how much we've been through together, you and I. Says she couldn't expect me to even consider starting again."

"But she loves you!" I exclaimed.

"She says she does," that grim laugh again.

"What are you going to do, Dad?"

"I don't know. I just... don't know."

We sat in silence for a while, sipping our tea, contemplating Dad's life without Dawn and listening to the gusts of wind growing stronger outside, squeezing and whistling their way in through the gap under the door.

I was shocked by Dad's news, but I didn't have a lot of time to worry about it because James and I had a trip away planned. We were going to a five-star spa hotel in the Lake District, and I had been really looking forward to it. It wasn't the kind of thing we normally did.

Neither James or I were particularly bothered about 'pampering' ourselves, in fact to be honest that word made me cringe a little.

However, Hazel had been to this hotel and it did really look fantastic. It was a new, smart building with huge glass sides, a spa pool tucked into a sedan roof, heated by solar panels, and an indoor pool with a waterfall. There were saunas and steam rooms, and each bedroom had a balcony from which to 'gaze at stunning, uninterrupted scenery', as the brochure put it.

I thought that James could do with the break because of his work, and I was not averse to three days relaxing. I knew that the hotel was right in the middle of amazing walking country so we could go out and explore if it all got a bit stifling.

Hazel had offered to pay for our break as an early Christmas present and as always she made it very hard for us to refuse.

"Look, it's not a problem, you two deserve a break," she said in answer to my initial protestation. "Jamie works so hard."

I didn't get a mention there, I noticed, but not to worry. The truth was, I didn't work as hard as James. However, I did work hard at my job and I also did everything around the house. All the shopping, cleaning and cooking. I didn't mind, I really quite enjoyed it, but I knew that Hazel looked on it as menial.

Anyway, we accepted her offer after a short while and I had begun to really look forward to our trip.

The day before we were due to go away, Dad came to pay me another visit. James was working late as always so I was glad of Dad's company. Right from the outset, however, I knew there was something on his mind. I wanted to let him come to it in his own time though.

"Do you want something to eat, Dad?" I asked. I had been cooking a sweet potato and aubergine curry and my mouth was watering. I hoped he'd say yes as it would give me a good excuse to eat early. Often by the time James got home, my stomach was tying itself in knots, but I usually felt like I should wait for him.

"No, you're OK thanks Sarah."

Damn.

"Cup of tea then?"

"Yeah," he sighed.

"OK Dad," I said as I put the kettle on, "What's up? Are things still bad with Dawn?"

"No, they're... they're much better actually," he answered glumly.

"OK... that's good isn't it?"

"Yeah," he sighed again.

"Is she going to stay?" I asked hopefully.

"No, well, that's what I wanted to talk to you about, love." Dad rubbed his eyes and pinched the skin on the bridge of his nose. "Things are better, much better, but nothing has really changed for Dawn. She still wants to go back to Canada."

"Oh no, Dad," I said. "I'm so sorry."

"Yeah," he said slowly and looked down at his cup of tea. "The thing is, shit, sorry, I don't know how to tell you this."

"What?" I asked, my heart beating rapidly as I wondered what he was about to say.

He looked at me, straight at me, "I'm going to go with her."

This took a moment, more than a moment, to sink in. I was desperately searching inside myself for the correct way to react.

"Oh... wow..." I said weakly.

"Hmm, wow," Dad laughed without humour. "I have been dreading telling you, Sarah. Dreading it. You have no idea how many times I've gone back and forth to make this decision. I don't want to leave you, you must know that, but I don't want to lose Dawn and you're happy with James and Hazel's right there in the next village..."

Well yeah, I thought, *she is, and she's OK, but she's James' mum, not mine.* She was always generous to me, but I was under no illusion that if anything ever went wrong between me and James, I'd be out of the picture without a moment's thought.

Dad, on the other hand, was mine. My dad. The man who had looked after me from the moment I was born, who was absolutely, unconditionally, always going to look out for me. Mum had died, Grandma was always there for me but, well, Dad was my dad. How could I possibly do without him?

Of course I didn't say any of that. What I said was, "Yeah, don't worry, Dad, I'll be OK. What about your work though? And the house?"

I thought I should turn the conversation to practical matters as soon as possible. Dad was no fool; he could see I was upset and he had a concerned look as he played along with my game, pretending that these were the important details.

"Well I've got a sabbatical from the university, starting just after Christmas," he said, "And I'm not going to sell the house. I'll try and rent it out. In fact, I was wondering whether you and James might be interested..?"

Oh God, I thought. I hadn't even told him we were buying this place. It was my turn to look sheepish.

"Ah, thanks Dad but, erm, we're actually going to buy the cottage. The owner offered us first refusal."

"Well that's great!" Dad looked surprised, "Can I do anything to help? Do you need some advice about mortgages? A loan for the deposit? I don't mean to pry, I know you're both earning, but it's hard getting a deposit together."

"Thanks Dad, but Hazel's helped us with the deposit, and to find a mortgage. It's a really good one," I added this last bit brightly, knowing that he might feel a bit put out he hadn't been consulted on this, or even informed of it.

The truth was, I didn't feel it was appropriate to tell him about it the time that he came round to tell me things were not good with Dawn, and then everything had moved so fast. I just hadn't got round to telling him.

"Have you told Grandma?" I asked, changing the subject. She would miss Dad too.

"She's next on my list," he sighed.

We both sipped our tea contemplatively. I felt cold, perhaps with the shock that Dad was going overseas. How would I get to see him now? I wondered. What part would he play in my life? But I was happy for him, genuinely happy, that he and Dawn had worked things out, because I knew she was good for him.

He didn't stay much longer. I think we had both gone into a sort of lockdown, preoccupied with our own thoughts and unsure of what to say. It reminded me of how things had been between us when I was a teenager. I had never really known how to broach important subjects with him and he, eaten up by grief, had seemed equally unsure.

When he left, however, we hugged for a long, long time.

"I love you, Sarah," he said into my hair.

"I love you too, Dad," I said, my face pressed into his jacket. When we pulled apart, I hoped he wouldn't notice the damp mark my tears had left.

The next day, James and I were on our way to the Lakes.

I had told him about Dad's news when he'd returned from work the previous night. His reply had left me fuming inwardly.

"Well at least we'll get good holidays. I've always wanted to go to Canada."

I couldn't believe my ears. What an insensitive, ridiculous thing to say. From the man (boy?) who lived within five minutes of his mum. I didn't speak. I turned away, filled the kettle at the sink. Tried not to respond as I knew that, if I did, it would not be pleasant.

"Are you OK, Sarah?" James asked eventually, coming up behind and putting his arms around me.

I felt my shoulders tense.

"Yeah..." I gulped against a hard lump of hurt in my throat, "It's just a weird thought. Dad being so far away. Not being able to see him."

"I know, it must be," he said soothingly, "but we'll go out and visit them. And surely he's going to come back here from time to time? What about his job? And his house?"

"I dunno," I shrugged, even though I did. I didn't want him thinking that those details were important.

"You'll be OK," he said. I hoped so.

By the time that we were in the car on the way to our hotel break, I had forgiven James. How would anyone know the right thing to say? I reasoned. I wasn't even sure of it myself. I had spoken to Dad a couple of times since the Monday, and apologised properly to him for not telling him about us buying the cottage. He sounded relieved, I think he was happy that he had told me, and pleased that we were OK, and I hope he was also at least a little bit excited about the prospect of moving to Canada.

"I can't wait for this," James said excitedly, squeezing my knee. I had made him promise not to bring any of his work paraphernalia – phone, laptop, etc. – with him, to make sure that we had a proper break and some time together, without anything else getting in the way.

The drive over was really good. The sun was shining, casting a glow upon the trees in their autumnal colours. We had the radio on loud, and I sang loudly along, casting off worries and sadness along the way. We turned down the volume as we drove into the village which housed the hotel. When we rounded a corner, we saw the place – resplendent on the top of a small hill. We smiled at each other.

It was amazing. The hotel staff were friendly and welcoming, and I was surprised by one of them taking our luggage from us and handling it onto a trolley. I was used to lugging my own bags around. I felt quite aware that my bag was a bit battered and worn, unlike James' which he had borrowed from Hazel.

Despite the price of the place and the fact that many of the clientele were surely far better off than us, there was no element of snobbery, from the staff at least. The porter led the way to the glass lift which whizzed almost soundlessly, it seemed, all the way to the top floor.

We followed the man wordlessly until he got to a door, slid the key card through the scanner, and handed it to James then flung the door open.

"The penthouse suite," he said.

"The..?" I said, thinking that there must be some mistake.

"Mrs Poole said to tell you it is her treat."

My jaw dropped. The room was enormous. More than a room. It had a living area with two vast plush settees and an enormous flat screen TV. The bed was all the way over on the other side of the room, and it was a monster of a thing. There were floor-to-ceiling windows along one side of the room, opening out onto a balcony, beyond which the unique scenery of the Lake District spread itself out as if solely for our pleasure.

"In the bathroom you'll find your own spa bath, one each," the man was saying, opening a further door to a bathroom the size of our lounge in the cottage. This too had enormous windows with far-reaching views. James squeezed my hand.

"I don't mind sharing," he whispered.

In the fridge was a stock of cold drinks, and snacks, and these were all to be taken whenever we liked, the porter said, there was no extra charge. He then gestured to a table with an ice bucket complete with champagne and two glasses. I was overwhelmed. He carried on talking, explaining where things were, how they worked, and what we were to do when we wanted a treatment at the spa downstairs.

"I'll leave you to it," the porter said, and as soon as the door swung shut behind him, I ran across the room and flung myself onto the bed.

"Oh my God! I can't believe this!" I giggled, "We need to ring your mum to say thank you. This is soooo nice of her."

"Mum can wait," James said, landing on the bed next to me. I raised an eyebrow. That wasn't something James would often say.

He pulled me close to him and drew me into a kiss then he picked up a remote from the bedside table and pressed a button. The curtains began to close and a soft light came on as the room was enveloped in darkness. I pulled him back to me and we lost ourselves.

Afterwards, we pulled on the dressing gowns which were provided by the hotel and sipped glasses of champagne.

"OK?" he asked me, smiling.

"Just a bit," I said, grinning.

"I just wanted to say," James said, "that I am sorry about your dad going away. I'm sorry if I didn't sound it last night."

"Don't," I said, not wanting to think about it right then. "It's fine. I'll be OK."

"I'll look after you," he said and I smiled at his earnest expression.

"In fact," James continued, "I was going to wait till dinner to do this but I can't. I just can't. This is too perfect."

Something about his tone of voice made me look at him sharply and before I knew it, he was down on one knee.

"Sarah Marchley," James said, "Would you do me the honour of becoming my wife?"

He pulled a small box from his bag and I opened it to see a beautiful ring, sapphires in platinum. Understated and shining like a promise.

"Yes," I said. "Yes of course."

We smiled at each other disbelievingly then laughed out loud. He put the ring on my finger and we collapsed next to each other on the settee, taking it all in.

Chapter Eleven

The weekend in the Lakes seemed like a milestone in my life. I was still smarting from the idea of Dad going abroad but now I was engaged. I was taking the next step into the world of grownups. I knew that James and I were young but I reasoned that Mum had been younger than that when she married Dad, and he had only been a little older.

I was the first of my friends, by a long way, to be considering such a life-changing decision. Rachel was living with her boyfriend, and Jenna from university had recently bought a place with her partner Daisy. That was about it though. Everybody else I knew was prolonging the student lifestyle, albeit most with the unfortunate inconvenience of having to work five days a week.

I wondered what people would think when I told them but I pushed everybody else out of my mind, and decided to concentrate solely on myself and my husband-to-be, and to give this pampering lark a go – see what all the fuss was about.

As it turned out, it wasn't too bad at all. That first night, we went into the rooftop pool when most of the other guests were having dinner, so it was just the two of us for a while. The night had long since turned dark and the mist had thickened so that the steam from the pool rose and mingled with it. Lights were placed discreetly around the decking and under the water's surface, projecting ripples onto the walls and metal handrails.

There were loungers around the outside but it was far too cold to use them. Instead, we cuddled up in the warmth of the water, and swam a few lengths before another couple came up the stairs, laughing loudly, and we decided it was time to return to our room. We ordered room service and ate at the dining table, listening to music and chatting.

"I can't believe how lucky I am to have met you, Sarah," said James, looking at me almost shyly. "I always wanted to get married. You know me, I'm not interested in playing the field. I just want to settle down, have a good job, a nice home, and a family."

"Steady on!" I laughed, "I think we can wait a little while for the last one of those things!"

"You do want children, don't you?" he asked, and I saw the worry on his face.

"Yes I do, of course I do," I said, "Just not yet. I'm only 23."

"Nearly the age your mum was when she had you." James looked at me.

"Yes," I said, "but she was already a teacher by then. I still need to get my career going. There's no rush."

After dinner, we collapsed onto one of the vast settees together and James put on the real-effect fire. I leant on him and looked at the ring on my hand.

"I can't believe this!" I said, "This is so exciting. Getting married. Me."

"Yes you, why not you? Of course you!" James exclaimed, and kissed me.

I leaned against him and in a short while felt myself getting drowsy. I must have drifted off, and the next thing I knew, James was carrying me over to the bed.

"Careful!" I smiled at him, "I don't want you giving yourself a hernia!"

"You're as light as a feather!" he smiled at me, then pretended to drop me on the bed. I lay back against the pillows, my sleepy mind struggling to take it all in. Somewhere downstairs music was playing but up there it was quiet and I could hear an owl somewhere close by.

We lay together in that bed, and even though I had been asleep just moments before, I found myself wide awake as James dozed off. He had his arm around me and I was getting uncomfortable but I didn't want to disturb him. In time, I moved his arm away and I carefully moved myself onto the floor. I made a cup of tea in the kitchen and took it onto the balcony, wrapping myself in one of the throws from the settees.

Outside the air was cool but the mist had thinned a little so that I could make out the odd star in the otherwise black night. There was the occasional bleat of a sheep, and a few owls now calling out into the stillness, but other than that it was quiet.

I sipped at the tea and contemplated all that had occurred that week. I was losing my dad, or I felt like I was. That thought came to me uninvited. I didn't want to think of it like that but, if he stayed out there in Canada then that was essentially what would happen.

He would always be my dad, I would always love him, but he would be completely removed from my day-to-day life. I felt tears spike my eyes as I thought of this. What would I do without him? He was truly my one constant.

On the other hand, I was about to move on in my own life. Get married. Be Mrs Poole. One day, have children.

I wanted Dad there when I got married. I wanted him there when I had children. But I couldn't expect him to miss his opportunity at happiness just for me. Realistically, I knew he would be there when I actually got married anyway. As if I would have a wedding without him. It would be something more to think about, I supposed, but James and I had not got as far as talking about when we would get married.

I think James had sensed that, although I had accepted his proposal, I was still fairly surprised by it. The details could come later, I hoped, and we would just enjoy our break away together. We could tell our parents face-to-face, whenever we next saw them.

Eventually, I returned to our warm room and thought of Hazel and how kind she had been to book this for us. I hoped she'd be happy when she heard our news. Dad would be happy because I was.

I thought of telling Chloe, and wondered what she would think. She and I were living such different lives, would she think I was mad for settling down so early? I thought not but I knew it was not something she would ever do.

The rest of our time away was better than I could have imagined. We came close to an argument when I discovered James checking his work emails, on his work phone, which he had promised not to bring with him. I had gone for a body wrap at the spa and James had said he was going to read the paper in our room. When I returned, however, there he was, his guilty expression illuminated by the light of his phone.

I must have looked annoyed but I was having such a good time, I really didn't want it ruined. Also, I reasoned that I had to accept him as he was. If he was so into his work, so be it. He switched his phone off again anyway and he seemed to really enjoy our walks, swims, and the wonderful food in the hotel restaurant.

I wished I'd taken a photo of him when we arrived and one the day we were leaving, as his face looked so different. He had colour in his cheeks and shining eyes. His jaw was no longer tensed up. He just looked so well.

As we left our room, I looked longingly back at it and put my arms around James' waist.

"Do we have to go?"

"'Fraid so," James kissed me on my forehead.

"We should drop in and see your mum on the way back," I said, "To thank her for this and to tell her our news!"

"Yeah, definitely," James replied, "She'd love to see us, and what the ring looks like in its rightful place."

"Oh," I said. "She's seen the ring?"

"Yeah, of course! You don't think I could have chosen that on my own, do you?"

Chapter Twelve

I was not looking forward to Christmas. Although it would be my first as a homeowner and a real life fiancée, it also coincided with Dad leaving for Canada.

Dawn had already gone and they were to spend Christmas apart so that James and I could spend the day with him. The plan was that he would fly out on 29th December, to start the new year in his new home. I knew that for Dad, and especially Dawn, this would have some positive significance – a new start, turning over a new leaf, etc… so I was trying to convince myself I should also begin the new year the right way. I had decided that I should busy myself with planning the wedding. This would give me plenty to think about while I got used to Dad being away.

Once we had returned from our Lake District break and told our family and friends our news, I had felt a bit flat. I knew it was because of Dad leaving, and I reasoned that I should have something to focus on. So, although James had not been in much of a rush to set a date, I decided it was the best thing we could do and that the sooner, the better.

We discussed it with Hazel, who seemed delighted. She offered to help in any way she could with the planning and I graciously thanked her.

"We've got a few ideas, haven't we, James?" I asked, smiling at my husband-to-be. I really did appreciate all that she had done for us but I was very keen that this wedding should be ours. Mine and James'.

Dad, who I suspected had thought it was a little early for us even to be getting engaged, had reacted cautiously to my suggestion of getting married the next year. I had in mind a summer wedding. Mum's birthday had been in June and as it was going to be a Saturday the following year, I thought we could get married on that date. I also knew that would make it easier for Dad to come back as it was well within the summer break.

"Wow," Dad said when I told him. "What's the rush? Not pregnant are you..?"

He was joking when he said this but as the words came out of his mouth, I saw him think a little harder about what he was saying. Knowing Dad, he was worried firstly that he would have hurt my feelings with his quip but also that it might possibly be true.

"No, Dad!" I rolled my eyes and laughed, "I just can't see the point in waiting. Will you be able to come back though? You will won't you?"

"Of course I will, Sarah, as if anything in the world would stop me. I hope you're not arranging this to fit in with me though. I would work something out to suit any date you and James chose. I do think that your Mum would have been so happy to think of you choosing her birthday though."

We were both quiet for a while.

"You don't think Dawn will be upset by it?" I asked.

"No, she won't, I'm sure she won't. Why should she? It's not like she thinks she's your mum, Sarah. She will completely appreciate the idea, I'm sure."

He was right. I told her myself when she came home later that day and she just gave me an enormous hug.

"I'm sure your Mum would have loved that idea," she said, "And I'll be there to celebrate with you. Assuming I'm invited, of course…"

"I should think so," I said, "I am going to miss you, Dawn. I hope you know that."

"I do," she said, squeezing my arm. "And I'll take care of your father, you know. I wish it wasn't like this, I really do, I'm not trying to prise him away from you."

"I know that," I smiled. "Life's just complicated sometimes, isn't it?"

"It is."

At the end of November, Dawn left, and December was a whirlwind of Christmas parties, packing up Dad's belongings and sorting through my own old childhood stuff.

In the attic were so many boxes from our past. It took us a whole weekend to go through them. Many were marked with Mum's careful handwriting.

We tried to be ruthless and pragmatic, just assessing what we did and did not want.

I took away my old toys and a few other boxes. Two of them were labelled 'Pregnancy and Baby'. A brief look revealed a lot of clothes, some soft blankets and a few books. I decided that I would take those too. Dad gave me a look.

"For the future!" I told him. "Hopefully I'll need them one day."

"I'd think they'll be a bit old-fashioned for you," he replied.

"Well maybe," I said, "But I'd quite like to have a look through them."

I could see it was painful for Dad at times so I tried to lighten the mood and keep him focused on his plans for Canada.

We talked about where he would live, just outside Toronto, and when I would be able to visit him. James and I had already discussed maybe May time, to have a break from the build up to the wedding.

"Five months," Dad said wistfully, "How can I go five months without seeing you?"

"It will go fast," I said, not looking at him, "You'll see. Then we'll get a full two weeks with you as well! We can do loads of tourist stuff."

"That's true," Dad said, "It'll be fun exploring with someone who's not a native."

"That's the spirit!" I said, grinning; something he always used to say to me as a child when he was trying to cheer me up.

Soon, Dad's house – my home, Dawn's home, Mum's home at different times, but always his home – almost felt like somebody else's. Sparsely furnished, with just the bare essentials necessary for the remainder of his time in the UK.

On my last visit there before Dad's departure, I wandered around the place listlessly, trying to recall as many memories as I could. With Dad going to Canada, I knew that this house could be out of our lives forever and, although I knew it to be just a pile of bricks really, it was always more than that. It was my last material link to my mum and I felt it held some kind of memory of us in its walls. I realised that, as I walked, I was listening hard, trying to hear echoes of our past, desperate for some kind of message from Mum. I realise that sounds crazy but I wanted to feel that she gave us her blessing to move on. I felt like we were betraying her.

I would never have mentioned that to Dad, of course. It was lucky that he came in when he did, and called my name up the stairs. I was sitting on my bedroom windowsill, picturing the cherry blossom tree in bloom and trying to remember all the times I'd sat in that exact same place before.

I told myself to get it together and called back to Dad. Splashing water onto my face, I ran downstairs to greet him. I was being ridiculous. Dad had Dawn to think of. I had James. We both had futures and lives to live. I would always miss Mum and I was sure that Dad would too but I couldn't expect Dawn to want to live forever in the home of her partner's late wife. Really, it was amazing that she had done for so long already.

I said a mental farewell to my home then Dad and I walked out together. I could have spent many more hours in there, but I knew it would all be futile. Now it was time to focus, on making the most of Christmas and my last few days with Dad before he left.

The plan was that we would spend Christmas at James' and my house, and Hazel would come to have dinner with us. Not something I was that thrilled about; I had really hoped to have some time with just Dad, and Hazel did have a tendency to take over pretty much any conversation she was within earshot of, but all of James' brothers were apparently otherwise engaged, so as usual it fell to us to make sure she was not on her own.

Dad stayed with us on Christmas Eve and came with James and me to Midnight Mass in our village church. I loved this. The magic of Christmas was alive and well in the old stone church, with its candles and organ and small choir. James and I knew a lot of our neighbours and most of the villagers came to the service even if they didn't usually bother with church. It felt very warm and comfortable to be there that night.

Outside, a frost had crackled its way across the grass and the windows of cars so that when we walked out into the chill night air, our breath puffing from our mouths like tiny clouds, we were greeted by a twinkling, crisp landscape and a cold, hard ground to crunch across on our journeys home.

Back at our house, James went to bed while Dad and I reminisced about Christmases past.

"I always loved Christmas when I was a boy," Dad told me, "but they were nothing compared to when you were little. I just loved it, your face all rosy and pink with excitement at the thought of Father Christmas having been. Your mum and I used to stay up late every Christmas Eve, wrapping your presents, and then you'd have us up at about five the next morning but it never mattered."

"Dad, do you remember what Mum got me that last Christmas?" I asked him.

"I do, Sarah, I do."

I was glad. I had never mentioned it to him. The last Christmas with Mum had been extra special. I felt it at the time but didn't really register it in my consciousness. Mum had clearly made it her job to ensure everything was perfect. I was too old for Father Christmas but we kept up the pretence of it anyway, with a stocking left in my bedroom and a sack full of presents downstairs. That year I had the usual books, chocolates, socks, pyjamas, etc., but I also had a special gift from Mum which Dad had not known about. She had bought me a lockable diary. A very nice, leather-bound green book which had a lock on it and a matching green pen which slipped inside the internal pocket. I loved it immediately.

I had recently read *The Diary of Anne Frank* and I thought that this must have prompted Mum's purchase.

"That's yours, Sarah," I remember her saying. "It's your book, it's your space, you can write whatever you want in it – anything – and nobody is going to read it unless you want them to. We won't look, will we, Tony? Not even if we find the key."

"No, of course not," said Dad, "I didn't know we'd got Sarah that, though."

"Ah, no," said Mum, "It's my little surprise, as is this…"

She pulled out a small package from behind one of the cards

on the mantelpiece and gave it to Dad. He opened it to find a chain with an oval pendant.

"What's this..?" said Dad, puzzled.

"It's St Anthony, your namesake," Mum had replied. "St Anthony of Padua." She extracted a little slip of paper from the jewellery case and read from it. "His life is meant to be a great example of courage in facing the ups and downs of life, the call to forgive and love, concern for others' needs and dealing with crises of all sizes."

"Wow," said Dad, "I don't think I knew anything about him."

"No, nor me," said Mum, "but I was just looking for something a bit special for you this year."

"Ah thank you," Dad pulled her towards him and hugged her. "I'm afraid I only got you the usual bits and pieces though."

"That's fine," said Mum, "I just thought you might like it."

"I love it," Dad had said, "My turn to get you something special next year."

Mum had just smiled.

"So did you ever use that diary?" Dad asked me.

"I did," I said, "Every day, pretty much, for the full five years of it. Then I went out and bought an identical one when I was sixteen. I've not replaced it this time though."

I had used my diary less frequently as time had gone on at university, until I no longer really felt a need to express my thoughts in that way. When I had begun that first book, each new page felt like a chance to be me, to express my thoughts and feelings. The matters I wrote about were relatively trivial – what had happened at school, having friends around for tea, any arguments I may have had with Mum and Dad. However, within months the entries had changed dramatically. This of course was in line with Mum dying. There was a good gap of nothingness when I was too shocked, too numb to even remember I had a diary. Then there were short entries when I had felt I'd wanted to write but once I'd got the pen in my hand, had no ideas as to what I wanted to say. Gradually, the writing filled the pages once more. Strangely, there are few mentions of Mum. There are clear references to feelings, e.g. 'Today has been awful' and allusions about my circumstances, e.g. 'I don't have anybody to talk to' but very few specific references to Mum.

Dad makes many an appearance, from the mundane facts of

days spent together to the more plaintive 'he doesn't understand me, he doesn't understand anything' and the usual teenage angst.

I rarely refer back to the pages and pages of scrawl, however, knowing now that the diary was a great tool for me to vent my feelings, in complete and utter privacy, where I could be honest and dramatic about things and say what I liked without hurting anybody. Mum would have known all of this when she bought that first diary for me. She would have known that I'd need that when she died and just while growing up. This gift was a practical way she could help me in those years after she had gone.

"Well I kept my promise and never read it," Dad said.

"I know, Dad, I know that."

"She was great, wasn't she?" he said.

"Yes, Dad, she was. Have you still got your pendant?"

Dad fished around inside the collar of his shirt and pulled it out.

I smiled. "Doesn't Dawn mind?"

"Not at all, I offered to remove it – though I didn't know if I wanted to, it just seemed the right thing – but she insisted I keep it. She says it is part of me, that your mum was an important part of my life, and that it's not right to put things away just because they're from the past."

"She's pretty great too, Dad."

It was his turn to smile.

Christmas Day passed as I had hoped, with lots of fun and drink and food, a wintry walk in the afternoon, and a lazy evening watching Christmas TV.

Hazel had been OK – even she could see that this day was important to Dad and I. Anyway, soon he would be gone and we would be all hers to do with as she pleased.

In bed that night, I lay thinking about Dad, and how life might be without him nearby. I was going to be brave, and grown up, and get on with things. I would apply for the teaching course, I would stand up for myself with Hazel as I knew she would turn up her nose at this career choice, and I would go for it. If successful, I could start the following year. In the meantime, I could carry on enjoying life.

I thought again of my diary, and how much it had helped me

when I was at school. There was nobody I could talk to, really. I know now Dad would have listened if I had asked him to but he was struggling so much with coming to terms with things that he had never actively sought me out. Something I knew he felt bad about. My school friendships had never developed into deep and meaningful relationships, as I had been aware of my friends' inability to cope with my change in circumstances. Again, not really their fault, they were just very young themselves, but at the time it had made me resentful to a degree. Aunt Elizabeth was overseas, my grandparents were another generation on. I turned to my diary with my secrets.

I thought about my entry when my periods had begun. I remembered this one well. 'I started today, and it bloody hurts. Really, really hurts. I have been in bed crying all day, and Dad doesn't know why. Or he might do. I've got the things Aunt Elizabeth left last time she was here but I don't know if I'm using them right. I just want this to go away.'

I thought again. My periods! James sighed in his sleep next to me, rolling over as he did so. I turned onto my back, imagining my eyes wide and cartoon-like in our dark room. I desperately tried to recall the last time I'd had cause to use those 'things' I had referred to that day.

Chapter Thirteen

I was a bit of a wreck after Dad had gone. On the morning of his departure, I drove him to Manchester Airport but I didn't hang around. I had to get on with it, as did he. We had a quick coffee, quite lost for words, then hugged tightly. I couldn't look at him; every time I did, I felt choked.

I could sense him shaking as we hugged.

"I'll just... I'm going to just go," I spluttered. "I have to."

"OK," he managed to get out. "I love you. You know that, Sarah? I love you so much."

"I love you too, Dad. I'll see you soon," I managed to squeeze out a smile before turning away and rushing off. I had hoped I'd make it back to the car before I broke down. I hate crying in front of people but on this occasion I couldn't hold it back.

I was attracting sympathetic and curious glances from passers-by, which I ignored as I rushed to the relative privacy of my car. There, I sat sobbing for I don't know how long, until I felt drained and my eyes ached. I closed them, against the drab December day and the darkness of the car park, and slowly I calmed down.

Onwards and upwards, I told myself, or onwards at the very least. I was steadfastly ignoring that seed of possibility that had lodged itself firmly in my mind. Could I be..? I could, I knew it, but I really couldn't believe it. I determined to see in the New Year at Hazel's house party, as planned, go back to work, as planned, and then in a couple of weeks if there was still no sign of my period I would test to see if there was something going on which was certainly not planned.

Of course in reality I couldn't wait that long. I bought pregnancy testing kits on New Year's Eve and I was in the bathroom, about to peel open one of the strange, silvery packages, when I heard the phone ring. Then James' voice. Then a scurrying up the stairs.

"Sarah! It's your dad!"

I couldn't help but smile at James' voice. He sounded excited for me. He knew I'd been waiting for this call. I'd had an email from Dad to tell me he'd arrived safely but I had not yet spoken to him. Although it was only a few days previously, it seemed like weeks since I'd seen him. I hurriedly stuffed the testing kit in with my boxes of tampons.

"Thanks," I smiled at James and took the phone from him. "Dad!"

"Sarah, love!" Dad's voice was full of relief. "How are you?"

"I'm OK, I'm fine thanks," I said happily, having absolutely no intention of letting him know what was on my mind. "How's Canada? How's Dawn?"

"Great, just great," he said, and it struck me that we were now being shy with each other. Unsure of what to say in this unfamiliar situation.

"What time is it there?" I asked, kicking myself. I may as well have asked him what the weather was like.

"It's early... Dawn's still in bed. I just couldn't wait to speak to you. It's about... 6am..."

"That's so weird!" I said. "It's about lunchtime here."

"Oh yeah, that's right, I guess you're going over to Hazel's soon?"

"Yeah, we're going to help her get everything ready for tonight."

"I bet it's going to be quite a party."

"It should be, yeah, of course her friends in high places can't make it," I laughed.

"Funny that," Dad chuckled. It wasn't very kind of us but Dad and I had a bit of a joke between ourselves that Hazel was making up these 'friends' who included a couple of very, very high profile retail magnates and a hugely successful businessman famed for his hot air ballooning exploits. I certainly had never seen any sign of them.

"What are you doing for New Year's?" I asked.

"We're going to have a quiet one," he said and I smiled. He and Dawn must have missed each other a lot over the previous few weeks. I was sure they would just enjoy an evening in together.

"I'd better go actually, Dad, Hazel'll be waiting for us. You get yourself some breakfast. I'll ring you tomorrow."

"Alright then, have a good time tonight. Don't drink too much!"

"I won't," I said, and I knew that I wouldn't. I had a feeling I shouldn't be drinking at all.

Hazel's party was 'quite a party' as Dad had put it. She had caterers in and waiting staff so that all the guests were never more than ten feet from another glass of bubbly or a canapé.

The food was delicious and I realised I was ravenous. Those tiny little scraps of cheese and sunblush tomatoes on miniature pancakes just weren't hitting the mark. I longed for dinner but it was a long time coming. I had really hoped to be sitting by James at the table but Hazel had done that thing of mixing her guests up. She had seated me by the wife of one of her colleagues and, mercifully, at the end of the table by the window with nobody on my other side.

I smiled at my neighbour and we introduced ourselves. She was wearing enough make up for all of the 33 guests, and her hair was bleached and straightened to within an inch of its life. As she smiled insincerely at me, I realised that the same could be said for her teeth.

"So, how do you know Hazel?" she asked.

"I'm engaged to her son."

"Ooh, which one?" she asked.

"James," I said, pointing him out.

"Jamie?" she exclaimed, "Lucky you! I've heard all about him from Gordon, he reckons he's the best thing since sliced bread. Bit of a spunk too, isn't he?"

"James?" I asked, surprised, and then felt bad.

It may sound awful but I didn't really think of him that way. He was… James. I loved him, I found him attractive of course, but I had not really considered other people doing so. I looked at him then, across the table, all clean shaven and smart in his new shirt, and saw what she meant.

He caught my eye and I smiled widely at him. He grinned happily back. Then I realised I had subconsciously placed my hand on my stomach. Hmm.

Liz, my neighbour, turned out to be pleasant enough, although I thought only superficially so. When she found out I planned to be a teacher, she said that she had hated all her teachers then she giggled, realising that may have sounded quite rude. I just smiled.

Luckily she knew the man on her other side quite well as he had worked with Gordon some years before, apparently. From what I could see, the world of Retail was very incestuous, as most of the people there either worked together, had done in the past, planned to in the future, or a combination of all three. There was certainly a lot of back-slapping and mutual appreciation going on amidst the guffaws and boasting. I soon tuned it out and concentrated on eating as much food as I could.

Liz 'couldn't manage another bite' of the chocolate brownie she had sliced the smallest corner from. I happily slid it over to my plate and devoured the lot. I thought I detected mild distaste from her at this point but I couldn't care less.

When the cheese and biscuits came round, I avoided the soft cheeses and blue cheeses as I thought I'd heard somewhere these could be bad for unborn babies. However, I had about three servings of the cheddar, a good number of biscuits, and became slightly obsessed by one of the chutneys.

After dinner, coffee and chocolates were served.

While the other guests had had their fill and wandered away from the dining room, I surreptitiously hoovered up the uneaten chocolates.

My appetite sated, I went to find James, who was outside having a cigar with one of his senior colleagues. I raised an eyebrow internally at the cigar. Since when did James smoke anything, never mind cigars? I didn't have long to wonder this as the first waft of the smoke hitting my nostrils caused my stomach to lurch and I had seconds to run to the bushes and throw up. So elegant.

I turned, embarrassed, to James, who looked half-annoyed, half-concerned, and his colleague, who looked amused.

"Had a few too many, eh? Not to worry, it's New Year's Eve!" he said merrily.

"Are you OK?" asked James.

"Yeah, I'm... I'm fine," I said, "But I think I need to go and lie down. I'll be back soon."

I was relieved we were staying at Hazel's. I made my way inside, praying that I wouldn't meet anybody I would have to talk to. I forced smiles on people as I pushed past them as politely as possible and then I had made it to the staircase. Each step filled me with relief and finally I made it to our room. I sank onto the cool covers and pulled a blanket over myself. I would just rest a little while, I thought, closing my eyes.

"Sarah... Sarah..." James whispered his drunken breath across my face, smudging a kiss across my cheek. "Happy New Year!"

I opened my eyes groggily. "Shit. Did I fall asleep?"

"Guess so!" he hiccupped happily. "Don't worry about it. Are you feeling better?"

"Erm... I think so..." I answered cautiously, unwilling to commit myself either way until I'd woken up a bit more. I was happy to find I was feeling much better. Suddenly quite wide awake, in fact. I heard a couple of car doors slam outside and realised that the chatter and clatter I'd heard down below when I'd been drifting off to sleep was gone.

"Have I missed the party?" I asked.

"Well, the end of it, I guess, but don't worry!" James reassured me again. "It was pretty much shop talk most of the night anyway. You would probably have been bored."

He stripped off his clothes then got under the covers. I realised I was still fully clothed so I followed suit, getting under the super-soft duvet with him. It felt like the bed sighed around me.

"I love you," I said.

"I love you too," James replied, "And I love New Year's Eve because it always reminds me of the night we got together."

He nestled into my shoulder and was snoring moments. I thought of his words, and I thought of what I knew by then was going on inside me. I thought it would all be OK.

Chapter Fourteen

On New Year's Day I woke up to a very hungover James, who was hanging over the en suite bathroom toilet (all Hazel's four bedrooms had en suites, of course) and looking very sorry for himself. Unfortunately this brought on an immediate reaction in me and I had to dash to the sink and follow suit.

"Uargh..." James groaned, "You look like I feel. I didn't think you drank that much last night though?"

"I didn't," I lamented, "It must have been something I ate."

"Yeah, that would make sense, it must have been something I ate too."

Mmm, I thought. *Not the wine, beer, whisky and cigars, then.*

I sat on the edge of the bath until I felt better then I persuaded James to get back into bed while I, suddenly ravenous, went in search of some breakfast.

Downstairs I found a distinctly bright-eyed Hazel. I remembered her trick when throwing parties, which was to fill everybody else's glass as often as possible whilst remaining stone cold sober.

"That way, Sarah, you're a step ahead of the rest," she'd told me. "People are much more honest when they're drunk, and you can get a lot more out of them."

I'd just smiled but I did wonder how anybody could go through life being so cold and hard-nosed.

On that particular morning, however, despite her bright and breezy appearance, I got the distinct impression I'd rattled her somewhat. Upon the appearance of a slightly flustered-looking Gordon (husband of Liz, my neighbour from the previous evening's dinner) from the conservatory – which, if I was not very much mistaken, Hazel had not long since vacated - I started to form an idea of why this would be.

"Morning!" I said cheerily, giving no clues as to my suspicions. "Sleep well?"

"Oh lovely, thanks Sarah," Hazel had quickly recovered herself, "You met Gordon last night didn't you?"

"Oh yes," I said innocently, "I think I was sitting next to your wife, wasn't I?"

"Oh were you? I'm not sure." Gordon stammered.

"Gordon was right next to me, weren't you?" Hazel boomed, "I put Liz next to Sarah because Sarah's so lovely and easy to talk to."

From most people this would be a compliment. Not Hazel. Who, after all, would want to be lovely or easy to talk to when there was so much more to be gained by getting one up on someone?

"I'm starving," I said, "Do you mind if I get something to eat?"

"Just help yourself, love, you know where everything is. I was just showing Gordon my garden."

I'm sure you were, I thought.

"Well I'll leave you to it," I said and went through to the kitchen.

I could hear their hushed voices but I didn't want to know. It was, after all, none of my business what my mother-in-law-to-be got up to. I wasn't worried on her behalf as she could clearly look after herself and I didn't know Gordon or Liz enough to care particularly about the state of their relationship. I wondered idly if James had any idea of what his mother got up to.

In the kitchen I helped myself to a bowl of cereal, which I ate standing up so that I could easily pour myself another. I made a cup of tea and I looked around for some bread. I needed toast, and lots of it.

As I was eating my fourth round of toast, Hazel came in and looked at me. I merely smiled innocently and carried on eating.

"Alright, Sarah?" she asked.

"Fine thanks," I said, aware that she was still looking at me closely. I started to feel slightly unnerved as I contemplated whether, instead of her being concerned about my catching her and Gordon out, she was actually aware of a change in me. Did mothers instinctively know when somebody was pregnant?

Could she see a change in me? I concentrated on my toast.

"Did you and Liz get on OK last night?" she asked conversationally and I breathed a sigh of relief. She was concerned only for herself. Of course. I should have known that, really.

"Erm, yeah, I guess so," I said. "It was a lovely dinner."
"It was good, wasn't it?" Hazel beamed, no doubt congratulating herself on having hired just the right caterers.

"Did you have a good time?" I asked.

"Oh yes, it was fine thanks, just another New Year's Eve, you know. Lots of shop talk." She always laughed a phony laugh at this phrase – 'shop talk' – they worked in Retail – get it?

"Gordon seems like a nice bloke," I couldn't resist it.

"Oh yes, he's OK," she actually had the good grace to look slightly abashed and I smiled inside.

Later that day, once James had slept it off, we returned to our cottage. It was cold, and the Christmas decorations seemed to have lost their gleam.

"Let's take all this down," I said to James, "Let's just get on with this year."

"Are you OK?" he asked, looking concerned.

"Oh yeah," I said, "It's just … Christmas has been and gone. Dad's gone. The New Year's here. Let's get the house back to normal and make life feel normal too."

I put the heating on and, once we'd taken down the tree, and the cards, James lit the open fire in the lounge. Nevertheless, my teeth were chattering when I went into the bathroom. I dug out the testing kit, locked the door, and ripped the packet open. I could wait no longer to confirm what I really already knew.

As I waited for the three minutes advised, I wrapped my arms around myself. I rinsed out the cup that we kept the toothbrushes in. I wiped the sink clean. I read some instructions on the back of some lavender bath salts. 'Not suitable for pregnant women'. That surprised me.

One minute in, I looked through all the bottles on the shelf, taking down any which were nearly finished. Two minutes.

I hummed to myself. I looked at my watch. I sneaked a glance at the test. Was that a blue line? I looked closer. It was. A blue line. I re-read the packet just to make sure that I had it the right way round, before I went into shock.

Even though I had known it, I wasn't really prepared for the news. I was pregnant. I was going to be a mum.

After a few moments to myself, I went back downstairs. It felt like I was walking into a different life.

I opened the door to the lounge and saw James reclining in his favourite position, slouched on the settee with his legs stretched out so that his feet were toasting nicely in front of the fire.

He was watching some New Year's Day animated film on TV and didn't even look up, just put his arm out for me to snuggle up next to him. I did so, pulling the fleecy throw over us both. He kissed me on the forehead.

"I feel so much better," he said, "Happy New Year!"

"Happy New Year," I squeezed my arms around his middle, feeling decidedly strange.

Which words should I choose to break the news to him? How was he going to react? We both wanted children, I knew that much, but in my head I was going to be nearing 30 before we took that next step.

"This is the year we're getting married, Sarah! Next time it's New Year's Day you'll be Mrs Poole!"

I gulped.

"Don't seem too excited then!" he laughed and looked at me. "Ooh, are you sure you're OK? You still look a bit pale. Are you feeling sick again? Maybe it really was something we ate. I'm going to ring Mum and tell her that her caterers are crap!"

"No, no, I'm fine, I'm. Well, I'm..." *Come on Sarah*, I told myself, *spit it out*. So I did.

"I'm pregnant."

Silence.

"You're..?"

"Pregnant, yes."

"With... with our baby?"

"Yes, I believe that's how it works."

"You're... you're pregnant! Fucking hell! How did that happen?"

"Well, when a mummy and daddy love each other very much..."

I could see the news was not entirely unwelcome to him and

suddenly I felt an elation flood into me. I could take the piss out of James, because he was happy about it. And I was happy about it. We were going to be parents! Totally unplanned but totally happy.

He laughed out loud and pulled me closer.

"Yeah, yeah, very funny! Oh my God, Sarah, we're getting married and we're going to be parents. All in the same year. This is amazing!"

I felt tears rolling down my face.

"You're happy about it then?"

"Yes! Yes I'm happy!" James said. "Of course I am! I'm over the moon!"

"So... so am I!"

"Oh my God. When did you find out?"

"Just now, only just, I did the test upstairs. You don't mind that I didn't tell you before?"

"No, no of course not. Oh, and is that why you were sick last night...?"

"I think so. And this morning. So I don't think you can blame the caterers."

"No, although I was still..."

"Come on," I said, "I suspect that may have had a little to do with the vast amounts of alcohol consumed last night."

"OK, perhaps you're right about that," he conceded.

"So don't tell your mum that the caterers were crap. She'd probably put them out of business!"

"OK," James laughed, "I can't wait to tell her she's going to be a grandma, though."

"Do you think," I said, "That you can hold on till tomorrow?" I badly wanted it to be just me and him that night, and our tiny, astonishing parcel of human life which I was holding within me.

Chapter Fifteen

The new year suddenly looked very different to me. Yes, Dad had gone to Canada and I couldn't say I was anything but devastated by his absence but on the other hand I had two huge things to focus on – the wedding and the baby. Although we had really, really not planned to start a family at this stage, both James and I were so happy at the thought of becoming parents that the timing didn't seem to matter. If anything, I thought it was great as I had in one sense lost one of the most important people in my life, but now, all being well, I was also to gain one.

I went to the doctors' and it was very strange. We were registered at the practice in the next village to ours, where Hazel lived, and I was praying I wouldn't see anybody. Somehow I had convinced James to hang on, just a few days, before we told his mum. It helped that she was out of town at some kick-start conference or something. She rang James every day but I knew he would want to tell her face-to-face anyway.

Going into her village, where she seemed to know everybody, I was just hopeful that I might not be recognised. I was being ridiculous, I told myself. Even if I was recognised, and seen going into the doctors surgery, how was anybody to know what I was going for? I just felt so aware of being pregnant that I thought it must be obvious.

As it happened, I was lucky. I'd gone for an evening appointment so that I wouldn't have to take too much time off work. In the dark nobody would have recognised my car, and the surgery waiting room was nearly empty when I got there, stamping my feet to shake off the snow which had not long since started to fall.

I had hoped James would have been able to make it but he

couldn't get out of work on time. I didn't really mind – this was just a preliminary appointment to register as pregnant and find out what exactly I was meant to do next.

Doctor Painton was kind and considerate.

"Congratulations!" he said when I told him my news. "So I take it you've done the home pregnancy test?"

"Yes," I said, "Do you need to test me as well?"

"No, that won't be necessary. The home test kits are pretty reliable. Do you have any idea of how far along you are?"

"Erm…"

"Can you remember the date of your last period?"

"I can't really, but I think late September."

"Late September?" he raised his eyebrows. "Well that would make you around twelve or thirteen weeks pregnant, I think."

I took this in. I'd been trying to work it out. I had thought maybe ten weeks, as that was when James and I had been in the Lakes and perhaps been a bit careless with our contraception.

"Which," Doctor Painton continued, "Means we need to get you a midwife appointment and a scan date, sooner than later. Twelve weeks is the standard time for your first scan."

I started to worry. How stupid I was! I was about three months pregnant and had not even realised. Doctor Painton must have read my expression.

"It's nothing to worry about," he said, "This happens a lot. It's quite normal – some women don't keep track of their periods, some have very irregular cycles and some just have a lot going on in their lives! It's not a problem, it just means you get jumped to the front of the queue. Like a VIP pass."

I smiled.

"Scans are amazing," he said. "I'll never forget my kids' scans. You'll love it, I'm sure." He gave me a load of reading material and he called the community midwife team, explaining my situation. Before I knew it, I had an appointment with them booked for the Friday and a scan the following Tuesday, to determine exactly how pregnant I was.

"Thank you," I smiled at Doctor Painton as I left his room, "Thanks so much."

"It's not a problem," he smiled back, "Enjoy it!"

Yes, I thought, *I am going to enjoy this*. I just knew that I would. Surely this was what life was about.

Back at home, James had lit the fire and made tea. He ushered me into the lounge where he'd laid out the coffee table with a cloth and put out a couple of glasses and a bottle of fruit juice.

"How was it?" he asked me. I could tell he was half nervous and half excited. Like me, really.

"Oh fine," I said, feeling the advantage of having talked about this big, slightly scary, life-changing event with a professional. Which James could have done too if only he'd got out of work on time. "Doctor Painton thinks I may be about three months pregnant though."

"Three months? No way! That's... a third of the way already."

"Shit, I guess it is," I said. "Which is why I've got to see the midwife on Friday, and have the first scan on Tuesday."

"Wow!" James said. "The scan. Andy at work was on about that. Him and his wife are having a baby in April. He said the scan was brilliant. They've paid to have some kind of 3D one as well."

Excellent, I thought. *Something else for them to get competitive about.*

"I didn't even know you could do that."

"No, nor me, he can't shut up about it though!"

"So can you come?" I asked.

"What to – the scan? I think so, I hope so. I want to see what this little bloke looks like."

"Oh it's a bloke is it?" I said, laughing, catching sight of the snow swirling outside, glowing in the light of our window against the pitch-black backdrop of the winter night.

"You know what I mean!" James said. "I'll check with work tomorrow."

"Hmm, I'd better tell my lot what's going on as well," I said, "It will just make life easier if they know why I need time off."

"You're going to tell them before I've told Mum?" James asked, a little put out.

"It's just a practical measure, James," I said, irritated. "Dad doesn't know yet. If it makes you feel better, I'll wait until you've told Hazel before I tell him. If you could wait until Tuesday, we could surprise her with a scan picture."

"I don't think I can wait that long!" James said.

I didn't think he could. I wasn't bothered though, I thought that the way he looked out for his mum would be a good example to our child. *Our child*, I thought. I smiled and touched my tummy. It had never been flat but I knew now that it was changing and I knew of course why. James went out to the kitchen to bring in our tea and I settled back on the settee, watching the snow fall thicker and faster, listening to the fire crackling in the hearth, and imagining the tiny heart beating away deep inside me.

I felt really nervous going to see the midwife. James had told me not to be daft but said he would come with me if possible. The 'if possible' alerted me to the probability he wouldn't make it, but I didn't mind, it was much more important for him to come to the scan.

My work had been brilliant when I'd told them, Bex getting all excited for me and saying it made her feel old as she and her husband Martyn had only just got married themselves and were not even thinking about a family yet. Although she was being lovely, it did make me think for a moment. She was nearly ten years older than me, 31 or 32. What was I doing, having a baby so early in life? Of course, at 24 – as I would be by the time the baby was born – I wasn't that young, not really. The same age Mum was when she had me. I suppose Bex had put so much into the business, children just hadn't really registered on her 'to do' list at that time.

"I think it's great," she said, "Really. And we will do whatever we can to support you so just yell when you need some time off or you just need to take a break for a little while during the day. My sister's got three kids, I know how tired she was during pregnancy. Just let us know if we can help at all. And thank you for reminding me that life is not all about work!"

She surprised me with a hug and left me feeling great. Dad may have been overseas, Chloe too for that matter, and Mum of course long gone, but I had a good support network of lovely people who cared about me. I knew I was very lucky.

The midwife, Sandy, also turned out to be lovely. She took my blood pressure, and a blood sample, and talked to me about pregnancy – how it affects everybody differently and the warning signs to look out for.

"When will I feel the baby move?" I asked, holding my stomach.

"Well possibly in the not-too-distant future," she said, "if we've got our dates right."

I was looking forward to that. And the scan. Up until then, we only had that pregnancy test which I had done to prove that I was pregnant. I even had moments of doubt; maybe I'd got it all wrong. I would go for the scan and all we'd see would be what I'd had for lunch.

I joked about this with Sandy and she smiled.

"Don't worry, everybody says that! It is weird, but you know. I bet you knew before you did the test. You'll have been picking up on things subconsciously, and your body will have been feeling different. You'll have been feeling different too; all those hormones surging around. You'll be tired and you might have mood swings but your body is doing something amazing. Enjoy it!"

Her words echoed Doctor Painton's. I loved hearing these professionals imparting those particular words of advice. It reinforced in me the feeling that pregnancy was something incredibly special. I was really, really looking forward to the scan.

At the weekend, we went to Hazel's house and James broke the news to her. She did something I had never seen her do before. She cried.

"Oh James, oh Jamie," she said, "I can't believe you're going to be a daddy. Oh and Sarah, congratulations love, are you feeling OK?"

"Yes thanks, Hazel," I said, not quite sure what to do in this unprecedented situation.

"You look well, you look great, let me give you a hug." She did so and then she patted my belly, which made me jump a bit. I had not been expecting that.

"Hello little man," she cooed.

"So you think it's a boy as well?" I asked.

"Oh well, I mean, boys are very strong in our family," she said.

"Well yes," I replied, "But I'm not sure it works like that, and besides, my mum and dad had a girl. Obviously."

"Oh, but they only had one," the words gushed out before she had time to contemplate what she was saying. She looked at me.

"Yes, they did, they would have liked more but as you know, Mum's illness meant they couldn't. So who knows – maybe they'd have had five more girls. Or one boy? I don't know, I don't care. I don't care if this is a girl or a boy. I really don't."

"Of course you don't," Hazel soothed, "And neither do I. I am just so excited. It really is the most wonderful news."

"How was your conference, Mum?" James asked, I think trying to steer the conversation in a different direction. He could see how close Hazel had come to upsetting me.

"Oh, fine," she said airily.

"How did Gordon's presentation go?" he asked.

I caught Hazel glancing at me. Oh, so Gordon had been there; that was interesting. I said nothing.

"It was very good. Very motivational. I think he introduced a few new ideas for alternative positions."

"I imagine he's very good at that," I murmured, just loud enough for Hazel to hear.

We stayed for our dinner then I said I was getting tired and we should get going.

"I need to catch Dad before he goes out for the day, tell him our news too."

"Ooh, doesn't Tony know yet? Tell him I'll take good care of his daughter," Hazel squeezed my shoulder and I felt my annoyance with her resurface.

"I'm fine," I smiled through gritted teeth, "I can take care of myself, thank you."

We crunched our way through the compacted snow to the car.

"Take her arm, James," Hazel called, "You don't want her falling over and hurting the baby."

James did as he was told and I took a deep breath. Somehow I felt like I had become the 'baby carrier' in the space of just a couple of hours. I couldn't wait to speak to Dad.

Chapter Sixteen

It seemed as though, within just days of officially finding out I was pregnant, my body decided to let the secret out. My clothes suddenly felt tighter, particularly the waistbands of my work trousers, and when I went swimming the newly developing shape of my abdomen was clear to see, or at least I thought so.

"You look lovely," James said when I mentioned it to him, "Perfect."

"Oh I don't mind," I told him, "I like it. It makes it seem even more real. I'm proud of being pregnant. I want people to see!"

"That's great, babe," James said, his eyes on his laptop screen. I wasn't sure where 'babe' had come from but it had recently started creeping into his speech and I wasn't sure I was that keen on it.

"Busy?" I asked him.

"Always," he sighed, although I knew he relished his work and was happy that it kept him so busy.

He had recently started going to the gym on his way back from the office, even late in the evening, so sometimes I wouldn't see him until 10pm at the latest. Because I had been so tired with my pregnancy – I had been having early nights for a few weeks before Christmas without suspecting a thing – I often didn't see James apart from mornings and weekends. I didn't really mind; I have always been happy with my own company, but I worried about the effect that giving his life over to work would have on him.

As I had reached the end of my first trimester, I was looking forward to having more energy, as the books and websites suggested I would. I was determined to stay up a bit later, make the most of the time with James before this baby came along and knocked out any chance of late evenings, as it surely would.

I was jealous of James in some ways; he was still the same person he had always been. Free to work, go to the gym, go out with friends as before. I was becoming more and more aware of my limitations; not just in terms of energy levels but the list of things I was no longer allowed to do, as well as those things I just really didn't feel like doing. I was determined to keep on swimming, throughout the pregnancy. Already I could appreciate the lightness I felt in the water. I could only imagine how great that was going to be when I was really heavy.

When I had told Dad I was pregnant, he'd gone quiet.

"Dad? Are you there?" I asked, thinking how typical that our connection had been knocked out when I had just told him this momentous news. "Dad?"

I heard a sniff.

"Sorry, sorry, Sarah, it's just... wow... I wasn't expecting that. You're going to be a mum! My little girl's going to be a mum!"

"And you're going to be a Grandad!"

I choked a little on my last words.

"Oh..."

I laughed, trying to make light of our emotions.

"I can't believe it!" Dad said, "I can't take it in!"

"Are you pleased?" I ventured, having worried that he would think James and me too young.

"Pleased?!" he exclaimed. "Of course I'm pleased, I'm delighted! It will be hard work for you. I know you know that but you'll be fine. I've always known you will make a great mum, just like your own was."

I felt my eyes fill suddenly, and I began to sob.

"Sarah? Sarah?" I could hear Dad's worried voice, coming to me from all those miles away, across the sea, from another country; another continent. It only made me cry harder.

"Sorry. Dad. Sorry." I managed to force the words out.

"Don't be sorry," he said, "I just... I wish... I could be there with you. Give you a hug."

This made me cry even more. I was glad James was out, working late of course. I had made sure I had the house to myself when I rang Dad as I had feared this might happen.

"I wish you could too." I sniffed but I began to pull myself together. "And now, well I only just thought of this today, I don't know if we'll be able to come out and see you."

The thought made me snivel.

"Sarah, don't even worry about a little thing like that. We'll come and see you."

"Will you really?" I sobbed, "But can you do that?"

"Yes, Sarah," Dad said emphatically, "We'll come back. It's four months until May, though. How can I wait that long?"

"It'll be fine," I said, pulling myself together and blowing my nose, covering the mouthpiece as I did so. "Don't worry. I'll be massive by then, though! Mid May; I'll be about seven months by then!"

"Oh my God, that really makes this distance seem too far. I guess usually a few months doesn't make much difference in any of our lives but you will change so much in that time. You'll grow, and I don't just mean physically."

I marvelled at Dad, at his words and his ability to express himself – and emotions – so much better these days. It was down to Dawn, I knew that. Maybe he had been like that with Mum as well; I just couldn't remember. I had memories of Dad before her death; plenty of them of course, but the Dad who I knew, or thought I knew, was the grief-stricken man, unable to communicate or, seemingly, to comprehend much more than what was right in front of him.

Dawn had helped him to develop, perhaps re-develop, this emotionally intelligent side and I loved her, and him, for it.

"What do you think Dawn will say?" I asked him, aware that she had wanted a baby of her own. Would it make her feel bad, I wondered, hearing about my pregnancy?

"I'm sure she'll be as delighted as I am," Dad said. "I'm sure she will."

"I'm going to see Grandma tomorrow too, I hope she'll be OK."

"I don't think you'll have anything to worry about there, Sarah. She might be a bit surprised, I suppose. She'll be glad to see you, anyway."

I often felt some guilt about my Grandma, knowing full well that I didn't see her enough. I resolved to make sure I saw her more often, and ensure she was involved in the baby's life.

"Are you still enjoying it out there?" I asked him suddenly.

"I am, I think. Work seems good, and I really like the people I've met, and the lifestyle. You'd love it too. It's amazing for outdoorsy stuff," Dad enthused, "You'll love all the walking and the winter sports but, oh, well I suppose you won't be visiting any time soon."

The realisation hit him; something I had already thought about. It wasn't just while I was pregnant that travel was going to be a problem. Although people told me that travelling with a small baby was far easier than, say, a toddler, I really couldn't imagine going all that way with a baby in tow.

"We'll see," I said, "I don't really know anything at the moment. Let's just see how it goes."

"Sure, of course," Dad said, "I'll just have to make sure I come to you as often as I can. Don't want my granddaughter growing up not knowing me."

"So you think it's a girl, do you? James and Hazel are sure it's a boy!"

"Oh yeah, I said granddaughter didn't I? Must be because you're my daughter! Are you going to find out?"

"Yeah, I think when it's born they'll probably tell me. I think it's best I know really."

"Oh yes, very amusing, Sarah," said Dad. "Good to see you're still practising having a sense of humour."

"I know, I'll get there eventually. I don't think we will find out beforehand though," I said. "I don't want to, and I don't think James does. We could find out at 20 weeks but I do like the idea of a surprise. I don't care anyway, I really don't. What difference does it make?"

"Well obviously I prefer daughters, but I'm biased. Oh Sarah, I am so pleased for you. Just take care of yourself, OK? I wish I was there to take care of you."

When I went to visit Grandma and tell her my news, I asked James not to come. I don't think he particularly wanted to anyway but I needed to do this alone. I bought her a bunch of flowers and took round a cake. We sat in the lounge of the house she had once shared with her husband and daughters, and I looked around me while she was making a pot of tea.

There were photos everywhere. Mum – dead, Grandad – dead, Elizabeth – overseas, Dad – overseas, me – pregnant.

Surprise! Soon there would be a new person to have photos of. However, the house felt lonely to me. The room felt too big for Grandma and I thought, as I often did, how much better it would be for her to live somewhere different. It was hard to let go of memories though, I knew that.

When she came back, she sat down and I decided the best method was to be upfront.

"Grandma," I said, "I've got some news for you."

"You're pregnant?" she said, taking a mouthful of cake.

That stumped me.

"Er, yes," I said, feeling slightly put out that I hadn't been able to tell her the news properly.

She laughed, "Oh Sarah, that is such wonderful news."

"But how did you... how did you know?"

"I didn't," she said, "But you're already engaged. You've bought your house. What comes next?"

It was my turn to laugh. "So you're not disappointed?"

"Disappointed? Heavens, no, I'm delighted! You'll be a lovely mum. And I'll be a great-grandma! I'd better try and remember how to knit. I made some lovely things for you when you were a baby."

"Well, I can't tell you how relieved I am. I thought you'd think I should be older, or married at the very least."

"Sarah, you must know, I've watched you grow up. I've seen you cope with your mum's death. You've got a degree, a good job, a nice young man. Even if you didn't have any of those things though, you could never disappoint me."

She clinked her mug against mine, her face in sharp focus, contrasting against those photos on her wall. I smiled and felt endlessly lucky.

As the weeks went on, and I was approaching a whole seventeen weeks of pregnancy, I did start to feel more energetic. I had also been aware of my baby's movements inside me, which was better than I could ever have imagined.

I loved walking along, knowing that it was just me and this little tiny person inside me. Not a secret exactly, as my ever-expanding stomach was beginning to be a giveaway, but something that really was just mine.

"I wish you could experience this," I told James, "It feels

wrong that you can't. It's amazing."

"I'm OK, thanks," James grinned, "I'm happy to leave it to you. I think I'd find it a bit weird!"

"It's not, it's really not," I said.

"Yeah but I wouldn't be able to go to the gym, would I? And I'd have to stop work when it was born."

"Well, only for a while," I said.

"But you're not going to go back to your job, are you?"

I looked at him. "Why not?"

"Well it's not like it's a career or you're earning big bucks or anything, is it?"

I felt my shoulders tense and almost a chill as his words hit home.

"What, so you think that because I'm not on some graduate fast track scheme or earning 'big bucks' that my job's not worth anything?"

"No, I..."

I didn't let him finish his sentence.

"I love my job," I said, "And I don't think that just because I'm going to be a mother, I have to give it up. Loads of women work after having children. Look at your mum!"

"Yeah, but that's different..."

"Why?" I exploded. "Why is your mum different? Because she's some hard-nosed high flyer who put her work before her family? I won't be doing that, by the way, but I will be working. Just so you know."

James' face was a picture and I was regretting my words even as they expelled themselves from my lips.

"No she didn't," he said, "She didn't put her job first."

"No?" I said, "OK, fair enough, that's not why your dad left, then? Because he'd had enough of being a poor second to his wife's job? In fact no, let's make that third, because I think she probably did care about you boys a bit more. You, anyway."

"What do you mean?" James demanded. "Don't talk about Mum like that, or Dad. You don't know anything about their relationship. Or how hard Mum worked to look after us."

"Was that why she was working so hard, though?" I asked, invested in the argument by that point. "Was she doing it for you? Or for herself? Did she employ nannies to look after you so she could earn more money? Surely from what you've said about me packing my job in, you're suggesting it's better for a woman to stay at home and look after her children than go out and earn a wage? And if your mum hadn't employed those nannies, she could have saved a lot of money, I'm sure."

"Right," James said, "Well I had no idea you felt that way about Mum."

"And I had no idea you felt that way about me, or my work, or how I am clearly just no good for anything but being a mother."

"That's not what I said!" James shouted. "Oh forget it, I'm going out."

"That'll make a change," I spat the words out, "Work or the gym? Or are you going to your mum's to tell her how mean I am?"

He answered by slamming the door behind him and I sat, trembling with indignation, anger, and a sudden, tingling fear. I was emotional, hormonal, very possibly irrational, and I should certainly not have said what I did about Hazel, even if it was what I thought. Seeping into me, though, trickling into my consciousness, was a very real doubt about the situation I found myself in.

Chapter Seventeen

The argument with James about Hazel had not come completely out of the blue. I knew what was behind it all. Never afraid to stick her oar in, she had suggested to us both over Sunday dinner at a nice pub ("My treat," she'd insisted as always) that we postpone our wedding.

"I don't think so," I'd said, "I don't see why we should. We're having a baby for goodness' sake, I think it's even more important that we get married now."

I turned to James. He was hesitating, his eyes flicking between me and his mum.

"I... well, I can see Mum's point," he said.

What point? I wanted to ask. She hadn't really made a point, just voiced her opinion. As always.

"Like you say," Hazel filled in for James, "You won't be in any fit state to wear that lovely wedding dress you'd spotted."

I didn't say that, I thought, *and just because you put 'Like you say' at the beginning of the sentence, it's not going to convince me that I did.* However, I kept quiet and let her continue.

"Sarah will just be too tired, so close to the due date. And what if the baby comes early? You'd have put all your guests to the trouble of coming to your wedding and then let them down. Think of Natasha and Graham, coming all the way from Dorset. They will be so disappointed if they organise a trip up here for your wedding only for it to be called off because of the baby."

Now we were getting closer to honesty. Natasha and Graham were Hazel's friends, not ours. In fact I'm not really sure they could be called 'friends' of hers. I had certainly never met them. Graham was a vaguely well-known British entrepreneur whose notoriety as an uncompromising businessman was just beginning to grow. Hazel had apparently worked with him in the past and she gushed about him, his (third) wife Natasha and their 'simply gorgeous' children.

"Well I don't mind if they would rather not come," I said, "I've never met them and I don't think you have, James?"

James shook his head then cast a slightly worried glance towards his mother.

"Our friends are mostly local," I continued, "We've tried to make this wedding the easiest possible thing for them to attend. The only people who are coming a really long way for it are Dad and Dawn, but if the baby comes while they're here that can only be a good thing. I don't think they would be disappointed!"

I mentioned Dad and Dawn because Hazel had clearly not given them a moment's thought. If she had been really clever she would have cited their travel as an excuse, not a couple of people who really only had to travel up the country to get to us, who probably would do so by private plane or helicopter or some such ostentatious method, and who I wasn't really convinced would be coming anyway.

I knew that Hazel was desperate to impress these people, and all the other guests as well. I also knew that she did not approve of the wedding plans we had made so far. Because we wanted to keep it low key, we had asked only about 40 guests; our respective parents, Dawn, Grandma, some shared friends from uni and a couple of schoolfriends. I knew that this was not enough for Hazel; her idea of an event was tied up with glamorous corporate affairs, which was the absolute opposite of what I wanted for James' and my wedding.

"We'll think about it," James responded to his mum and I glared at him while she looked satisfied. She even glanced over at me, slightly victoriously. Both she and I knew that, where James was concerned, her views would always hold more sway than mine.

I seethed silently and vowed that this was one battle she would not win. However, on our way back home, James began arguing the case for his mother's viewpoint.

"Don't you think it would be nice to get married when we could have a honeymoon?" he asked.

"Well yeah, that would have been good, but it's not the end

of the world. We've got the week in Cornwall in May..."

"With your Dad and Dawn," James scoffed.

"Yes," I shot him a sharp look, "Who we haven't seen since December and who we won't see again until the summer, and after that, who knows?"

Unlike your mum, I thought, *who we see every week at least once, usually twice, sometimes three times.*

"I wanted us to go somewhere special, though... the Caribbean!"

"I know, and that would have been lovely," I said, turning to my fiancé and putting my hand on his knee. I didn't really want to argue with him. It wasn't really him I was angry at, although he could definitely grow a pair as far as his mum was concerned, but his loyalty was something I loved about him so I couldn't really get too cross.

"Things have changed though, James, haven't they? And even if we put the wedding off for a year, we still couldn't go on honeymoon to Barbados or somewhere."

"Why not?"

"Why not?" I arched an eyebrow. "Well there is the small matter of an eleven-month-old to worry about."

"We could leave him with Mum."

What? I screeched inwardly.

"Erm, I don't think so," I said, "I'm not leaving my – our – baby for a couple of weeks to go on holiday. How relaxed do you think we'd feel, being away being away from him *or her*?"

"Mum would be great, she's already said she wouldn't mind."

Ah, so those two had been having this conversation already, behind my back. That did not surprise me. I could feel my anger growing and my hackles rising. I didn't want to get upset though, so I took a very deep breath.

"I'm sure she wouldn't, but I would. And anyway I might still be breastfeeding at that point."

"Not at nearly a year! Mum said she stopped with all of us at two months."

I knew that was the stage when Hazel had gone back to work after having her babies. I was not about to do that, and even when I was back at work I knew I could still be breastfeeding if everything was going well.

"I know, and that's fine, but I might not want to stop that soon. Or I might. I might not even be able to breastfeed at all. Who knows? I do know that I don't want to make that decision right now."

I could sense the argument spiralling.

"Look," I said, "let's just think about all of this. I know your mum would like things to be just so, but it is our wedding, and I think it would be really romantic to get married before we have our baby. I know I'll be massive and I won't be able to wear that dress, but you know me. That kind of thing doesn't really bother me. And Graham and Natasha... well they're welcome as your mum's friends, but we don't know them, and they will just have to take us as they find us. Anyway, the wedding's a full month before the due date so with a bit of luck it will all be fine."

I related all of this to Chloe over a Skype call one day, when James had left early for work and I had woken with him. I didn't mind, as I knew I might catch Chloe at that time of day.

"So where have you got to with it all?" she asked me.

"Precisely... nowhere. I don't think either of us particularly wants to return to the subject but we're going to have to soon because the venue needs confirmation before the end of this month, or else they'll have to make that date available again."

"You're going to have to sort it out, Sar," Chloe said.

"Sar?!" I exclaimed. "Is that an Aussie accent I detect?"

"Don't change the subject – although no it is definitely *not* an Australian accent, thank you very much – you need to get it sorted. I'm sure his mum means well and all but it's not her wedding, is it? Although having said that, if you do leave it to the following year I'll be able to come and be your bridesmaid and everything!"

"True," I said, "I know I decided not to have bridesmaids but if it meant getting you into a hideous dress for the day I might change my mind. I would love it if you were there though, Chloe. That is probably the only benefit I can see to delaying. But I can't give in to her, Chloe, I can't."

"I know, and you definitely shouldn't. I wish I could be there for your big day but I guess our lives are just a bit different at the moment. I will be thinking of you though; you know that, don't you?"

"Of course," I felt myself welling up; bloody hormones, "I'm always thinking of you."

"Oh right, well I don't know how to tell you but I'm not really into girls. Sorry."

I grinned. "Idiot."

"I know, but look, I've got to go. Let me know how you get on."

"Will do."

A week later I was able to tell my friend exactly how I had got on.

"You don't sound too happy," Chloe said. "Don't tell me, you're not getting married."

"No," I said angrily. "Apparently not. Not this year anyway. Honestly, I could kill James at the moment. Why could he not, just this once, side with me and not his mum?"

"Because he sounds like he's a bit scared of her?" Chloe suggested.

"Yep, apparently so, pathetic isn't it?"

"I don't know, she does sound pretty scary."

"Yeah well she's a dragon, that's for sure. I just can't believe it. Well I can. But I can't. Know what I mean?"

"I think so."

"I am so, so, so pissed off. But I can't get too annoyed, I've got this little person to think about."

I patted my stomach and stood up so Chloe could get a view of my swelling belly.

"Ah wow, Sarah, that is really, really amazing. I can't believe you're going to be a mum. I just... well, it's just brilliant!"

"I know," I couldn't help smiling. "It is. But I really wanted to be married before this little one comes along. And perhaps even more than that, I wanted James to stand on my side. After all, I am apparently going to be his wife one day. I know he loves his mum, I'm glad he does, but we're going to be his family now."

"Well I'm sorry, Sarah, I really am, but maybe it will be for the best...? At least you won't have a wedding to stress you out when you're heavily pregnant."

"I know," I said, "but the whole point was that it wasn't meant to be stressful. Now that we've got a year's delay, that's even more time for Hazel to apply the pressure and make it into the wedding she's always dreamed of. And how stressful is it going to be getting married with a baby in tow? At least while it's tucked away in here, it can't cry or need feeding. It's very portable!"

"You'll be OK," said my friend, smiling directly at the webcam so it felt as though she was really looking at me, "don't sweat it."

"Aha! 'Don't sweat it'! You are turning into one of them."

"Oh my God!" Chloe exclaimed, "I think I might be? Still, I'm not turning into one of 'them' so if you're delaying this wedding in the hope it will give me time to change my mind, I'm sorry. I wanted to let you down gently but I just don't fancy girls."

"Idiot."

"Thanks. At least I can be your bridesmaid now."

"We'll see."

So really, the argument James and I had over his mum had been brewing for a while. When James had left the house that evening, I sat trembling, and trying to hold back the tears, but then I thought *What the hell?* and let the floodgates open. Clutching a pillow to me, I felt sobs wracking my body. I suddenly felt really alone.

Dad was so, so far away. Chloe was on the other side of the world. I felt I had got myself entangled in James' and Hazel's world, and I had allowed myself to be trapped there. Living in the village next to hers, in the house she had chosen for us. My closest family and friend abroad, I had to rely on these two people who apparently cared nothing for me and for what I felt or thought about things.

However, as the sobs gradually died down, I became more calm and rational. I made myself think of James. The gentle boy I had met at university who now, although engrossed in his career, was still a kind, thoughtful partner who I thought would make a lovely dad.

Hazel was, undeniably, overbearing and often thoughtless, but I knew that somewhere, deep down, she had a warm side and that, despite her own focus on her career and reputation, she would always look out for her family.

I made myself a drink of warm milk and took myself off to bed. When James and I had rowed before, one or the other of us would leave a note or come to find the other, apologising and wanting to smooth things over. I wasn't sure yet how to end this particular argument as I knew it was based on some genuine resentments and an issue we had to get past, but I also knew that I did want to end it.

We had a baby to think of; that was far more important than a wedding.

I set my mug on my bedside table and went to close the curtains. Outside, I could see nothing except a small square of lawn illuminated by the kitchen light, which I'd left on for James' return, and then thick, soft, dark night stretching on into the distance.

Chapter Eighteen

When I saw Dad again, it was the strangest feeling. I realised that I had been focusing on the moment when I would see him, for the previous few weeks really. I had been almost nervous about the whole thing, which was ridiculous.

I had missed him so much though, and although it had been only a few months – not even five – since I had last seen him, so much had happened. My bump had ballooned, for one thing. I'd had my 20-week scan, and refused the chance to find out whether it was going to be a boy or a girl. James had managed to miss this scan too. I was not happy about it.

However, that had been back in March and it was now May. Dad was coming back from Canada for a visit and we were all going to Cornwall.

The baby was just weeks away from being with us and I had been lucky that the pregnancy had gone smoothly. However, it didn't stop the occasional anxiety. Like when I'd fallen over because I'd been trying to tidy up a load of boxes we had in the spare room. James was late at work again, when he had promised to be back to help, and I had decided I would just get on without him. When I fell, I managed to stop myself with my hands to some extent, but even so, I had shocked myself and I had to sit down for a while as I was shaking. I rang the midwife, who reassured me that if I had not fallen on the bump the baby would be fine. Even so, I realised finally that I should limit what I did whilst pregnant. It wasn't forever. There was no loss of face in admitting that some things weren't right to do when carrying a baby.

Anyway, all of that was in the past. James had explained the predicament he'd had when it came to missing the scan. It seemed that there was some emergency with one of the stores for which he was now accountable; apparently it had flooded so he had to get stuck in and help out. God forbid that sales should slip for one day.

I did sympathise to a degree. I knew that he got a hard time in meetings and on the weekly conference call if his figures weren't good. His boss seemed like a nightmare to me. It sounded like he had no problem having a go at his 'team' in the middle of a meeting. He had reduced some of James' colleagues to tears on more than one occasion.

"Why don't you find another job?" I'd asked James a few times. "Then you could tell him to piss off."

"Yeah, but I really love my job. It's a buzz. And I know he's a bit of a wanker but you need to be strong in Retail. You've got to, to survive, to kick the competition in the balls."

I hated James talking like that. "OK, maybe you have got to be strong in Retail, but I'd say the same for any job. And acting like a complete dickhead isn't being strong. It's being a dickhead."

"Ah, he's alright really, he's a good laugh on nights out."

"I'm sure," I said sceptically but I left it at that. James' career was his concern and I wasn't going to interfere.

However, it did annoy me that he was missing appointments like the scans. For his sake as much as mine. He wouldn't feel that lump in his throat as he saw the shape of our developing baby. He didn't get to gasp in amazement at the sound of the tiny, determined heartbeat whooshing along.

I had long since suspected that much of the child-rearing was going to be my responsibility. The way things were going, James just wasn't going to be around. However, I was so very, very happy at the thought of being a mum, I was sure that I'd be OK managing on my own when I had to, and that whatever help James could give would be a bonus.

Anyway, back to Dad. I didn't meet him at the airport. He insisted that I stay at home and that he would come to me. As he had let his house out, he and Dawn would be staying at our place and using it as a base for a few days while they caught up with friends and colleagues before we went for our longed-for holiday in the South West.

Their flight was due in at 8.35am on a Saturday morning.
Ever since that time had shown on my clock, I'd been waiting.
Even though it was two hours' drive from Manchester airport.
And they would have had to wait to get their luggage, get
through customs, etc...

I didn't know where to put myself. I tried reading a book but
I realised I was scanning the words without taking them in.

I went up to the spare room and straightened the duvet about
20 times, until James came in and asked what I was doing.

"I don't know, I'm so excited, I don't know what to do with
myself!"

"It must be weird," James mused, pulling me gently down
onto the bed next to him, "I can't imagine not seeing Mum for
four months."

"Nearly five," I corrected him, "And no, I can't imagine you
not seeing your mum for that long either."

James looked at me. "What does that mean?"

"Nothing!" I exclaimed, thinking that I had not meant any
offence. "Just that she's an integral part of your, our, life, isn't
she? I mean, she helped out with getting this place, she knows
most of the people you work for, and we see her a couple of
times a week at least. It's not a criticism. It's just how it is."

"I guess so." James hugged me to him then put his hand on
my bump. "Is it kicking?"

"No, I think it's having a snooze," I said.

He poked my side gently. "Wake up, little Poole."

"Hey, it's not a Poole yet!" I said.

"What do you mean?"

"We're not married yet!"

"Yeah but, it's still... it's still my... You're not thinking it
will have your surname?"

Oh shit, I thought, we hadn't had this discussion. In my head,
until I had married James, the baby would be a Marchley. OK,
maybe that was in part pettiness due to my anger at his going
along with his mum rather than me when it came to our wedding
date. However, we weren't going to be married when the baby
was born and I wanted it to have the same name as me.

"OK," I said, "We'll work it out. Maybe we should just wait
until the baby's born and then see what we think."

"Right," James said, and pulled back from me. Shortly, he

left the room then came past with his gym bag.

"You're going out?" I asked. "Aren't you going to stay to see Dad?"

"I should be back before he gets here," James spoke tersely, "and I've got a whole week with him next week."

I chose to ignore the potentially unflattering way he had put this, and just smiled. "I know, I can't wait!"

James didn't reply but tripped off down the stairs and out of the door.

Ah well, I thought. He'd come round. I didn't really mind about the baby name thing, deep down, as we were intending to get married anyway, but there was – if I was very honest – a little part of me that wanted it to keep my name until I was Mrs Poole, just to stick the vees up at Hazel.

I lay carefully back on the bed and wondered how long till Dad and Dawn arrived. Then, after three attempts, I managed to sit up again, went downstairs and made a cup of tea.

Chapter Nineteen

As we rounded the corner, the view of St Ives was breathtaking. Laid out before us, the streets tumbled towards the sea. A vast body of bright turquoise water, shimmering and glittering in the May sunshine, inviting me in.

"Wow!" I said to James, who didn't respond, his eyes on a truck in front of us. A truck which appeared to have taken a wrong turn and which was now steadily reversing towards our car. James sounded the horn. The lorry driver waved his arm out of the window good-naturedly, letting us know he was aware of us. He pulled back a little more then corrected his path and chugged off down the hill, disappearing around the corner as we took the turn he had taken by mistake. We drove up a steep narrow street, moving away from the sea and up towards that brilliant sky. I glanced back and smiled, knowing I would be down there in those waves later that day.

"Which way now, Sarah?" James asked. I consulted the directions Dad had printed out for us.

"I think we're... Oh, I think that was it," I said as we drove past a building I recognised from the website.

James sighed. We were on a one-way system and now had to find our way back around it. I patted his arm.

"Sorry," I said.

It had been a long journey and he'd insisted on driving all of it himself as it was getting to the point where it was uncomfortable for me, sitting in a car for hours on end. I had the seat belt tucked away beneath my bump, but the baby and I seemed to be engaged in a battle for space. Each wriggle it gave made me want to wriggle or, worse, want to wee. Not what you need on a lengthy journey.

Dad and Dawn had come down the previous day, setting off at some ridiculously early hour to make the journey in one day. We had opted to take our time and break the trip in Bristol, staying at a hotel overnight. I was itching to get down to Cornwall but it wouldn't have been fair on James to make him drive all that way in one day. He had been up working till the early hours to try and get everything done before we left. I could tell he was still fretting about it when we were at the hotel so I took myself off for a swim in the hotel pool while he got out his laptop (which I had really hoped he would leave at home) and went to work in the Starbucks in the hotel lobby. After my swim, I had gone to find him but he'd been busy on the phone and had held his hand up to me. *Not now.* I fought back my irritation. If he could get all this done before we went to Cornwall then I supposed it would be worth it. He could relax and we could spend some time together. Something we hadn't done in a long time.

I had gone back to the hotel room, made a cup of tea and lain on the bed. Before long, I felt my eyelids beginning to close so I just let myself sleep. James woke me at about 6pm, with a kiss and a fresh cup of tea.

"Oh... wow! Thanks," I said, trying to get my head straight. "Did you get your work done?"

"Yeah... well most of it," James said, lying on the bed next to me and resting his head on my belly. It was actually really uncomfortable but I didn't want to tell him that so I stroked his hair, willing the baby to give him a kick.

"I am so hungry," I said. "I could eat a horse."

"OK, I'll check the room service menu," James said, shuffling off the bed. "Nope, no horse, sorry."

Instead we ordered pizza and chips, a bottle of beer for James and a sparkling water for me. We ate the meal in bed, feeling slightly guilty but relaxing for the first time in a long time, it seemed to me.

Shortly after eating, James was asleep but because of my long nap, and because the baby had decided to wake up and begin spinning around in my belly, or so it seemed, I was wide awake.

I watched my fiancé sleeping and felt really happy we were going to have some time together. OK, it was with Dad and Dawn too but they would do their own thing a lot of the time and

I hoped James and I would be able to just hang out together. All I really felt like doing was eating, ambling about, lazing in the sun, and a bit of swimming. I knew that a week off would do James some good and I realised I had missed him. I was very good at being self-sufficient and I enjoyed my own company but I didn't want to be on my own all the time.

I breathed as deeply as I could and imagined that baby inside me. It felt like a frog sometimes, I thought, or a whale. Some aquatic creature, kicking against me or slapping its tail down, splashing around. I placed a hand on my belly and switched on the TV. There was nothing good on but it was nice to watch rubbish. Despite myself, I soon found I was drifting off so I turned on my side, placing the pillow I'd brought with me under my bump, and soon had joined James in a deep, dreamless sleep.

In the morning we had an enormous breakfast. Cereal, yoghurt, pancakes, pain au chocolat. I couldn't help myself. Well actually, I could and I did. I helped myself to everything that took my fancy. The problem was, I had an enormous appetite but limited space inside for all this food to go so I soon felt full. I waited for James to finish his full English then I waited in the lobby while he got our bags. We checked out and we were on our way, driving against the onslaught of traffic heading into Bristol to offices and shops.

"See you later, losers!" I laughed. "We're off to Cornwall!"

James laughed and smiled at me and that smile lit up my day. I hadn't noticed how little he'd smiled lately, until then.

However, it was still a long journey down so by the time we'd reached St Ives and bypassed our apartment, James' smile had worn away again. It was OK though, I'd have been the same. It inverted into a distinct frown as we found ourselves in the midst of the traffic nightmare of St Ives. A small, old fishing town, it was clearly not designed to cope with the sheer volume of traffic we found ourselves caught up in. James manoeuvred his way around the tiny streets whilst I tried to find a GPS signal to get some directions. I tried very hard to concentrate and not be distracted by the different views of the town and glimpses of golden beaches and crashing waves as we took different twists and turns. Eventually the phone worked and we were able to navigate our way back to the road we had come in on. This time we made it into the driveway of the building and found our allocated parking space. I was dying for a wee but didn't want to mention it as James looked pretty hot and bothered. It had taken us a further 45 minutes to get back there. Oops.

As I stepped gingerly out of the car, Dad appeared in the car park.

"You made it!" he said, giving me a hug. "We thought we'd seen you about half an hour ago..."

"Shush!" I said, "We won't talk about that!"

"Oh, OK... Hi James!" Dad said, as James came around the side of the car. They shook hands and James gave Dad a smile.

"Hi Tony," he said. "This looks great!"

I was grateful to him for bringing his good humour back so quickly. Dad had chosen this place to stay. I knew it had cost him quite a lot of money but he had waved away our offers to pay for any of the rental.

"It does," I said, taking in the gardens and the view across the town.

Dad and James started unloading the car and I went in, up the four flights of stairs to the top floor flat. I greeted Dawn quickly then made my excuses and headed to the bathroom. It was beautiful – a huge bath in one corner, a walk-in shower in the other, and decorated in blue and cream. A large model ship adorned the windowsill. I could hear the sea through the small open window and some gulls crying nearby.

Once I'd relieved myself, I took a tour of the apartment with Dad. He showed me the room I was to have with James. It had a huge king-sized bed, and through the window a panoramic view of the town and the sea.

The lounge and dining room were open plan with sloping ceilings and two balconies taking in different views of St Ives. We could see the harbour in one direction, a couple of small vessels beyond its walls, waiting patiently for the tide to come in. Through the other window was an amazing view of the Island, with the tiny St Nicholas' Chapel balanced atop its grassy slopes.

I stood and looked across the town, then up at the lone gull circling leisurely overhead.

Dawn handed me a glass of squash and Dad cracked open a beer for James.

"You're on holiday!" he said. "And for that matter, so am I."

He took another bottle for himself and we all sat down.

Dad and Dawn told us about a restaurant they'd been to the previous night and Dad said he'd been swimming in the sea that morning.

"I can't wait to get in the sea!" I said.

"Oh yeah!" James grinned.

"What?" I looked round at him. "What do you mean, oh yeah?"

"Well you're not going in the sea when you're pregnant, are you?" he looked to Dad and Dawn, who looked at me.

"Why on earth not?" I said. "I can't come to Cornwall and not go in the sea."

"Yeah but you don't want to get swept off in a current or something."

"Well no, I don't," I said, "But I don't want to get swept off in a current when I'm not pregnant. It'll be fine! I'm a strong swimmer."

"Right," James said, and took a sip of his beer.

I had a slightly uncomfortable feeling deep inside. I knew this had annoyed James but I wasn't about to back down. I would be fine. I wasn't intending to go swimming far. I knew my limits and I wasn't going to push myself or risk the health of our baby. I just hoped that he'd get over it quickly.

"So we thought we'd go out and get some food in later today," said Dawn, sensing the slight shift in the atmosphere. "You two can make yourselves at home, and we'll get out of your hair for a bit."

"Sounds good!" I smiled at James, who gave me an unconvincing smile back. I groaned inwardly, hoping we weren't heading towards an argument. We'd only been there two minutes.

We went about unpacking with a kind of uneasy peace between us. It felt like a small storm was brewing but I chose to ignore it. It was really important to me that we had a good time on that holiday. It would be our last before we had the baby, and it felt like I had hardly seen James during the preceding few months, he'd been so busy at work. It seemed like our last chance to be just 'us' and I had hoped that the holiday would remind us exactly what that meant.

I'd read and heard plenty of stories about the strain having a baby could put on a relationship and I wanted to be ahead of the game in creating the strongest relationship into which to introduce our baby.

A sort of uneasy peace had settled over us since the night we'd argued and James had walked out. I'd stayed awake for as long as I could, wanting to see him and make things right, but eventually I must have dozed off. The next morning I'd woken as he was getting up for work, and had tentatively asked if he was OK. He'd answered an abrupt yes then gone off for the day, and had rebuffed any further attempts of mine to talk about it.

I decided that the swim could wait and instead suggested that we took a walk into town. That was the best thing I could have done, as it turned out. We meandered down the steep hills and steps, my arm through James', and came out at the harbour, next to the Lifeboat station. We strolled along the promenade, mingling with the other tourists, and stopping to eat ice cream on one of the many benches. The sun warmed my face and I leant against James, feeling something like relief from a stress I had barely been aware of. His arm went around my shoulder and I closed my eyes to enjoy the moment.

The very fleeting moment, as it turned out. My reverie was broken abruptly by a sharp peck at my fingers, and the disappearance of my ice cream cone. A bloody gull had nicked it!

"The little..." James exclaimed.

We looked at each other and laughed. I saw the gull a little further up the harbour sands, greedily pecking at my ice cream whilst trying to guard it from other scavenging sea birds.

James shared the remainder of his ice cream with me then we wandered on, up through the little cobbled streets and rounding the bend to the splendour of Porthmeor beach.

This was pure open wild seaside. The waves were topped with numerous slick, body-suited surfers, and the shallows glistened and sparkled in the sunlight. At the far end of the beach were rugged rocks and cliffs adorned with lush green grass. At the near end was the Island, with the chapel of St Nicholas, patron saint of seafarers, keeping a watchful eye over the waters from its lofty position above both town and sea.

We wandered onto the sands and I took off my shoes, letting my toes wriggle in the rough grains. I wanted to run. I always have that instinct when faced with an expanse of beach, but I knew that running when seven months pregnant would not be quite so much fun. Instead, I took James' hand and we walked the length of the beach, mostly in a not uncomfortable silence.

Back at the apartment, Dad and Dawn welcomed us in with a bottle of bubbly. I had a small glass and felt a little tipsy from it. They then insisted they would cook us dinner so I sat, slightly swollen feet up on a plush footstool, and gratefully accepted being looked after. I was tired by nine so made my excuses and went off to bed, feeling the warm wellbeing that only a day in the sun by the sea can create. I didn't even bother opening my book but fell gratefully in between the crisp white sheets and laid my head on the pillow.

The following day we spent lazily, around the apartment and then back into town. I thought I could feel James relax, and I was happy – for him and for me. The swim could wait another day, I thought.

We ate out that evening with Dad and Dawn at a tapas restaurant and Dad raised a toast to the four of us – no - *five*, he corrected himself, looking pointedly at my very round belly, and our holiday.

It was clear how happy he and Dawn were, and I felt happy for them. If not quite happy that he lived in Canada, because I missed him too much for that, happy that they still had their life together. I knew it was the right thing.

On the third day I was a little restless and had suggested to James that we visit the Barbara Hepworth Museum and the Tate Gallery. He had seemed keen on the idea the previous evening but when I mentioned it at breakfast time, he went quiet. I felt myself tense up.

"You do still want to go, don't you?" I asked, determinedly upbeat and light-hearted.

"Yes, of course I do. It's just that…"

"Just what?" I asked, irritated and knowing what he was going to say.

"I just, I've got some work…"

I banged my teacup down in its saucer. I couldn't look at him, I was so incensed.

"This is a holiday, James, do you know what that means?" I stood up and left the room.

Shortly afterwards, I announced my intention to go to the Hepworth Museum myself. I said I would phone James at lunchtime and hoped he would have finished his work by then so that we could go to the Tate together. I didn't look at him to see his reaction to this. I made myself believe that I had faith in him to take the not very subtle hint and realise how important this was to me. How important it should have been to him.

In the Hepworth garden I calmed down. I don't think it would be possible to be anything but calm there. It had taken me a while to locate the museum, having a ridiculous aversion to asking for directions. In the end I happened upon it quite by chance. However, the steep incline of the hill had me red-faced and panting by the time I got through the door. The lady working there offered me a chair and told me to take my time. She brought me a glass of water and I sat back, looking at the story of the Yorkshirewoman who made her home in this Cornish town.

She looked from the pictures to be somehow stern – I guess she had to be very strong to survive and succeed as a female artist at that time.

Once I had caught up with myself, I thanked the lady and wandered up the staircase into a room full of small sculptures. There I saw a work called *Mother and Child*, and learned from another museum employee that this was a recurring theme with Barbara Hepworth. I stood looking at the model, admiring its smoothness, unwittingly stroking my own smooth, round belly as I did so. It was only when I noticed another woman watching me, smiling, that I realised what I was doing.

I wandered out into the garden and was amazed. So close to the centre of the busy town of St Ives, this place could have been miles away. Shielded by masses of tall bamboos and other leafy, expansive plants and trees, it felt like a paradise. I could hear the sea, I could hear the gulls, and I could see why and how the artist was so inspired there.

I stood for a while at the door to her workshop, left untouched since her death. I imagined what it must have felt like when arthritis started to take hold of her hands and how that must have left her frustrated and bereft, not to have control of the two most essential instruments of her work.

In a small shed was a little bed, with thin faded covers which reminded me of visiting my paternal grandparents when I was small. I thought of Barbara Hepworth lying there on a hot summer's evening, new ideas blooming in her mind and keeping her awake.

Sitting alone on a bench and watching the other visitors wander around the plants and sculptures, I felt myself fall in love with the place. Not just Dame Hepworth's garden but St Ives itself. The light which people always talk about when they discuss the art in St Ives. It was magical. Majestic. Life-affirming. I felt clichés flooding my mind but I didn't care. I already knew clichés came from truth and I thought that day, sitting alone on a bench in the sun, I had found the truth. I determined to forgive James for being crap and to let him off this one morning of work. I wanted to enjoy being there with him and to fulfil those hopes I'd had of a happy holiday together before we became a Family of Three.

Chapter Twenty

It took me a while to get back up the hill to the flat. I had read about the shortness in breath I was likely to experience at this stage in the pregnancy but it seemed to me that the baby was getting bigger every day, pressing against my diaphragm and ribs. Taking a deep breath was not really an option.

People smiled at me as they passed by, kindly, I think, not laughing at my pathetic red-faced state. I stopped frequently to let my body catch up but I enjoyed knowing the reason why I was not exactly at my physical best. I could lay my hand on my bump and know that in there was the little person I was longing to meet, and that we would be together properly very soon.

Despite my eagerness, I still hoped that we would last the full term of the pregnancy. There were things I wanted to do at home, now that I was on maternity leave, before the baby turned up. One of them was to sleep. Another was to look a little more into teacher training, with half an eye on the future. I knew that I wouldn't be up to that kind of thing for a while after the baby had been born.

For the time being though, I had a week by the sea, with my partner, my Dad, and my sort of stepmum. A golden opportunity which I should not waste.

By the time I reached the flat, all annoyance at James had dissipated. I was excited again by the holiday and slightly emotional, which I put down to pregnancy hormones. I had never been so easily moved to tears before. As I climbed the steps (slowly) to the flat, I realised I had tears in my eyes at the thought of all these people I cared so much about.

"I'm back!" I called in a sing-song voice into a quiet, echoey flat.

I listened hard. I could hear James' 'work voice' and realised he must be on the phone to somebody. I went to the bathroom, and then into the lounge where he was standing at one of the windows, talking seriously. He looked round, gave me a half-smile and a half-wave. I blew him a kiss and wandered off to our bedroom to look for my book. I fancied a lazy afternoon on the settee with the open windows letting the fresh sea air blow across me.

At the door of our bedroom I stopped. On the bed were James' bags, packed. I raced back to the lounge, as much as it was possible for me to race anywhere.

"What's going on? Why are your bags on the bed?"

He held up his hand to me, apologetically, listening to the person on the other end of the phone.

"Yeah, look, sorry Bill, can I call you back? I'll ring you on the way."

"On the way?" I nearly screeched once he'd ended the call. "On the way where?" Though I knew the answer to that question.

"I'm so sorry, Sarah, I really am, but something's come up and I've got to get back."

"Come up? What's 'come up'?" I shouted at him, incensed.

"Shh..." he gestured to the floor, indicating the flat below. He was always too concerned with what other people thought.

"I won't 'shhhh'! Why should I? Why shouldn't they know that you're ruining our holiday? I can't believe this. We've only been here a day and now we've got to go again because of your *work*." I spat the last word.

As well as being more emotional, I had definitely found pregnancy was making me more irritable. Or was it just having a spineless, work-obsessed fiancé?

"No, no, I spoke to your Dad, they'll bring you back with them. You don't have to come back now. I wouldn't ruin your holiday."

"Yeah but... you have." I sat down, deflated, my eyes suddenly filling with tears. "You have."

He sat next to me and put his arm round me, kissing my shoulder. I couldn't look at him.

"I'm really sorry, Sarah, I really am. But it is an emergency. One of my store managers has fucked up, big time, and apparently Andy's sticking his nose in. If I don't get up there and sort it out it's going to reflect really badly on me and push him further up the ladder."

What ladder? I wanted to ask, but I kept the thought to myself. I'd had enough of this. His stupid job, his obsession with beating Andy, his need to please his mum by following in her footsteps. The James I had fallen for wasn't this James. He was kind and funny, a little unsure of himself. Now he was turning into an arrogant, obsessive and competitive idiot. I only hoped he would change when he met our child.

In the meantime though, I must admit I was relieved that I could stay on. I would have been uncontrollably angry if I'd had to pass up this chance to have time with Dad and Dawn.

I sighed and stood up.

"I'll make you a sandwich to take with you."

"No, no, don't worry about that, I just need to get going."

"OK," I said flatly.

James hugged me tightly.

"I'm sorry, Sarah, I really am. I love you."

"Love you too," I said into his shoulder, feeling the bulk of the bump between us.

Once he'd gone, I made myself a huge sandwich, got a large bag of crisps from the cupboard, and plucked an apple from the bowl. I sat on one of the settees, looking out to the sea, and watched the boats on the waves as I tucked into my food. I felt like I could look at that view forever.

I thought through the situation with James. I didn't want to be angry with him but I could feel it there, burning slowly and surely away deep within. I wondered what Dad and Dawn had thought when he'd told them and felt embarrassed that this was the kind of thing my partner would do.

As it turned out, they were sympathetic – not just towards me but to James too.

"Poor bloke," said Dad, "That job sounds like a nightmare."

"Yeah," I grunted, "It is."

"I hope they let him have his time off for paternity leave without any interruptions."

"Well if he'd turn his bloody phone and laptop off they wouldn't be able to interrupt him, would they?"

"Don't be too hard on him, Sarah, I know you're disappointed. We are too," said Dawn. "Some of these companies are so hard to work for though, and I've heard Retail can be a nightmare. I've got a friend who worked in that sector for a while but she quit because of the bullying and the egos."

"Well... thanks for being so understanding," I said, "But I'm annoyed with him for your sake as much as mine. I can't believe he's missing our holiday."

"Hey, don't worry about that." Dad hugged me, "We've still got you. And look at this beautiful weather. Let's just enjoy ourselves, eh? Now, can we get you some lunch? You must be starving."

"Mm... yes please," I said, pushing my empty plate under the settee with my foot.

After my second lunch had settled, I changed into my swimwear, pulled a dress on, grabbed a towel, and stepped into my flip flops. Now it was time for my swim.

I took my time wandering down to Porthminster, as it was really warm. The heat only served to make me all the more keen to get in the water.

On the beach, I found a spot near the café where I felt I could safely leave my things. I'd brought just a few pounds with me and a key to the flat, tucked into a small bag. I placed the bag beneath the towel, took off my dress and flip flops and made my way confidently towards the water.

There were families everywhere; building sandcastles, playing beach tennis, running towards the waves with newly acquired body boards, and children shrieking and splashing in the shallows.

I smiled at a little girl as I strode purposefully past her, determined to get my shoulders under the water as quickly as I could. The water was bitingly cold against my ankles, and I gasped, but I carried on. Into the gentle waves I went; one deep breath and I was in. I felt a sharp kick from the baby at precisely that moment and I wondered if it was protesting at the chilly sea.

There were fewer people further out so I swam a short distance until I felt I had the space I wanted. Then I took a few strokes back and forth, getting thick salty seawater in my mouth and feeling my hair spread out behind me. Within minutes the cold was no longer bothering me.

I floated on my back under the strong afternoon sun, letting my ears submerge so I could not hear any other people, just the deep underwater sounds. I closed my eyes momentarily and I realised that I was feeling something I hadn't in quite some time. I was relaxed.

Above me, the sky was that optimistic spring blue, and what few clouds there were just sparse, translucent cotton wool drifting aimlessly along as I floated below them.

From time to time I would check my position and make sure I wasn't getting pulled by the current but I was a strong swimmer and still able to touch the seabed with my toes if I needed to. Despite James' fears, I was fine and I stayed in the sea for I don't know how long. I didn't want to get out, but eventually I reasoned that I had to. I made my way up the beach, salty sea tears racing over my round, smooth belly.

I would swim every day for the rest of the holiday, I decided as I dried myself off, then I bought a hot chocolate which I sipped at, enjoying its scalding heat, as I sat and watched the happy families and couples enjoying themselves.

Aside from James' absence, the rest of the holiday was just what I needed. Even though I loved my job, it felt like a huge relief not to have to get up to get into the office in the morning and the prospect of a full twelve months without the daily work commute seemed like bliss.

The weather was glorious, every day without fail, so that we were getting up to blazing sunshine, eating breakfast with the balcony doors wide open, and spending leisurely days around town, on the beaches, or just lazing in the apartment.

I loved having Dad and Dawn there and I was fighting the feeling that each day we spent together was a day closer to their return to Canada.

"At least we'll see you again in a couple of months, when the baby's here," said Dad.

"I know," I said, "I can't wait already."

"We'll try and come for at least two weeks so we can help out when you need it," Dawn said. "Maybe we should time it for the end of James' paternity leave?"

"That would be great," I said, "Though I would love you to

be there the day the baby's born. In fact, please come then. I'll need you. I want you to meet the baby – your *grandchild* – as soon as you can."

I looked at Dad and grinned but thought of Dawn. Did it feel strange to her that she was going to be, sort of, a grandmother without having had children of her own? I didn't know how she and Dad had settled things between them but they certainly seemed happy. However, I worried slightly that one day she would start to resent him for not providing her with a family of her own.

Life can be so bloody complicated.

During that holiday, the baby started waking me up in the early hours. I didn't mind. I could make up for the lack of sleep during the day. I would get up and go into the lounge, watching the town come to life as the sun rose over the horizon. Clouds of seagulls would rise against the skyline, screeching and announcing the new day.

I would see delivery vans and street cleaning trucks make their way through the unusually empty streets down below while I sipped an orange juice and munched through a plateful of toast.

One day towards the end of the week, I decided I would go down to the town myself; explore it in this early morning solitude.

I left a note for Dad and Dawn and carefully, quietly, closed the door behind me. They had been out for a meal the night before while I'd had an early night. I'd been vaguely aware of them coming back, giggling like a couple of teenagers.

I tiptoed down the stairs so as not to wake the other holiday makers and then I was outside. The air was slightly chilly so I pulled my hoodie around me and began the determined descent to the heart of the town. With every step my mood lifted higher. Each glimpse of the sea boosted my spirits and I realised I was grinning widely, walking with a spring in my step, loving this place and this holiday.

I walked along the harbour front, watching the boats bobbing up and down as the sea made its creeping way across the sands, slowly and subtly raising the vessels from their resting places. Around the corner and down some stone steps which took me to Porthgwidden Beach. I passed a jogger on the steps, whose grin seemed to mirror my own.

Down onto the beach. I took off my shoes and pressed footprints firmly into the sand as I walked, then up some more stone steps to a bench where I put on my shoes then sat back and rested awhile. One hand stroked my bump, feeling the baby kick and wriggle. Perhaps my uncustomary morning exercise had woken it up.

I could see a man running along the shoreline of the beach, and I knew it would not be long before the town started to fill with people again. I pulled myself up, determined to visit the chapel while nobody else was about. As I stood, a plaque on the bench caught my eye.

'May you find what you want in life, know it when you see it and have the good luck to get and keep it. We did. This place was our Shangri La.'

I stopped and read the words again, wondering about the person who wrote them. Their name was below them, just initials and a surname. A man or a woman? I thought a man, though I was not sure why. There was a 'we' mentioned so I imagined a couple who had come on holiday to St Ives, fallen in love with the place and never looked back. Did they move there, or just return as often as they could?

I looked across at the other benches. Each of them adorned with a plaque. I decided I would read them all. Somebody somewhere had made the effort to have each plaque made. Somebody had felt enough to want to share their thoughts or commemorate a person here, in this beautiful place.

The plaques were poignant, and every single one made me think.

'For Mum and Dad, who loved this place'. A happy thing, a child or children wishing to remember their parents and celebrate their lives in the place they loved.

Then there were grief-filled, heartbreaking words of parents to their daughter, their 'smiling angel' who died aged 23.

Tears dropped quickly from my eyes when I read this. Their daughter. They lost their daughter. I was not (quite) a parent yet but I knew already something of the love they must have felt for their girl. And how wrong it must feel to have a child die before you. I knew how it had broken my grandparents' hearts when Mum died.

I breathed deeply and closed my eyes, thought of Dad back at the flat, and wanted to hug him.

All the people the plaques commemorated, and the people who'd had them made, would have argued with each other; been cross, irate even, at times. Probably this girl and her parents had the usual teenager-parent arguments; she rebelling and they struggling just a little to see her grow up, grow away from them.

But with death comes truth; the truth of love, and all of these plaques spoke the truth about life. When you find what you want, recognise it. Cherish it. Do all that you can to hold onto it. And always, always appreciate it.

It made me think about James. I knew I had a fierce love for this baby I had yet to meet but as I wiped the tears from my eyes and my vision cleared, I looked out over the miles of sea and I knew this was not the case for James.

I continued my walk up to the chapel and there I sat, thinking about everything. Mum, Dad, James, Dawn, my baby, Dawn's wish for a baby, Grandma all alone in her family home, and Elizabeth over in America. Chloe – young, free and single and halfway across the world. Impending motherhood.

Suddenly I felt very tired. I'd wanted to walk the length of Porthmeor as well but decided a rest would do me more good. I wearily made my way back down the Island and into town, stopping to pick up some almond croissants to take back to the flat. I ate one on my way home, which gave me a much-needed sugar boost, and eventually arrived back at the apartment with sleep on my mind.

When I got in, Dad and Dawn were clearly up and about. I was greeted by the smell of fresh coffee and the sound of happy voices from the lounge.

"Good morning!" I called out, coming through and dumping the bakery bags on the table.

"Hello Sarah!" Dad came and gave me a hug and I looked over his shoulder to see Dawn beaming at me. "We've got some news for you!"

The thought of a baby briefly crossed my mind but Dawn was coming towards me, holding her left hand out.

"I'm going to be your stepmother!" she laughed loudly.

I laughed with surprise and pleasure and I hugged them both.

We celebrated with champagne, though I had the feeling they'd had a fair bit the night before. I had a small glass and that was enough for me. I congratulated them again then made my apologies and went through to my room for a lie down, exhausted by my early morning walk and the emotional start to the day.

Chapter Twenty One

There was one day left in Cornwall then we were faced with the prospect of a long drive home and, for me, return to life with James. I had spoken to him every day since he'd gone but, despite my trying to shake the annoyance I'd felt, I knew there was resentment within me and I found it hard to think of anything to say.

I could sense he was struggling too. His head was filled with work but he knew that if he talked too much about any of that stuff it would wind me up.

So we made small talk, about the weather, about what I'd been doing on holiday. I told him about Dad's and Dawn's engagement.

"That's great," he said, "isn't it? Are you OK with that?"

"Yeah, of course I am," I made out there was no reason I would feel otherwise.

I was not looking forward to going back home. I knew it but I didn't want to admit it. It meant the end of Dad's visit. It meant long days alone whilst James worked and most of my friends were at work too. I had antenatal classes to attend, which I was looking forward to, and through which I hoped to maybe meet one or two people, but other than that my time was my own.

While that was usually an appealing prospect, I had to admit to myself that I was starting to feel lonely. Something I was not used to. James and I should have been preparing together for what was going to be an enormous change in our lives but I was beginning to admit to myself that I didn't think James was going to let it be an enormous change to his. He would still be working, and I knew now how much. I could see the future with some clarity.

Although I had never had a baby, I knew it to be very hard work, and I had read plenty about women feeling isolated, facing day after long day of life alone with a demanding baby, coupled with sleep deprivation of the highest order. Realistically, how much help was James going to be?

I didn't want to think about it but I had to.

However, I was determined to enjoy my last day in St Ives. I decided to have a wander down to Porthmeor beach as I had missed it previously, then agreed to meet Dad and Dawn for lunch at the Tate Gallery café.

The two of them were unendingly happy, it seemed, although I had caught Dad casting slightly worried glances in my direction. I knew he was thinking about missing me when he went back to Canada. I also knew he was worrying about me. It was obvious that James was not in my favour and I think Dad wanted me to sort that out, for James and I to go into parenthood together, strong and united.

I smiled when I caught one of these looks. He smiled back.

"I'm going to miss you," I said.

"I know, I'll miss you too, but I'll be back soon," he responded brightly.

"You'll be busy planning your wedding!"

"I guess I will," he said, "It's weird isn't it?"

"No, not really," I said, "I mean, I guess it must a be a little strange for you but it makes perfect sense. I think you and Dawn are meant to be together, and if that means you being in Canada, I'll just have to live with it."

"Well thank you Sarah, that means a lot to me, it's not easy, though; I'm torn thinking of living so far away from you. Especially when I should be here to help, with the baby and everything."

"I know. I wish you were closer. But life is complicated. We know that. I know you're always there for me, and that's better than anything."

"Dawn feels guilty about it too you know."

"Well she shouldn't. She mustn't. She has her family in Canada. One of you is always going to lose out, aren't you? I'll be fine. I'll just have to come and visit you as soon as I'm used to being a mum."

"That would be great," Dad kissed me, and looked up as

Dawn came through wrapped in a towel. His feelings for her were written clearly across his face. How could I possibly begrudge him the happiness he'd found?

Down on Porthmeor there were a lot of us. Adults with shoes and socks off, trouser legs rolled up even though the weather that day was not particularly warm or sunny.

Maybe trying to regain some sense of childhood; sand sliding between toes, conjuring memories of idyllic family holidays. The annual arguments, sulks and tantrums – from parents and children alike – forgotten in a memory awash with sunshine, mucking about in the sea, pasties and KitKats with an extra crunch of sand thrown in for good measure.

People trying desperately to make the most of every remaining moment there by the sea. The wondrous, breathtaking, living sea. A force of nature we humans could do little about. Just marvel at its sheer strength and size.

Making the most of those moments in the knowledge that the following week meant a return to normal, landlocked, office-entrapped life. Suits and smart shoes, meeting rooms, computer screens, artificial striplights casting an orange, headachey glow.

For me, however, despite my fears of long, lonely days, I knew that I was also returning to something exciting and so I faced the end of the holiday with a mixture of dread and thrill. I breathed in the sea air, closed my eyes in the sunshine and hoped for some kind of strength, some kind of blessing, for the months that lay ahead.

Chapter Twenty Two

It was countdown time, and suddenly I couldn't stop finding things to do.

'Put your feet up,' people would tell me, or 'rest now, you won't be able to when Baby comes'. (I found referring to the baby as 'Baby' really irritated me).

If I didn't make the best of the time I had, I wouldn't get any of the things done which I really wanted to.

I wanted to prepare all my teacher training stuff – I was not going to apply right away but if I had it all together then, when the day came that I wanted to do it, I wouldn't be starting from scratch. I wanted to get the house in order. Chuck out all the old stuff we'd collected over the years. Hoover and dust every last inch of the place. Get the cot put up, empty out a chest of drawers for 'Baby'. Wash her – or his – clothes and fold them in readiness. Get that hospital bag packed: nightdress, maternity pads, breast pads, toiletries, underwear, slippers, dressing gown, newborn vests, nappies, sleepsuits, sheets, blankets... I didn't want to forget anything and I didn't want to leave it too late, just in case things happened earlier than expected.

Rest? Pah. Who needed rest?

I decided to start with the chest of drawers. I had really been looking forward to getting the clothes out and looking through them again. I had tried not to go overboard but I had bought a few things, as had Hazel, Dawn, and even Jess and Bex. It seemed that the imminent arrival of a brand new human being brought out the shopping instinct in us. The little vests and body suits were so tiny. I could just sit and look at them for ages, feeling the soft material against my fingertips and marvelling that soon James and I would have a tiny little person to wear these things.

I had asked James to get the boxes of baby stuff I'd retrieved from Dad's down from the loft as well. I wasn't sure what to expect from these, imagining that any clothes would surely be yellowed with age, or possibly moth-eaten, but I really wanted to see if anything was salvageable.

I began with the new things, though. Should I wash the clothes first or not? I decided that yes, I should wash them all. It seemed best to ensure that the baby would be in completely clean clothes and I had bought some new washing powder and fabric conditioner so they would all smell lovely-wovely-woo. Yes, I had done what I'd sworn not to do and got a bit over-excited about the baby. I was not yet obsessed but I had found out some surprising things about myself. I had never been one for cooing over baby clothes but now the sight of scratch mitts could almost reduce me to tears. I needed to get a grip.

So, I washed all the teeny tiny baby clothes and loved hanging them on the line outside. It took ages because there were so many of them, but seeing those freshly-washed, immaculate scraps of material swinging in the breeze in our cottage garden filled me with joy. I stood and looked at them, slowly rubbing my belly. I had taken to doing that a lot as well. I hoped the baby could feel me doing it. It was meant as reassurance that when they had to escape their dark, warm, cosy world, there was somebody out there just waiting to look after them.

I went in, and made a cup of camomile tea. I was in truth delaying the next stage. The boxes from Dad's house. I wanted very much to open them but something was putting me off. I stood leaning against the counter and enjoying the mellow smell wafting up on the steam from my teacup.

I took my cup in my hands and carried it upstairs, setting it down on the carpet. Then I lowered myself to the floor – I was beginning to find this kind of movement increasingly uncomfortable – and opened the first of the boxes.

There, at the very top, was a yellow knitted blanket. It seemed familiar and I was sure I remembered wrapping my dolls in it. I opened it out and a little note fell to the floor:

'Knitted by your dad's Grandma, just for you'

It was Mum's handwriting and it gave me a shock. I picked up the paper and gazed at it then placed it carefully on my bed. I had not been expecting that and wasn't sure how I felt about it. Had Mum written that knowing her fate or just at some point decided to label these memories? She had always been very good at writing on photos – who, where, when – I think that kind of thing was just very important to her.

Then there were five lilac flannelette cot sheets. No note with these. I guess they were self-explanatory. I put my face into them, maybe hoping to catch a whiff of Mum; a magical glimpse of the past, but they just smelled a bit musty. I put them with the blanket, to be washed.

The rest of this box contained clothes. Tiny dresses and tights which must have once been mine. They too went in the washing pile. I opened the next box.

This time I really had to catch my breath. There was an envelope, addressed to me, in Mum's writing. I started to shake, not knowing what to do. Did I want to open it? Of course I did, although I was sort of scared of doing so. I took it with trembling fingers and hauled myself up, then went to the bed and sat down on it. Slowly I pulled open the flap at the back and retrieved two sheets of writing paper. I unfolded them and began to read.

Dear Sarah,

I have thought long and hard about whether writing this letter is a good idea or not. I hope that when you read this you will understand why I decided I should. I am scared that it will upset you and that is the very last thing I want.

I'm hoping that you are reading this because you are expecting a baby. I am very much hoping that you decided to have a look through your old baby stuff, and that you and Dad haven't just passed it straight on to a charity shop (in which case, somebody else is reading this letter which would be very strange).

Anyhow, assuming that:
> *a)   it is you, Sarah, reading this*
> *and*
> *b)   you are having a baby,*

I wanted to say congratulations and how much I wish I could be there with you. Having you has been the very, very best thing I could ever have hoped for in my life. I can't put it into words very well; you will know, I hope, what I mean, when you hold your own baby in your arms. You'll understand even more as that baby grows and the two of you get to know each other. Because I have loved you more and more every day you have lived. I always knew I wanted children but I could never have imagined quite how utterly life-changing an experience it is. For something so commonplace and natural, having a child is incredible.

But I shan't witter on. I had promised myself I would keep this succinct. But I must be sure you know just how very, very much I love you and how becoming a mother has completed my life.

I also want you to know that being a parent is hard. It is magical, wonderful, and all of that, but on a day-to-day basis, it is very hard work. You don't have time for yourself. You can't leave the house in the morning having just rolled out of bed and eaten a quick slice of toast. An uninterrupted cup of tea becomes a luxury. Reading a book; a whole book, in less than a month – two months, even - forget it, at least until your child is about three years old. There are tantrums to deal with (these may be yours or your partner's) and the inability to do anything or go anywhere with any sense of urgency, so prepare yourself for having the same conversation again and again, and again. Particularly when it comes to getting to school on time.

Oh, but it is brilliant. All of that is brilliant. Never lose sight of the fact that your child is a person. Not there for your own convenience. You may be able to train them to sleep through the night. You might even be able to coerce them into doing what you want with some kind of bribery but at the end of the day, your child is a human being who is developing every day and who, just like you, will want to do things their own way. (This doesn't mean you always have to let them, by the way!)

I am not a fount of knowledge about children. I have only one. I wish I could have given you a brother or sister. But I am your mum and I wanted to find a way to pass on a little of what I have learned about being a mum, for a time when you will (I hope) find it useful.

Loads of people will tell you that your child will be grown up before you know it. In some ways this is true but in others it's not. One single day can seem like forever when you or your child, or both of you, are ill. Or if you've been up all night then your baby wakes you at five. It can go back to sleep when it wants but you still have all those 'things to do' rolling around in your head like marbles, which won't let you rest.

Then you see your child start school and are amazed that day has already come around. They start to lose their baby teeth. To stay at friends' houses without you. You miss that time you had when they were tiny and much of the time it was just you and them. But you love seeing them grow and learn and enjoy life.

I just wish, so very dearly, that I could be there with you now. I know you will make such a very lovely mum, if that is what you choose to do with your life, and I hope that you have a strong, supportive partner as I have been so lucky to have had with your dad.

I could go on forever, Sarah, but I won't. I hope that you don't mind I wrote this for you. And don't worry about keeping it or cherishing it forever. Things get lost, or broken. This letter could get soaked by a spilled cup of tea. Accidentally thrown away. It doesn't matter. What really matters is that you remember this: I love you, Sarah. Having you in my life has made my life. I know I will be dying sometime soon, it breaks my heart to leave you, but you have to know that I consider my life fulfilled by having had you. Other people may live to 100 and never be so lucky.

Take good care of yourself and my grandchild(ren) and of course your amazing, lovely dad who loves you just as much as I do.

If there is something after all this then I will be watching out for you.

Love forever,
Mum xxxxxxx

In the quiet of the house, my sobs accompanied my reading. My watch on the bedside table ticked along, marking the time as I read and re-read these words which were coming to me from a time, and person, long past but not ever forgotten.

So she had known that we would find out about her own

knowledge of her illness. I suppose it couldn't possibly have stayed hidden. She had known but she had chosen to make our last months together normal. There had clearly been signs that we had overlooked – our special Christmas presents for instance, and some of the things she had said to us – but Dad and I had no reason to have realised their significance. There we were blithely living our lives – work, school, petty arguments with friends, irritations with traffic – while Mum lived on with the deep, probably terrifying, secret of her illness.

I tried to read the letter again but I couldn't stop crying and my vision was blurry with tears. I thought of her words instead and I felt the love of what she had done – not just in the letter but in concealing from us what was happening to her.

I don't know how long I sat there but eventually the tears dried up and I was left with a slight numbness, a surreal feeling as if I was looking at myself from a distance. That, I told myself, was what it meant to be a mum, and I swore then that I would do the same for my child. Whatever life threw at me, I would do my best to do right by my child.

Eventually, I picked myself up. I put Mum's letter carefully away. I knew what she meant by not worrying about keeping it – she didn't want me to break my heart if something happened to it – but I couldn't help but cherish it and would do everything in my power to keep it safe. I wouldn't re-read it again that day, though. I decided I just needed to get on. So I tipped out the rest of the clothes from that box. There were some knitted jackets, hats and bootees in there, each with a little scrap of paper telling me who had made them – grandparents, neighbours, even Aunt Elizabeth, who I really couldn't imagine with a pair of knitting needles in her hands.

I took them all downstairs and sorted them for washing then I went outside and unpegged the other clothes from the line. Methodically I folded them, placed them in the basket, then brought them upstairs to put in the chest of drawers.

All the while Mum's words ran through my mind and, slowly, I felt the shock dissipate and a calm, comforting feeling slowly seeping into me.

PART TWO

Chapter Twenty Three

I was on the hospital ward for a total of three days before even having the baby. It may not sound like long but believe me, when you are stuck in hospital, for whatever reason, one day feels more like a week.

For me, I was constantly impatient as well. I wanted my baby! I had come in because I was overdue and I was going to be induced. In my naivety I had believed that I would go in the afternoon I was booked in for, get induced, go into labour, have the baby probably that night or at the very latest the next morning and be back home within a day or two.

That seems laughable now.

I had arrived at the ward with James. We were both nervous, believing that within the next 24 hours at the most we would officially be parents. He carried my bag in and we located the ward where it was all to happen.

A lovely midwife called Teresa welcomed us in and showed me my bed. There were five others on the ward, only one of which looked to be vacant. One woman about my age was sitting on an exercise ball, looking fairly uncomfortable. A bored-looking older woman lay on her bed, flicking through a magazine. The bed opposite mine was vacant and the one to the other side had a full-sized suitcase laid carefully on it. It appeared to be at an exact right angle to the mattress and it looked absolutely immaculate.

The bed next to mine was shielded by a curtain but I could hear some hushed discussion between, presumably, its occupant and a medical professional of some description. I tried hard not to eavesdrop on the conversation.

"Right, get yourselves settled in," said Teresa, "and I'll be back soon to get the basics done. In the meantime you could do a wee for me in this."

She handed me a weird kind of bowl made from egg carton-like material. I looked at it.

"The toilets are up there," she said, scribbling my bed number on the bowl, "You can leave it on the shelf in there and I'll pick it up."

She bustled off and I looked at James. He shrugged.

"I'll see you in a minute, then," I told him and duly went to the toilet and followed Teresa's instructions. I wasn't that enamoured with leaving a bowl of wee on a shelf but I guessed it was merely the tip of the iceberg where dignity and having a baby were concerned. I'd already endured a so-called 'sweep', firstly by a trainee midwife and then by a qualified one. They had asked if I'd mind the trainee 'having a go' and I just thought, why not? She had to start somewhere.

I wondered what else I should expect and I was glad that I didn't know. It must be harder when you've been through it before. I was nervous, but riding on a wave of exhilaration at the thought of finally meeting this little person who'd travelled around inside me for so long.

James and I sat, anxiously, not speaking. The ward was so quiet, it felt like the minute either of us said anything, it would attract the attention of the other occupants. I wanted to know about them, their stories, and how long they had been waiting. We were about to go through a momentous experience; if not exactly together, in unison. Our babies would very likely have the same birthday.

After a while, Teresa returned. She expertly whisked the curtain around the bed and asked a few questions which she noted down the answers to. She took my blood pressure and explained that she would need to give me an internal examination before they could apply the Prostin gel which should kick-start my labour.

She explained a lot, but to be honest I don't think I really took it all in. I just wanted to meet my baby.

I think Teresa mentioned then that the gel might take a while to work but I didn't think to ask how long 'a while' might be.

We just did as we were told, James and I, being young and polite, and unsure of ourselves, then sat back and waited.

In time, James had to leave while we 'ladies' had our tea. He kissed me on the forehead and promised he'd be back later.

"I'll go and have tea at Mum's," he said.

"Good idea," I smiled. "James... we're going to be parents! Can you believe it!"

He looked a bit pale, I thought, and put it down to nerves. I didn't blame him one bit.

Dinner was served on trays in the common room which housed the TV. The ward itself consisted of six rooms similar to mine so in total there were 36 beds. About 15 of us were eating and I took a seat next to the woman I recognised as bouncing on the exercise ball.

"Hi," I said, and smiled.

"Hiya," she said, "Just in, are you?"

"Yeah, just this afternoon. How about you?"

"Two bleeding days," she said, and winced.

This was news to me. Two days?

"What – have they not induced you yet?"

"Oh yeah, they induced me alright. I've had two lots of that bloody gel now, I wish they'd give me some more to be honest."

I took this in. I had not planned on being there for two days. Dad was set to visit the following day and I'd imagined him arriving to hold his grandchild in his arms.

We introduced ourselves, between her pains. She was Olivia; Liv, she said, and her husband was coming in later. Like me, she was approaching two weeks past her due date and so they had decided to induce her.

"I tell you what, it's bloody boring on that ward," she said. "The staff are nice and everything but it's the last place I want to be. I wish they'd let me go home but once you're induced, that's it. You're in. Have they done you yet?"

"No," I said, "After tea I think."

"Ah well good luck," Liv said, "It may be totally different for you. Who knows, you may even have yours before me!"

I smiled at her and when we'd finished our food (spaghetti in a not-bad tomato sauce followed by a watery rice pudding), I walked back to our room with her slowly. The curtain was still drawn around the bed next to mine and I looked at Liv. She mouthed 'teenage mum' at me, and then withdrew to her side of the room and back to the exercise ball.

I sat on my bed and read some of my book. The same few words of it, again and again. I had just started it and I couldn't make sense of the opening paragraphs. I don't suppose I was thinking straight really. Every time there was movement at the door I looked up, expecting to see a midwife, only to be disappointed.

Visiting time began. Liv's husband, Simon, turned up. She introduced us and he went off to make us both a cup of tea. He was lovely, really smiley and upbeat. They drew the curtain around their bed, talking and laughing quietly, and I looked around at the other occupants.

The bored-looking woman now had her partner with her. She was still looking at the magazine, though, while he sat in the chair next to the bed, playing with his iPhone. The owner of the immaculate suitcase was now in place as well, and had an older woman with her. Both were beautifully dressed and made up, and I assumed they were mother and daughter.

I could hear crying from the bed next to mine, and a gentle, reassuring young man's voice. My heart went out to this girl I had not yet seen. I was scared enough; not just by the labour but by the responsibility which lay ahead of me. I wondered how she must feel.

In time, Teresa came through the door. I looked up and smiled.

"No hubby yet?" she asked cheerily.

"No, he'll be here soon though," I replied.

"Well listen, I'm sorry Sarah but we've had a few unexpected things happen this afternoon. It's taken me way longer to get to you than I'd hoped. I think the best thing for you is to leave off the Prostin until the morning. Get a good night's sleep tonight, eh? You'll need the energy."

"Oh," I said, and she could clearly see I was disappointed. More than that though, I just wished I was at home. What was the point of being there if they weren't even going to induce me?

My disappointment was compounded moments later when my visitor arrived. Not James, as I'd hoped. But, you've guessed it, his mum.

Chapter Twenty Four

To say I was disappointed to see Hazel would be an understatement. Disappointed but, sadly, not surprised.

"James sends his love," she said, placing a bunch of beautiful flowers on the locker next to my bed then leaning to kiss me on the cheek. "I told him to rest tonight. After he got your message saying they weren't going to do anything, we thought it would be best. He's so worn out from work, poor love. Retail will do that to you, you know."

Hazel often talked about the world of retail as though it was akin to brain surgery or space exploration. She couldn't hide the fact that she loved James following her into that field of work.

Her other three sons, James' older brothers, had evidently each disappointed in their own way. Neil, the eldest, was a vet. Now, I couldn't see anything wrong with that but I did sense that Hazel was not enamoured with animal care. She appreciated his earning capacity, of course, but there was the added spanner in the works of Neil being gay. No grandchildren from him, or so Hazel thought. I happened to know that Neil and his partner Alan had other ideas but James and I had been sworn to secrecy about that.

Next was David, the supposed black sheep of the family. He chose not to go to university, taking an apprenticeship instead with a firm of electricians. He had started his own, very successful, business but split up with his long-term girlfriend so was another disappointment on the grandchildren front.

The brother after David was Jason, who went to university and then went travelling, and had never come back for more than weeks at a time. Hazel always said Jason was a free spirit. I thought he was a freeloader. He seemed to go from (older) girlfriend to (older) girlfriend, across South East Asia. They were usually Westerners, maybe divorced, and he tended to live with them in their homes for a while until he got bored of them, or perhaps until they got fed up of him. He was quite charming, I could see that, but he didn't bloody do anything.

So it had fallen to James, the youngest of the brothers by some years, to fulfil their mother's dreams. He was doing just that, possibly to the letter, by: pursuing a career in Retail; being engaged to be married, to someone he had been in a relationship with for a number of years; making Hazel a grandmother.

James was extremely compliant with his mother's wishes, as demonstrated by the previous points, plus the fact he did not come to visit his fiancée in hospital when she was shortly to give birth to their first child. Not that I was bitter.

"Now what is this nonsense about keeping you in tonight, when they're not even doing anything?" Hazel asked, before I had even had a chance to thank her for the flowers. "Have you said anything to them? I bet you haven't. Never mind, Sarah, I'll go and see somebody."

"No!" I said sharply. Because I could be quite quiet, Hazel had it in her head that I was lacking in confidence and unable to stand up for myself. She was quite wrong.

"Oh," she said, and looked at me. "Are you alright?"

Well at least she's asked me, I thought.

"I am," I said, "I'm not enjoying being here, I wish I was at home, but this is a hospital. Things happen which they can't predict. It took them longer to get to me than planned and they don't particularly want me getting going in the middle of the night when there are fewer staff."

"Babies always come in the middle of the night," Hazel huffed. "All my boys did."

"Well yes," I said, "But all of yours came naturally, didn't they? There's nothing that can be done about that. But there is no point making a baby come in the middle of the night when it doesn't have to and it may be more tricky to deal with it, is there?"

Hazel actually conceded the point. She even appeared to relax a little. "I brought you some goodies," she whispered conspiratorially.

I could see a Waitrose bag tucked away inside her oversized

handbag. Whatever else you might say about Hazel, she was never less than generous. I was sure she'd brought me some lovely goodies, and was looking forward to tucking into them once she'd gone.

"Now then, what's all this?" Teresa the midwife said, arriving just as Hazel was passing the bag over to me.

"Not contraband, I hope?"

"I'm afraid so," I grinned and introduced her to Hazel.

"Ah, no young man tonight then, eh?" Teresa asked.

"No, he's, erm, working," I said, excusing my fiancé.

"Ah well, as long as he gets away in time for the main event!" Teresa said cheerfully.

"Yep, that's non-negotiable!" I smiled.

Teresa patted me on the knee and told me she was going off shift then but her colleague Amanda would be along later on in the evening to introduce herself.

Hazel showed no sign of going.

"How was your day?" I asked her, aware that she liked nothing more than a chance to talk about herself.

"Oh you know, I don't know what I'm doing at that godforsaken charity!" she exclaimed, "They have absolutely no idea of what it's like in the real world. Goodness me, their shops are staffed by *volunteers* for God's sake. People who can't get real jobs and just want to steal all the good donations. Not that there are many of them."

I had heard this many times before. Hazel had left her lofty position at the chain store (under slightly cloudy circumstances) and taken a position in the Retail arm of a fairly large charity where one of Gordon's mates had been working as a consultant. She clearly considered herself way above this. I hated to hear the way she would talk about volunteers, as though they were the lowest of the low rather than people who actually gave up their free time to help a good cause.

Still, I let her rant on a little longer. She had no confidence in the staff who worked for her, or in the Managing Director she worked for. Blah, blah, blah. At one point I looked briefly over at Liv, whose husband had gone. She gave me a little smile.

After a while I let slip a huge yawn. Oops.

"Oh sorry, dear, I shouldn't go on, I know."

I smiled, as if to say, 'No, not at all,' hoping that it hid my real meaning of 'Yes, please go.'

Still, I appreciated her coming to see me. I really don't mean to sound ungrateful. And she had brought all those thoughtful things for me. Mostly I just wished that it had been James.

I hugged her and said goodbye, reminding her that at some point in the next few hours she could be a grandma.

"Oh my God, I'm far too young for that," she giggled. "I'll give James your love."

"Are you going to see him now as well?" I asked, surprised. It was getting quite late and he'd need his rest in case he found himself getting up in a few hours for the 'main event', as Teresa put it.

"Oh didn't I say? He's staying with me tonight."

I should have known. I was away for one night and James had gone back to Mummy.

After the last visitors had gone, all was quiet on the ward. The immaculately dressed one had gone for a bath, and the older woman had pulled her curtains around herself.

I saw Teresa's replacement briefly as she hurried in to our room then straight past me and behind the curtains of the bed next to me. I could hear quite a lot of crying going on. I felt my heartstrings stretch. I had not even laid eyes on this girl, but I could only imagine what this experience was like for her.

Liv asked me if I'd like a drink.

"Don't be daft, I'll get them," I said, as she was clearly not feeling comfortable, and made her promise to stay put.

I brought back two hot chocolates and I sat on her bedside chair while she stayed firmly on that exercise ball.

"Was that your mum?" she asked me.

"No, my erm... not mother-in-law... yet. Although, actually she would have been by now if this little person hadn't surprised us."

"Ah, decided to wait until you could fit into your dress, eh?"

"Yeah, something like that. So how are you feeling? Do you think you're getting closer? I know that's a stupid question, I can't imagine I will have any idea!"

"Not stupid at all," Liv said, "and yeah, actually, I have a feeling it may not be too long now. It may just be wishful thinking of course but these pains are getting a lot stronger and far closer together."

To demonstrate this, Liv's body kicked in, requiring her to make a sharp intake of breath. I looked away until she spoke again, not wanting to intrude on her pain.

"I think I'd better try and get some sleep, if I possibly can," she said. "Thanks for the drink, no doubt I'll see you for breakfast in the morning."

"You never know..." I said and wished her goodnight.

I returned to my bed and swished the curtains around myself. I seemed to have done nothing all day yet I felt exhausted. However, predictably, once I had got myself ready and tucked up as well as possible on the slippery hospital bed, I could not get to sleep for the life of me.

I had never stayed in hospital overnight before and it was only then, when it was quiet and the lights had been dimmed, that I realised how close to eerie it was. And how strange to be sharing a room with complete strangers. Not only that but strangers who were also undergoing this most extreme and personal of experiences.

The crying had at last stopped in the next door bed and I soon heard a softly spoken, "Knock, knock." I wondered for a moment if it was meant for me, then a friendly face popped around the curtain. I smiled.

"Hi, Sarah," she said, "I'm Teresa's replacement, if there could possibly be such a thing. My name's Amanda and I'm here all night."

"Hi Amanda," I whispered, not sure if the others were asleep.

"So how are you feeling?" she asked.

"Oh, OK," I said, "Disappointed I haven't been induced yet but I guess I just have to wait till the morning. Nervous as hell as well."

"Of course you are. Well, listen. I've been through it four times and look at me. No need to worry at all." She crossed her eyes and made a gurning face.

"Yes, that's certainly put my mind at rest, thank you."

"Just press that buzzer if you need anything. Who knows, maybe your body will kick in during the night and you won't even need to be induced!"

Amanda went off to see Liv and I was alone again. I picked

up my book but again failed to make any headway with it.

One of the others in the room was snoring loudly. I was actually relieved in a way as I thought I had been snoring ultra-loud during this pregnancy, at least that was what James would have me believe. Still, it wasn't helping me get to sleep.

I lay back and listened to the sounds of the ward. As well as the snoring I was aware intermittently of a buzzer going off in one of the other rooms and was sure I could hear a baby crying somewhere. That gave me a bit of a jolt. I thought of why I was there.

Then I heard a loud gasp from the other side of the room. I was pretty sure it was Liv. A buzzer went off, and I half wanted to see if she was OK but I decided that would be weird. We had only met that day and this was an intensely intimate experience.

However, I couldn't help but hear the whispered conversation she had with Amanda

"I think my waters have broken."

"Let's have a look, oh yes, I see what you mean, don't think there is any disputing that."

"Oh my God, is this it then?"

"It certainly looks that way. Are you in pain? Do you want some relief?"

"Yes please, that would be great."

"OK, well stay put. I'll send Sophie along to sort out your bed for you and help you pack. Shall I phone hubby?"
"Yes! Yes please! Oh God, I bet he's only just gone to sleep!"

"Well it'll be good practise then, hee hee!"

I smiled to myself, liking Amanda more and more. I was pleased for Liv also, that it sounded as though things were moving along. When I heard them come along with a chair and a trolley for her and her stuff, I popped my head around my curtain and wished her luck.

"Thanks, Sarah... See you on the other side," she said.

They wheeled her away into the unknown and I was left with my thoughts. And the sound of a stranger snoring.

Chapter Twenty Five

In the morning, I found myself eating breakfast with the 'been there, done that' brigade. Having given birth to at least one child each, these women clearly knew everything there was to know about childbirth, caring for babies and, I assumed, life in general.I sat quietly eating my Weetabix and trying to look interested.

"Well I had an epidural with *both* mine," said one of them, pushing back her long straight blonde hair proudly, "And I don't care what anybody says. The pain was *excruciating*."

"Oh I didn't, I just had gas and air with Imogen," piped up her older, dark haired neighbour, competitively.

This seemed to set the tone, as all five of my breakfast companions tried to up the ante with their variations on pain levels, pain relief, and fighting to assure everyone seated that they had been through the worst labour and that their choice of pain relief and birthing method had been the best. I was relieved when the empty chair next to me was taken by the older lady from my room, the one who seemed more bored than anything.

"Hi," I smiled at her.

"Hello. Aren't you one of my cellmates?"

"Yep," I said, "I'm Sarah."

"Carole," she spoke abruptly, but not in an unfriendly way.

"We were just having a discussion about childbirth," I told her, "Well, some of us are. I'm not actually qualified, as this is my first time."

"Well this is my fifth," this brought about hallowed gasps from the others, "And I can tell you each time is different. I've had two caesareans, and my last came so quickly he'd pretty much slipped out before they could get me out of the car and up to the ward."

This information was readily digested by our fellow diners.

"Really?" said the woman with just two epidurals, as I now thought of it. "This is number three for me. I think we're going to go for six though."

Wow, I thought, *she's going to have three more children just so she can say she's got the biggest family*. I wanted to pipe up that I was planning on eight but decided to leave it.

"I tell you what, though," said Carole, "It's not the childbirth you really want to worry about. It's what happens after. You get the baby home, everyone's excited. Especially when it's your first. Then it's back to work for husband, and on to being bossed about – sorry, *advised* - by your parents and in-laws, screamed at by your baby, and trying to cope on five hours of broken sleep a night."

I wondered at the truth of this as, if it was really that bad, why was she in there having her fifth baby? However, I thought of Hazel and could easily imagine she was going to want to be very 'involved' with the baby. In fact I suspected she might quite like to wrap it up and sneak off with it, just to make sure it turned out exactly the way she wanted. No chance. I remembered her offer of James and I moving in with her 'just for a little bit'. I thought I saw James teetering on the brink, so I quickly said a polite 'thanks but no thanks.' She wasn't happy, but come on. We needed to be able to look after our own baby.

Sipping my orange juice, I tuned back in to the conversation.

"My Peter's mum is a nightmare," one of the women was moaning, "She looks after Amelia once a month and she always gives her sweets."

"Well *my* mother-in-law is round all the time, at least once a week, always wanting to take Charlie out. I just don't want her to, she's got no idea about kids."

"But I guess she brought your husband up?" said Carole, and I suppressed a smile that she had said what I was thinking. "What's he like then? A nightmare?"

"Ooh no," the woman giggled, "He's fantastic. He's really hands-on and so great with Charlie."

"I guess that was just good luck then eh, if his mum's so rubbish? I hope our kids' partners don't talk about us like this one day."

The woman's cheeks flushed a little and there was studious quiet around the table, soon followed by the scraping of bowls and piling of cutlery and crockery onto trays. The other five took their things and left the table. I sat with Carole while she finished her breakfast.

"Something I said?" she asked, grinning.

I smiled back. "I think you have a valid point."

"I tell you what, that's the worst thing about motherhood really – other mums! I don't know what happens to women, or maybe they're already like it, the child just gives them an outlet for that side of their personalities. I mean, I moan about my in-laws, and my own parents, but they are genuinely just trying to help. Yeah, they've got different ideas to mine and Mike's but I just tell them if they're doing something I don't want them to."

"I'm sure you do," I grinned.

"And it's fine! I appreciate their help and the kids love them. I'd hate my children not to have grandparents. What are your in-laws like?"

"I've only got the one and actually, I'm not married yet so she's not really 'in law'. I guess she's a bit of an 'in place of' actually; my mum died when I was eleven."

"I'm sorry," Carole said, "I bet you really feel that now. I can't imagine not having Mum around. She was my birthing partner for my second daughter! Mike was away with work and the little monkey came three weeks early so Mum came with me. What's your partner's mother like then?"

"She's alright," I said, "Her heart's in the right place. She's got four kids actually, James is the youngest. Four boys in fact."

"Ooh... bad luck!" said Carole, "I don't know what I'd do without my daughters. I love the boys just as much, of course, but they're not quite as interested in me as the girls. They love football and roughhousing, typical boys!"

I smiled but inwardly thought that I was not going to get into this 'typical boy, typical girl' thing. My child was going to be whoever and whatever he or she wanted to be.

"I think she quite likes it actually! They're all quite different but they all love their mum."

"Hmm, just like the Krays," Carole smirked.

We made our way back to the ward and Carole told me she had been waiting to be induced. And she was hoping that today would be the day. Her baby wouldn't keep still and seemed to prefer lying transverse. I discovered this meant it was lying sideways which was dangerous apparently, if the waters broke and the umbilical cord came out first, or a limb got stuck. I felt like I'd learned so much since I'd arrived there. Who knew there were so many possible complications?

"I've been here three days now," Carole complained, "and they keep on checking whether the baby's in the right bloody place. All it needs to do is get its head down and stay down. Then it can come out!"

"Well fingers crossed for today," I said, "Isn't the specialist due round soon?"

"Oh yeah, he's due round soon, but that doesn't mean he'll be round soon. Bleeding lunchtime yesterday, near enough!"

My heart sank a little. I was so desperate to get started. Still, I thought, at least I hadn't been there three days.

"Best go and show willing," said Carole, "I'm meant to be sitting on one of those huge bloody balls to keep the baby the right way round. I'm not sure it makes a difference really but I need this little bugger out soon! They started to suggest yesterday that if the baby's the right way round today they might send me home. That is not going to happen, I can tell you now! I am not leaving here till this baby's out."

I admired her forthrightness. I knew I could stand up for myself but in this situation, where I was new to the whole thing and very, very far from an expert, I could imagine I was going to meekly follow whatever instructions were given. I sat on the chair next to my bed and phoned James. It was not long till visiting hours so at least he could come and keep me company.

"Hi babe," he sounded a bit offhand, "how was your night?"

"OK," I said, not wanting to tell him how badly I'd slept. "How about yours?"

"Oh yeah, good thanks," I thought I could hear Hazel's voice in the background, "Listen, Mum's asking if there's anything you want today."

I thought that was nice of her, but surely James had already thought to ask that?

"You could bring in my headphones please," I said, "and some squash. And, erm, no that's about all, I'm being well looked after here, thanks."

"No problem, what time are visiting hours again?"

"Ten till twelve this morning, then two till four in the afternoon, and six till eight in the evening."

"Right, so your dad's here later, isn't he? I'll come and see you this morning, is that OK?"

Again I could hear Hazel's voice. I'm pretty sure she was saying 'Of course it's OK' – W*ho asked you?* I wondered.

"Yep, that's great, I'm looking forward to seeing you, it seems like a long time."

"It's only been a day, not even that!"

"Yes I know, but hospital days are long days."

"Do you want books? Magazines?"

I smiled at the sound of James' concern.

"No I'm OK, I've got my Kindle thanks. Just you, and the squash."

"And the headphones!" he reminded me.

"Yes, and them."

Ten o'clock came round slowly and so far there was no sign of the specialist. I sat in my chair, not wanting to leave my position in case the doctor did come around. I was determined I wouldn't be stuck on this ward for days like Carole and Liv had been. If they induced me that morning then I could be in labour by the afternoon. I could even have my baby that same day!

It was past eleven by the time James turned up.

"Sorry Sarah, I just had to help Mum with something," he said, placing a bottle of squash, my headphones and a packet of M & S biscuits on my locker.

"Oh," I said, not wanting to create a fuss in the public arena of the hospital ward. I was not happy though. Before I had a chance to think of anything else to say, another figure appeared at the entrance to the ward, accompanied by Teresa. The specialist! At last.

Carole also looked up eagerly and he went to her first, asking a few perfunctory questions and gesturing at Teresa to draw the curtains around the bed.

"That's the doctor," I told James quietly.

"You don't say!" he said, smiling and taking my hand, "So how are you?"

"Oh yeah, bored out of my mind really."

"Any pain?" he asked.

"No," I said ruefully, thinking there couldn't be many situations when it was actually disappointing not to be in pain.

"Not long now," he said, and squeezed my hand, looking a bit pale and nervous.

"No! No way!" I heard Carole's voice sound emphatically from behind her curtain. "I'm sorry but that is not going to happen. You've been telling me for the last few days how risky it is if the baby's transverse. What happens if I go home and it moves again? No, I am staying here and I want to be induced."

She was quiet as the doctor's voice talked in hushed, calm tones.

"Well I'm not going to ask for a caesarean! I've had two already, you know that. Yes I know it might take a while for the gel to work, but you're not getting rid of me now. Not till you've got this baby safely in my arms."

I smiled and looked at James, who raised his eyebrows.

"Don't you start acting like that!" he said.

"God, I don't blame her," I told him. "She's been here for days and nothing's been happening. Honestly, I wasn't joking when I said hospital days are long. I can't believe it's less than 24 hours since we got here. Seems like 24 days."

James had brought a paper with him and thumbed through it while I sat on the bed, nervously drumming my fingers on my tummy. After a while, the curtain around Carole's bed was drawn back and the specialist emerged with Teresa. Carole gave me the thumbs up and I smiled quickly then turned my attention to the medical professionals who were coming my way.

"Sarah," Teresa said, "This is Mr Godber, the consultant."

"Hello," I said and he answered back brusquely as Teresa handed him a thin file which he flicked through, nodding as she reminded him why I was there.

"OK, let's have a look, shall we?"

Teresa pulled the curtain around my bed and I found myself tensing up at the thought of an internal examination by this less than warm man. Particularly as James was with me. I know it was nothing to Mr Godber, who would have had his hand inside hundreds, maybe thousands, of women, but it was something to me. I was relieved when he suggested Teresa did the examination.

The two of them stepped to the other side of the curtain while I removed my trousers and underwear and placed a neatly folded white sheet over my bottom half. James looked even more pale, I thought. Tough!

"OK," I said more bravely than I felt.

Teresa smiled reassuringly and began the exam, which didn't take long. I breathed in deeply and closed my eyes, counting slowly in my head in a bid to relax.

"OK," she said, "No dilation to speak of, sorry Sarah."

"Right, I can't see any reason to delay," said Mr Godber.

"Does that mean I'll be induced today?" I asked.

"Yes," he said, "But it may take a while for things to get moving. Teresa will come back after we've finished the rounds and apply the gel."

"It may not be till after lunch," Teresa said apologetically, "But it will be happening today!"

Then they were gone. I dressed in silence, then looked at James.

"This is it!" I said, taking in his grey face.

"I guess so."

Chapter Twenty Six

I tried not to let James know how I felt about his not coming in the previous evening. I tried...

"So, you stayed at your mum's last night?"

"Yeah, it was the best night's sleep I've had in ages."
"Oh smashing, I'm really pleased for you."

"How was your night in here?"

"Erm, not the best night's sleep I've had in ages. Let's put it that way."

"I bet. These beds aren't very comfy, are they?" he pushed the mattress, which refused to give.

"Nope."

"Are you OK?"

"Yep."

"Did you like all that stuff Mum got you? She said you deserve some treats."

"Yeah, that was really nice of her."

He smiled then. He knew that I had a problem with his mum, yet really as time had gone on, I'd realised it wasn't Hazel I had the problem with. Yes, she was overbearing and unbearably thoughtless at times but it was James' inability to stand up to her that was the real issue; that and his reluctance to cut those apron strings.

"So are you coming back this afternoon?" I asked. "You'll be kicked out soon so that we ladies can have our lunch."

"Won't your dad and Dawn be here by then?"

"No, I don't think they'll make it till this evening."

"Do you want me to come?"

"Yes, of course I do."

Did I?

"It's just I've got…"

"Let me guess. You've got some work to do."

"Yeah, I – don't sound like that! You know I've got to keep up. I'm working at home anyway so you can just call if you need me and I can take paternity leave as soon as the baby's here, isn't it better to hang on till then?"

"Oh, so you are planning on taking it, then? That's nice to know."

"Of course I am. I mean, I'll probably have to keep an eye on emails…"

"Of course," I abruptly butted in. "No problem."

""What..? Don't be like that, Sarah. I can tell there's a problem. Look, this is our future I'm doing this for…"

I looked around the ward. Carole and her husband were chuckling at something in the newspaper. My immaculately-made-up neighbour, Lisa, looked like she was dozing (immaculately) on the bed while her mum quietly read a book. Liv's bed was still empty. To my right the bed was also empty and to my left, the curtains were drawn resolutely shut.

I decided to draw the conversation to a close before I began to make a scene.

"Yeah, OK James," I sighed, "OK. Do what you need to do. Just…. don't send your mum in this afternoon, OK? I should be finally having the Prostin and I want some privacy."

"Oh Mum wouldn't mind."

"DON'T let her come in," I almost snarled, and I saw Carole glance discreetly in my direction.

"OK."

James went to kiss me on the lips but I turned my head. I was so angry with him and the worst thing was, I don't think he had a clue why.

Lunch came and went. I sat with Carole again, and Lisa sat with us. The young girl from the bed next to mine was having hers alone; one of the orderlies had brought it round to her.

I noticed some of the people I'd sat with at breakfast chose another table. It didn't get past Carole either.

"Don't think I'm too popular here!" she laughed.

"Ah well, I wouldn't let it bother you."

"It doesn't," she said. "Believe me."

"How are you getting on, Lisa?" I turned to our other room-mate.

She looked at me and smiled.

"Oh I'm OK, thanks. I just want to get it over and done with. If you know what I mean."

"I do, I definitely do."

"Yep, I think we can safely say that's what we all want," Carole said grimly. "I need to get back to my kids. I'm not sure Mike can cope for much longer."

"Are they coming in to see you?" I asked.

"Well, assuming I'm not in the throes of labour this evening – and I bloody hope I am – the older ones are coming in then."

"That's really nice, I bet you can't wait to see them."

"I can't, to be honest. I'm missing them like hell."

"Is your... have you got a partner?" I ventured to ask of Lisa, wondering if that was the right thing to do.

"No. Not anymore." She laughed a bit grimly.

"Oh, I'm, I'm sorry."

"No, it's OK," she shook her head prettily. "He cheated on me, about two weeks after we found out I was pregnant. I was, it was... really hard but I knew I didn't want him around if he was capable of doing that. I'm lucky I've got Mum. And Dad, he's great too but Mum's my best friend. She's so excited about this baby too."

"Will she be your birthing partner then?" Carole asked.

"Yeah, isn't that great? I think I'm going to have to look after her though, she'll be so emotional."

"That is lovely," I said, "really lovely."

"Will your mums be visiting?" Lisa asked brightly.

"Mine'll be in once I've had the little'un," Carole said.

"My... no, but my dad and his fiancée are coming in tonight."

"Oh," Lisa said, "My turn to be sorry. Did your parents split up?"

"No, Mum died when I was at school. A long time ago." I tried to draw the conversation to a close right then and there but to my horror I found that tears were falling, unbidden, down my cheeks.

"Hey, oh God, I feel awful now," Lisa put her hand on mine. "Going on about how great my mum is."

"Don't..." I struggled to speak against a sob, "it's bloody pregnancy hormones. Honest... honestly, Mum died when I was eleven. It was awful, but it was a long time ago. I've accepted it. I think I'm just, this situation..."

"I know," said Lisa, and Carole patted me on the arm.

I cried a little harder at their kindness.

That afternoon, only half an hour or so after lunch, the visitors began to return. Then Teresa turned up, pulling a trolley with the heart monitor on it and swishing the curtains around me.

"No hubby?" she asked brightly but I could see a small crinkle in her brow as she busied herself getting the equipment set up.

"Fiancé," I corrected her, "and no, he's got to work this afternoon; he was in this morning though."

"Oh well, that's good then. Anyone else coming in this afternoon?"

"No, I don't think so. My dad and his girlfriend... sorry, also fiancée, should be in this evening though. They're living in Canada at the moment."

"Ah, I bet you miss him."

"I do, I really do. I can't wait to see him."

"OK. Let's get these monitors on you, shall we? I'm so sorry we're running so late again today but, assuming everything's OK, we can get that Prostin in you and get this show on the road."

"That would be brilliant," I said and she smiled at me.

"You may not feel quite the same once you're contracting!"

"I don't care," I said, "I just want to meet my baby."

"You will soon enough, you will."

Once I was strapped up to the devices and she could see that the readings were coming through clearly, Teresa left with the promise to be back 'in ten', with the Prostin gel.

I watched the numbers, marvelling at the thought that they were being caused by my baby. My hand rested on my stomach and I stroked the taut skin, knowing the baby was so close, just centimetres away but untouchable.

When Teresa came back, she scanned the paper printout.

"I'm happy with that," she said. "Let's get this show on the road, shall we?"

This was clearly her stock phrase but I liked it.

"Let's," I said.

"OK," she began undoing the straps which she'd fastened around my bump, "well I should warn you, this bit's not the most pleasant but you've already had a few internals, haven't you? No worse than that. I'll step outside for a moment, you can remove your bottom layers and put this sheet across you. Give me a shout when you're done."

I manoeuvred myself onto the bed and lay down, then had to sit up again in order to successfully remove my trousers and knickers. The sheet safely across me - though really, what was the point? – I told Teresa I was ready.

It was over within a minute.

"There you go," she said. "Let's see what that does for you."

"So what do I do now?"

"The same as before really," she said. "Try to relax but also keep active. Lots of walking. That can really help bring labour on. I'll come and see you a bit later."

She disappeared through the gap in the curtain, taking the trolley with her.

"Amy?" I heard her say, and a small voice answered.

I pulled my clothes back on and drew back the curtains. Carole and Mike were disappearing through the ward door. Lisa had a friend with her. She smiled when she saw me but the smile vanished quickly.

"Are you OK?" I asked.

"Yes, I'm fine, thanks, I think that lunch may have got my labour going, though. I've been having these pains. They must be contractions."

"Wow!" I said, "I'm jealous!"

"Don't be, they're painful."

"They'll be worth it," her friend said.

"I'm off for a walk," I told them, "I'm going to try and have my baby before you have yours!"

"It's not a competition!" Teresa's voice called from behind the curtain.

I laughed and walked slowly out of the door.

The maternity wing of the hospital was on its own, across a car park from the main body of the building. It felt strange being outside, in the almost-normal world. I didn't want to go into the other building. Instead, I walked the length of the car park, enjoying the July sunshine and the kind looks I got from passers-by. As I walked, I stroked my belly and internally willed my baby to start coming.

What was labour going to be like? Despite my antenatal classes, I had little idea. I hadn't wanted to know too much because it was going to happen, and if it was going to be awful surely it would be better to just find that out at the time, not spend ages worrying.

I wasn't ready to go back in when I got back to the maternity ward so I did the same walk again but by the time I'd finished I was desperate for the toilet so I returned to the ward. Something had changed. No, two things had changed.

Lisa's bed was now surrounded by a pleated blue curtain while the bed to the left of mine, for the first time since I'd been there, was not.

Chapter Twenty Seven

I looked with interest at the bed. The covers were ruffled and a stack of magazines were on the table, along with half a packet of Fruit Pastilles and an iPhone.

There was, however, no sign of the girl. I hoped she was OK but reasoned that she must have been, to have left everything as it was.

Carole gave me a cheery wave then gestured towards Lisa's blue curtain with her eyebrows raised. I had no idea what the eyebrows were trying to tell me so I just smiled and shrugged then I heard raised voices.

"I want him to be here, Mum."

"No," came a very firm, very well-spoken voice. "I won't have it."

"It's not up to you, Mum, it's... *owwww*..."

"Hush, dear, don't upset yourself. Just think about the baby. Oh, where is that midwife? She said she'd be back by now!"

There was some low groaning followed by a sharp intake of breath. I really didn't want to listen but there was no option, other than to leave again I suppose. Which I didn't. So maybe I was being nosy after all.

"Mum, it's his baby. I want Dean here. It's his baby."

"Well he should have thought about that before going off with that... that *whore*."

I looked at Carole. She looked at me. I could see she had a book in her hand but it was hanging limply. She wasn't even bothering to pretend to try and read it.

"Where is that midwife?" Lisa's mother exclaimed again.

I had seen Teresa when I came back in.

"Alright, love?" she'd smiled at me, but had looked distracted as she'd hurried off to answer the phone.

I was almost tempted to tell Lisa and her mum that I'd seen Teresa but I thought better of it. She surely would be on her way back any time. Also, it would have been clear that I'd been eavesdropping.

Sure enough, within moments, in hurried Teresa. She didn't bother with the 'knock, knock' bit but just slipped through the curtains to whatever scene lay beyond them.

"Now how are we..."

"Oh, so you're here at last," came Lisa's Mum's shrill tone.

"Yes, sorry about that, it's a... well, it's a bit awkward but..." Teresa lowered her voice so I couldn't hear the rest of what she said. Not that I was trying to, of course.

"No he cannot!" Lisa's mother sounded like she was set to explode.

At the same time, another "Oooowwwwwwwww!" could be heard.

"OK, it's OK love," came Teresa's comforting tone. "Most importantly, we'll get you to the delivery ward. I've asked Suzy to come along for your stuff, and I'll go and get the wheelchair. I don't suppose you feel much like walking at the moment."

"N... nnnno. I don't. Can I speak to Dean?"

"What?" said Lisa's mother.

"It's a bit tricky, love," said Teresa, speaking over the top of Lisa's mum. "I mean, I can't get the phone to you. You could ring him..?"

"Over my dead body!"

"Mum!" Lisa said, "Will you just shut up?"

"Well I never..."

"I'm sorry, I'm sorry Mum, I don't mean to be rude, it's just, well this hurts so much and... well I'm sorry as well, I never told you the whole story."

"What... what do you mean...?"

Carole's and my entertainment was halted for a short while as Lisa seemed to be overwhelmed once more by another wave of pain.

"Aaooowww... Ooooooooowwwwwwwwwww!! It wasn't just him, Mum. In fact if anything..." she panted.

Carole's book dropped to the floor.

"Where has Suzy got to?" Teresa popped her head out of the

curtains, perhaps to try and avoid this moment of drama and give Lisa a tiny bit of dignity at least. I busied myself with my phone and Carole scrabbled about, trying to look busy so Teresa wouldn't think ill of us. She did give me a small smile however, just as Lisa's mother's voice came shrieking from behind her.

"You did WHAT?"

"I slept with him, Mum."

"Darren? Dean's friend Darren?"

Teresa looked unsure of what to do. Then her eyes alighted on Suzy, cheerfully wheeling a trolley around the corner, fully oblivious to the fact she was about to enter a scene worthy of *Eastenders*.

"There you are!" Teresa exclaimed. "Lisa, Suzy's here! I'll go and get that wheelchair. Suzy, get Lisa's stuff as quickly as you can. We need to go."

Suzy slipped behind the blue curtains just as Lisa emitted another howl of pain, whilst her mother remained uncharacteristically silent.

Within moments, Teresa was back, Lisa was in the wheelchair, and the curtains were swooshed away so that Lisa could be taken to deliver her baby. She looked flushed and in pain and her mother didn't look much better.

"Good luck Lisa!" I called as the unhappy procession made their way through the ward doors.

"She's going to need it," said Carole.

Chapter Twenty Eight

And then there were three. Carole, my mysterious neighbour, and me.

What of my neighbour? Well, shortly after Lisa's exit, I set eyes upon her for the first time. She appeared in the doorway, looking flushed and uncomfortable. Extremely self-consciously, she quietly shuffled in her fluffy bunny slippers back towards her bed.

"Hi," I said, as she passed me, "How are you?"

She turned and looked at me, before casting her eyes downwards.

"I'm... OK..." she faltered.

"I'm Sarah," I said.

"I'm A-A-A...Ai..." she took a deep breath. "I'm A-A..."

I waited for her while she swallowed and took another deep breath.

"I'm Ai-mee."

"It's really nice to meet you," I said. "And that's Carole over there, you may have met already?"

Carole looked up, waved and smiled. I knew Amy was only a matter of a few years older than her eldest daughter. I'd thought I was young to be having a child but I looked at Amy and realised what 'young mum' really meant.

She still had braces on her teeth, and a slight touch of acne. Her face was all girl, though she'd clearly gone to some trouble to make herself up. Eyeliner, eye shadow, concealer, lipstick.

"We haven't met as such," said Carole, heaving herself up and coming over. "I think we were checked in on the same day, weren't we?"

"I-I-I-th-think so."

"That's right. Now everybody else has gone on. How long's it going to be till it's our turn?"

"Have you had any contractions?" I asked Amy.

"I th-think so, now," she nodded.

"Oh wow, not too long then," I wondered if that thought was any comfort to her. Of giving birth and being a mum for the rest of her life, which was the more scary thought?

"I hope it's not too bad," she said, as though reading my mind. "Me mum said it were awful wi' me but not so bad wi' me brothers."

"How many have you got?" asked Carole, "Brothers, I mean."

"Two. They're 15 and 13."

"You're making me feel old!" Carole exclaimed, "My oldest is the same age as your younger brother."

"Oh, y-you're not old!" Amy answered quickly and kindly, "Me mum's old, she's f-43."

"I'm 45," Carole replied.

"Oh, I, er, I-I-I..."

"Don't worry," Carole laughed, "I'm not offended. I am old, to be having a baby. This is our last one and a real surprise. I thought I was past it but... I guess not."

"This was a surprise too," Amy confided, though I don't think either Carole or I were shocked at that bit of news. "I'd just finished me period, I thought I'd be OK. But..."

"I bet it was a shock," I said, "What did your mum say?"

"She weren't best pleased but she's been great. Only problem is, she don't like Rob."

"Your boyfriend?" I asked.

Amy nodded, "Yes, she won't even come in here when he's here. That's why I've been so upset. I love him, and I love her."

Her eyes filled with tears.

"Sit down," I said, "Come on, let's all have a drink shall we, before we get any newcomers."

"I don't think that'll be happening," said Carole. "Teresa says they wind it down at the end of the week as there's less staff cover at the weekends. So I think it's just the three of us from now on. I wonder which of us is going to go first."

Chapter Twenty Nine

While we were sitting drinking our tea, Teresa came in.

"What a cosy scene," she laughed. "I'm glad to see you all getting on. How are you?"

"I think we're all OK," Carole took on the role of spokeswoman.

"Great. Any twinges?"

"None here," Carole answered.

"Nor here," I said.

"I-I-I-m-m-m," deep breath from Amy, "M-maybe."

"Hey, that sounds promising," said Teresa. "Sorry for you two, though. It will happen you know, I know it doesn't feel like it but you won't be here forever. By the time I'm back on Monday I want you to be gone."

"Oh, are you not on this weekend?"

"No, even I need a break sometimes."

I was surprised by how disappointed I was at this news. I barely knew the woman; after all, I'd only been in for a day, but I'd come to trust her and rely on her no-nonsense cheer.

"Well, OK then. I keep meaning to ask, by the way, how is Liv?"

"Liv?"

"Yes, Olivia, she was in that bed there," I pointed.

"Oh, yes," Teresa paused. "She's had her baby. I can't really tell you any more than that."

"Of course," I said, thinking I probably shouldn't have asked. There must be really tight rules regarding confidentiality. "Well great that she's had it, maybe I'll see her on the other side!"

"Yes, maybe," Teresa said, "Now it's nearly visiting time. Amy, before Rob gets here – or is it your mum this afternoon? –

I'd like to do an internal and just see how you're getting along. You two ladies, why don't you go for a walk or something? See if you can get things moving too?"

Carole and I looked at each other and shrugged.

"Why not?"

"Come on then love," Teresa ushered Amy to her bed and Carole and I eased ourselves up and out of the ward.

As we wandered up the path, an ambulance rushed by, lights flashing.

"Hospitals are fucking depressing, aren't they?" Carole said.

"Yep."

"Did you have to come and see your mum in hospital – before she died, I mean?"

"No, I – it was sudden."

"Oh, that must have been awful. Though it would have been equally awful if it was long and drawn out. I don't suppose there is an un-awful way to lose your mum. I don't know where I'd be without mine."

"Well I suppose I'm used to it now, I don't even know if I still miss her. It's so long since she was part of my life. I do wish she was still alive though. But, you know, Dad's got his new partner. Things move on."

"They have to."

"They do."

Carole winced.

"Oh my."

"Was that a..?"

She steadied herself on a nearby lamp-post. "Yes, if I'm not very much mistaken, I think it was."

"Wow!" I said. "I really hope so. You've been waiting long enough. Let me know when you're ready to carry on walking. Or would you rather go back?"

"No, no, let's walk, I think it's doing me good."

"Great."

We walked and chatted. Carole described her children to me, and her family; and her life before them. She had been a professional, a high-flyer, working for some American IT company.

"That was my life really," she said. "I mean, I met Mike at

work – he was married at the time, I know, don't look at me like that – but we worked together and gradually became closer. He left his wife for me and we carried on working together. Nobody at the company knew for ages."

"Wow," I said, thinking of Hazel and Gordon. Then James popped into my head. I knew how much of his time he spent at work. I could see how relationships could develop when you spent that much time with people, in fairly intense situations. Still, I'd had no reason to doubt James' fidelity. Just his ranking of priorities.

We stopped while Carole took a deep breath, her hands on her belly.

"I think this is coming on quite quickly," she said. "I'm sure that was worse than the last one. It's hard to tell though, really."

"Shall we head back?" I said. "Maybe Teresa will give you an examination too."

"Yeah, that's something to look forward to," Carole said drily, but agreed that it might be for the best. We turned round and walked back, returning smiles from hospital visitors. We must have looked a sight; two heavily pregnant women waddling along through the car park.

Back at the ward, Amy was sitting on her bed, flicking through a magazine. She looked up and smiled at us. I saw what a pretty girl she was, and I was happy to see her looking fairly relaxed.

"What did Teresa say?" I asked her.

"She said I were about four centimetres, but she says it m-m-m-m-might go quite quickly because I'm so young. Sorry," she looked at Carole, who laughed loudly.

"Stop apologising, love! That's only going to make me feel more old! I'm pleased for you, really I am, and actually you might have company down on that delivery ward. I think I'm ready to pop too."

It was only then that I realised with Carole and Amy gone, I would be alone in that room. I wasn't too keen on the thought. Still, I reasoned, I could very well be gone soon too, if the Prostin kicked in.

"I hope you both get those babies out nice and quickly," I smiled at them.

"Well you too," said Carole, squeezing my shoulder then

leaning heavily on me, and groaning.

"Are you OK?"

"Yes, I think – argh – that is definitely more painful."
I helped Carole lower herself into the chair by her bed and she
pressed her red button, summoning help.

Chapter Thirty

By tea-time, Amy had gone. Wheeled away in her trusty chariot, as Teresa put it. Carole and I looked at each other, she from her position perched on an exercise ball. I from my chair with my swollen feet propped up on my bed.

"Just you and me now, kid," she said.

"Yeah, but it's not going to be long for you, is it?" I asked, timing the words with another deep groan of pain from her.

"I guess not. I'm going to try and have something to eat first, though. Fancy sharing my last meal with me?"

"I think I'll get my own thanks, but yeah, I'll come with you."

We wandered along the corridor to the communal area, where the orderlies were waiting with their trolleys, menu cards and shiny steel-lidded plates.

"What's it for you tonight, love?" the oldest one asked me.

"Jacket potato please... with salad, and ice cream for pudding."

"Coming right up! And you?" she turned to Carole.

"The same. Thank you." As we took our trays to the table, Carole whispered, "Actually I ordered the shepherds pie but that was before I saw the look of that one there."

She gestured towards a pale-looking slop which was being picked over unenthusiastically by one of our comrades.

"You're disgraceful!" I laughed.

"Ah, it doesn't matter. They've always got the wrong things here because there's never the same people about who filled in the menu cards. Half of 'em have gone to..."

She broke off to groan. I looked at her, concerned. "Don't you think you'd better be going? That doesn't seem like long since your last one."

"Oh fuck, maybe you're right. You couldn't go and tell them, could you? I'll try and get some of this down me before I have to go. I always have a massive appetite when I'm giving birth."

"No problem."

I stood up and wandered over to the midwives' station, looking up and down the corridor. I spotted Amanda, who must have been coming on shift, and explained to her what was going on.

"Oh right, best get that sorted out then! Thanks Sarah. You go on back and eat your tea, you're going to need your strength soon as well, you know."

Back at the table, Carole was standing up, rubbing her back. Some of the other women were watching her, but pretending not to be. Still, she wasn't exactly trying to hide her discomfort.

"Shit... fucking hell... Oh myyyyyy God."

I just sat next to her but I couldn't pretend I felt like eating. Presently, Amanda appeared with a wheelchair.

"Hop in!" she said cheerily.

"Yeah, I don't think I'll be doing much... motherf... Help me out will you, Sarah? And Amanda, can you give Mike a ring?"

"It's already being done, no problem. Now watch your mouth, Mrs, people are trying to eat in here. Get in and behave yourself or I'll have to tip you out. Don't think I won't!"

I grinned at Amanda, and gave Carole's arm a squeeze.

"Your turn next," she said, wincing, and she was gone.

I sat at the table for a moment before unpeeling the foil lid from my plastic cup of orange juice, downing the drink in one, then tucking into my dinner in earnest. Now I was on my own there was nothing else to do.

It was strange walking back into an empty room.

Carole's bed was still wrinkled but already Amy's had been stripped and made up afresh. At least I knew Dad and Dawn were coming to visit. I checked my phone, which I'd left in my bedside locker. There was a message from Dad:

'We're here! ETA at hosp 1930. Need us to bring you anything?'

There was nothing from James. I nearly rang him but I was feeling stubborn. He could ring me. I was the one sitting on my own in hospital.

I went to the bathroom, sorted out my hair, and even put on a tiny bit of make-up. I had hardly even considered my appearance since I'd been on the ward but I decided I wanted to look nice for Dad. I wanted to appear in control and confident so as not to worry him.

Back on the ward, I rolled Carole's exercise ball over to my bed and sat on it gingerly. Maybe it would help get me going as well. I was busy trying to find a comfortable position when I heard a voice.

"Here she is!"

My dad! I nearly rolled off backwards.

"Hey, steady on!" he said as he rushed over and helped me up, hugged me, then stepped back.

"Well, would you look at you... you're fit to burst, I'd say."

"Tell me about it."

"You look great though! Glowing!"

"Hmm."

"It's true! Isn't it, Dawn?"

"Too right," she stepped forward, having hung back in order for Dad and I to say a proper hello to each other. I smiled at her and thought how well she looked. Usually quite skinny, her face seemed to have rounded a little and she looked all the better for it, in my opinion. Clearly her return to her home country had suited her well.

"So where can we get a drink?" asked Dad.

"If you're looking for a pint, you're going to be disappointed," I said, "but visitors can get coffee and tea back out in the foyer. I, however, can get my drinks over there because I am a resident of this exclusive ward. And mine are free!"

"Typical," said Dad, "So what do you want?"

"I'll have a cup of tea please."

"I'll go and get us something, Tony," Dawn said, "What do you want?"

"Are you sure..?" said Dad, squeezing her hand, "Can I have a coffee please? I'm guessing it may be too much to ask for a flat white?"

He looked at me.

"Yep. You can get white. Or black. With sugar. Or without

sugar. I think that pretty much covers your options."

"Just a white coffee please, Dawn," he said. "And I'll be back with your tea in just a tick, Sarah."

I couldn't help smiling. It felt brilliant to see them both again. Even though it had really only been a couple of months since Cornwall, I had really missed them, both of them. When Dad came back, I told him so.

"I'm so sorry I've not been here for you, Sarah. I wish I could have been."

"I didn't mean it like that, Dad. I just want you to know how great it is to see you and have you here now."

"I know you didn't, love, but I still wish I'd been here. And that I could be here longer to help you settle into being a mum. We'll be over for a good couple of weeks though, at least. And I'll be back again in October."

October. My baby would be three months old by then. It was hard to imagine.

"So you're still enjoying life in Canada?"

"It has its good points. But it has one particular bad point. You're not there."

"Don't, Dad, don't think like that. You're happy with Dawn, aren't you?"

"Yes, of course I am."

"Then that's good enough. More than good enough. You two have your own lives to live and you need to be together. You can't be here and there. Even if we wish you could."

"Thank you Sarah, it's lovely of you to say that. I know it's not been easy for you. Even with James and his mum about." I said nothing. "Actually, Sarah, I can't not tell you this for a moment longer. I, oh shit, I... I've been worrying about this."

"What?" my heart was beating suddenly faster.

"Nothing to worry about love, really, at least I hope not. I... we... Dawn's pregnant."

The words tumbled into the empty room.

"You're... she's having a baby?" I burbled stupidly, my mind working overtime to take in all the implications. My dad, a father again. Me, no longer an only child (sort of). My baby having an aunt or uncle younger than itself. Dad and Dawn having a baby. Dawn's dreams being fulfilled.

"Oh my God, Dad," I was crying. Again. Where were all

these tears coming from? "Congratulations! That is the best news." I flung myself at him.

"Really, Sarah? Do you really mean it?"

"Yes I do, I really do. I'm so happy for you two."

"Oh Sarah," Dad hugged me close to him, being careful not to squash the enormous bump, and stroked my hair. "I was so worried you'd be pissed off."

"No!" I exclaimed, "Why should I be? You two deserve to be happy. I know I haven't had this baby yet but I already know how important it is to me, and Dawn deserves to feel that too if she wants to. You two are meant for each other and this baby... my brother or sister," I laughed, "will help ensure that you're really, truly happy together."

"Sarah, I love you so much."

"I love you too," I saw Dawn hovering nervously by the doorway. "Dawn! Come in! Dad's just told me, and I am so happy for you."

"Are you really?"

"Yes!" I laughed. "I am. So, so happy."

I held back from saying that I only wished they were having the baby closer to home. That wouldn't have been particularly helpful. Dawn came and joined the hug and I laughed again.

The sound echoed in the otherwise quiet room.

Chapter Thirty One

When visiting time was over, it really was just me in the little ward. I wondered how Carole and Amy were getting on. I thought I didn't like sharing my space with other people but actually, now faced with the alternative, I realised that it was by far the preferable option.

The midwives and orderlies would come in and bustle about, chatting to me cheerily, but they couldn't stay for long unless I needed them to and I didn't. The Prostin appeared to have had no effect whatsoever at that point. It would, I knew it would. It had to, but I felt right then like I could be there forever, doomed to watch other mums-to-be come in, and go out, while my baby just continued to grow bigger and bigger.

I was reminded of U. A. Fanthorpe's poem *After Visiting Hours*. Something about after the visitors had left... the hospital was a ship, sailing its way into the night. It felt like that. We patients were captive passengers, tucked up safe in our allotted bunks, holding our collective breath and waiting for the morning while the staff – or crew – went about their business, trying to keep us on course.

There was something about the place; in the air, the smells and the sounds. If I'd felt it that first night, surrounded by other women – each tucked away behind their curtains, for all I knew equally as awake and uncomfortable as me – that second one, alone in the semi-dark, it was almost all I could think about.

Hospital. A place to make people better. A place to bring new lives into the world. A place of sickness and death.

I couldn't stop my mind from wandering to all the people who had stayed on that ward, in that bed, before me. What had happened to them? No doubt the majority had delivered their babies safely but what of those who hadn't? There were doubtless some who would have suffered the loss of their baby, or their own lives.

I'm not given to needless worry. I am well aware that it improves nothing, prevents nothing, and just brings everything down. The choice, as far as I'm concerned, is to try and hope for the best, making life as good as it can be while you have the chance, or spend time and effort getting stressed about something which may never happen. If the worst does happen, then you deal with it.

On that particular occasion, however, I couldn't help myself. Having sailed through my pregnancy physically and mentally, believing there to be no point in thinking too much about the birth, suddenly there it was, laid bare in front of me. I was going to give birth. One of the most natural things in the world, yes, but also one of the most dangerous, surely? I had avoided the programmes like *One Born Every Minute*, because I didn't see the point. I was going to give birth. It was going to happen whichever way it was going to happen. I had very little say in the proceedings or the outcome.

However, despite my best efforts to steer clear of too much in the way of birthing information (other than the practical advice given out at antenatal lessons), there were of course plenty of women who loved sharing their own birth stories, or those of people they knew and, somewhat surprisingly, to my mind at least, they seemed particularly keen on sharing the horror stories. With a woman who was going to have to give birth. I found it very interesting that this was deemed acceptable by so many people. However, I'd shrugged it all off, let the facts roll off me like raindrops off a duck's back. Or so I'd thought.

That night, in the hushed hospital, with only my thoughts for company, the stories started to return to me. The woman who'd had to have an emergency caesarean section after 72 hours' labour. The friend of a friend of a friend who'd died of a massive bleed shortly after giving birth to a healthy baby boy. The baby who'd become stuck and had been asphyxiated by the umbilical cord. The stillborn girl with lips icy blue.

Try as I might, I could hardly recall any stories about good births. Straightforward affairs with a bit of pain, sure, but still – a healthy baby, and a tired but glowing mother and father at the end of it. The majority of births must go well, I reasoned with myself; it was just that the success stories didn't seem to people tales worth telling.

However, as I lay there, propped up on that squeaky plastic-covered hospital bed, I felt myself tense up and my heartbeat increase as fear slowly ebbed into me. Why had the Prostin not yet kicked in? I wondered. Was everything alright in there? As often happened when I worried about the baby, I put my hand on my stomach to feel an almost immediate kick in response. I could have sworn that there was something going on there. That baby knew when I needed reassurance, even though it was surely my job to provide that to the baby, not the other way around.

I switched my light down low. I put my earphones in and switched my music on to Shuffle. I lay on my left side. I lay on my right side. I was hot and uncomfortable. In the end I put my light back on to full brightness and took out my book but the words swam in front of me, floating on tears. Before I knew it, great sobs were racking my body and I let them come, reasoning that there was nobody they would disturb.

It wasn't just the birth I was worried about. It was James. More correctly, it was our relationship. I had been so delighted to hear Dad's and Dawn's news, but seeing the way they were with each other only compounded what I already knew. There was something not right about James and me.

Dawn and Dad could barely stop grinning at each other, and Dawn was leaning into him. He was stroking her leg and she was holding his arm. They were proud of each other. Proud of what they had achieved together and excited about the adventure they were embarking upon.

James, though he had been pleased at first, had shown an increasing lack of interest in the baby, and in me. He had been to barely any appointments, had attended one of the four antenatal sessions, and had been about to protest about that until he'd seen my face. He'd not been in to see me that afternoon, or in the evening, when he knew very well that I could be going into labour. He had phoned but... so what? What was a phone call? There was something very wrong and I knew it.

I took out my pad and pen from the drawer next to my bed, still crying fairly loudly, and I was about to write down how I felt when I heard a voice from the other side of the curtain.

"Are you alright, Sarah?" It was a voice I didn't recognise.

"Yes," I coughed, not really sure I wanted to be disturbed.

The voice became a face, which poked in between the curtains. This was someone not much older than me. A plumpish face, framed by a dark bob and sporting a concerned look.

"Ah, what's up, love?" she asked and the word 'love' struck me as slightly odd, coming from somebody my own age, but I could see the kindness in her and it made me cry even harder. She let herself in and took the seat next to my bed, not speaking but looking at me. Waiting for me to be ready.

"Oh my God," I said eventually, "I am so sorry. I don't know, really, what's wrong. I just. I guess it's all a bit overwhelming. And really weird, being stuck here on my own."

"Oh yeah, I can imagine, it's not great is it? I don't think this happens very often but do you know what? Every time I've seen it; someone in here alone, I mean, they wind up just like you."

"Really?" I looked at her and sniffed.

"God, yeah! It's horrible, isn't it? You're waiting for your baby, you're waiting for the bloody Prostin to work, and you've seen everybody else go off to have their little bundles of joy. Of course you feel weird. Of course you do!"

"Thank you," I managed a small smile. "That actually really helps to hear you say that."

"Good," she said, "and it's true. Oh sorry, I should have introduced myself. I'm Peta. Well, most people call me Pete."

"Hi Pete," I said. "Are you a midwife?"

"Not yet, but soon... I hope! A midwife in waiting, shall we say? Now, let's get you sorted. How about a couple of slices of toast and some hot chocolate? I'll get it for you and we can have a chat if you like, or I can bugger off if you like. Whatever's best. Either way, I want you to relax and then get some sleep. You're going to need it. I just know that little one's birthday is going to be tomorrow."

I smiled, and thought that was the perfect thing to say. Pete had brought me right back to the reality of the situation and focused me on what was important. The baby. Suddenly I felt excited again. I was going to meet my baby soon, and it really could be the next day. I gratefully accepted her offer and she brought me the toast and hot chocolate on a tray, with a fresh jug of water. We chatted at length, discovering that we were the same age and that we had a few acquaintances in common. I talked a bit about my concerns regarding the birth and she was able to tell me what she had experienced to date, with the births she'd been involved in and the patients she'd looked after. There were a few difficult situations, but none catastrophic. I believed her and I felt a soft relief seeping into me. I was starting to relax again. I didn't mention James because I thought maybe I was just in a bit of a state. He and I were different to Dad and Dawn anyway. I couldn't expect things to be just the same and it was surely natural to think the grass was greener sometimes.

After a while, Pete was called away and I switched off my light. I felt suddenly exhausted so I turned onto my left side. My right hand held my bump lightly and I tried to send thoughts to my baby, as mad as that might sound. *I'll see you soon*, I thought, *and I can't wait. Come out safely and I'll be waiting for you. I'll look after you, you'll be safe with me.*

I was aware a couple of times of nearly drifting off but, annoyingly, I caught myself and for some reason made myself wake again. However, the next thing I knew, it was morning and Pete was pulling back my curtains. She had brought me my breakfast on a tray, which she wasn't really meant to do. As I sat up and thanked her, I felt a sudden and undeniable pain in my abdomen.

"Ow!" I gasped, surprised, and Pete looked at me with a grin.

"I think, Sarah, that you've just experienced your first contraction."

Chapter Thirty Two

What surprised me once they'd begun was how quickly the contractions began to escalate. I was in the bathroom, brushing my teeth, and I had to hold my breath for a moment as I leant on the sink. I looked in the mirror to see my flushed face wincing, a dribble of toothpaste at the corner of my mouth. Not the prettiest sight but I really couldn't have cared less. This was it! My baby was coming!

Back out on the ward, I was surprised to see a new face; somebody had been checked in and given Carole's bed. She looked a bit older than me and distinctly fed up. I smiled at her as I rubbed my back and padded softly back to my bed. She returned my smile but looked tense.

I opened my locker, pulled out my phone and dialled James' number straight away. It went to voicemail.

"Hi!" I said, suddenly so excited to be able to tell him the news, "It's me! It's coming! The baby's coming! It's..." I had to break off while a new wave of pain rippled through my abdomen. I breathed long and hard, and continued. "I'm having contractions! My waters haven't broken yet but this is it, this is definitely it! So give me a call and get your arse down here, as soon as you can!"

I grinned to myself, sure he'd be back on the phone as soon as he got the message. I rolled the exercise ball – which had found its way to the other end of the room – back to the side of my bed and sat on it, waiting for James to call back and for Pete to come and tell me there was space on the delivery ward. I didn't want to think about if there wasn't. Was I meant to have the baby there in that room?

After about two minutes, I tried James' number again but

again it just rang out. I tried our home number and got the answerphone so I left a message there too. Slightly less excited in tone. Where was he?

Pete appeared at the doorway and I looked up expectantly but she gave me an apologetic smile and went to the newcomer's bed.

"Be with you as soon as, Sarah, just keep doing what you're doing. Those balls are perfect aren't they?"

"Mm, yes," I smiled. Not as perfect as having a baby. Still, they were busy. They couldn't predict what was going to happen. I busied myself eavesdropping on her conversation with the new woman instead. Who turned out to be very brusque in her answers and, so it seemed, had two weeks left until her due date but her waters had broken and she hadn't yet had any contractions.

"Can't you just induce me?"

"No, well, it's not as easy as that," said Pete. "The best thing you can do is wait for Mr Donal the consultant and ask him about it. I do think he's going to say to wait, though. You need to get these antibiotics working for you first, at the very least."

"But I'm here now. This is where babies get delivered isn't it?"

"Yes, it is, well no – not 'here' as such but yes, in so far as this is a hospital you're right."

I could practically hear the frost cracking in the air between them. *Go, Pete. Who does she think she is? I've been here two days. I'm bloody well first in, anyway.*

"Yes, I gather that," the woman said, "I didn't actually think I'd be having it here on this ward. But it's ridiculous. I can't just sit around here for days on end waiting for this bloody baby."

"Well, I'm afraid you might have to so you're just going to have to get used to it. I do understand it's frustrating," I got the feeling this attempt at nicety was added through gritted teeth, "but I'm afraid that it's the way for many of the ladies in here. And you've come in at the weekend when there are just lower staffing levels. We can't predict who's going to walk or be wheeled through the door to the ward so we tend not to push a birth that isn't ready to happen."

"Well it's just ridiculous. I might as well go home."

"And that's up to you. I can't stop you. But you are in the

best place here and now your waters have gone, you should stay safe. You don't want an infection, it could risk your baby's safety, and yours."

The woman seemed to huff a bit but said nothing else. Pete busied herself attaching up the various monitors then drew the curtains around her and smiled at me as she exited the cubicle.

"Now let's get you out of here! I'll be back in a tick with the wheelchair, unless you feel like walking?"

"Yeah, I'll walk," I said. "Can I just phone James again?"

"Oh, haven't you got through yet? Of course you can. I'll come back with the trolley for your bags."

Pete disappeared up the corridor and I picked up my phone. As it was ringing out at James' end I could hear my new neighbour making a phone call, lamenting her terrible situation and then giving somebody – her partner? – a right earful. Thank God I was getting out of there.

James still did not pick up, however. I tried our home. Nothing. Then – of course!

"Hello Hazel, is James there?"

"Oh hello Sarah, love, how are you? Yes he's here, he's just having a nice relaxing bath."

He's what?

"Oh how nice for him. Please could you get him? You see, my labour's started."

"Oh my God! Has it? I'm thrilled. I'll get him to call you back once he's out of the bath."

"Actually, I'd quite like to speak to him now."

"Oh yes, of course, I'll just call him." I heard the sound of her hand going over the mouthpiece and a muffled, "Jamie love, it's Sarah. She's gone into labour... yes, I know... well I think she probably wants to... OK, I'll tell her..." the hand was removed, "Sarah, he said he'll be there."

"Oh, OK. Thanks, Hazel."

"No problem, you just take care now, keep that little grandson of mine safe won't you?"

I'm afraid I just hung up. I could always pretend I'd been having a contraction. Well if you can't be rude when you're going into labour, when can you?

Pete soon appeared with the trolley and we began our walk to the delivery ward. We had to stop a couple of times while the contractions came and went. They were definitely getting much closer together.

"Is that lad of yours on his way in then?" Pete asked.

"He'd better be! I'm just waiting for him to call back."

"He'll be here," she said, "They love it, these blokes. I can't believe they never used to let the men in to the delivery rooms. I mean, yeah they're useless pretty much, ooh, 99% of the time, but it's their baby too. It's their moment as well, seeing their little boy or girl into the world. I've seen the biggest, muscliest, most tattooed men cry like, well, like babies. It's quite wonderful to be honest."

As she said that, I thought of Dad, who had missed my birth but would surely be there for his new son or daughter. Mum had been the first one to hold me, the only one to experience the magic of their baby's arrival. All thoughts of irritation with James seemed to ebb away as I was flooded with emotion. I just wanted him there with me, right away, to experience as far as possible what I was going through. Not the pain; I didn't mind that I was going to be in pain. I just couldn't believe that soon our baby was going to be there, with us. We could hold our child at last.

The lift announced its presence with a ding, its doors opened and a woman caked in makeup walked out, smiling at us then clicking off on impossibly high heels.

"You'll be back in shoes like those soon!" Pete laughed.

"I can assure you I have never been, and will never be, in shoes like those," I said, grimacing as another contraction took hold.

"No, I don't suppose you would. Let's hang on a tick, shall we? I'll keep the doors open."

Once the pain was subsiding, we moved into the lift. As the doors closed in on us, we were enveloped by a horrible, cloying perfume, no doubt left by the previous passenger.

I tried to hold my breath but it was no good. As the lift started to move, my stomach surged and I threw up all over my bags and down the front of poor Pete.

Chapter Thirty Three

And then she was there with me. A small, incredibly warm and soft bundle of limbs which Claire, the Irish midwife, placed directly onto me after I'd moved aside the straps of my nightie.

My daughter. Blue-tinged, almost opaque skin, making a small mewling noise as she searched instinctively for milk.

"That's a good sign," Claire smiled.

Hazel, for once, was quiet, watching her granddaughter, whom she had been so sure was going to be a grandson, with tears in her eyes.

I touched my little girl's head and shushed her gently, my own tears now dried up as I let the reality of motherhood wash over me.

At the sound of her first yell, the tears had come. Maybe even before that, as Claire had been cheering me on, telling me what a great job I was doing – *big push now* – and I'd felt this slippery, unforgettable sensation as my daughter arrived into the world.

There was no going back.

She had yelled and Claire had neatly taken care of everything, snipping and clipping the cord, while I had sobbed deep, heaving sobs of complete joy and relief.

"Abigail," I said.

"That's what – that's what you're calling her?" Hazel asked me, clearly still choked up by the emotion. "Is that what James wants too?"

"He said he likes it, yeah," I said, and added with a sudden burst of feeling. "And he's not here now, is he? So yes, Abigail. Abigail Georgina."

Hazel had turned up on the delivery ward about an hour after I'd been there. The look on my face must have said everything when I realised it was her and not James. However, my labour had been getting underway by that point and I had just decided to concentrate on that. Somehow, although I felt disappointed, I couldn't pretend that it was a shock to see her.

She did at least have the good grace to look a bit abashed.

"Jamie couldn't come," she said. "I don't know if he's coming down with something…"

I let those words hang in the air. We both knew there was no truth in them. He had let me down, again.

Hazel took a moment to let her granddaughter's name sink in. When she replied, to my surprise, she wasn't fighting James' corner.

"He should have been here," she said.

"Yes," I said, "he should."

Chapter Thirty Four

Once the initial euphoria had worn away, I realised how exhausted I was. The labour had been a good few hours, Abigail arriving in the early morning, and as it had been overnight and following some particularly bad nights' sleep, I was absolutely whacked. Still, the adrenaline was flowing and I wasn't going to sleep, not for anybody.

Claire had disappeared to get me some toast and a cup of tea – and a coffee for Hazel. I had Abigail, now dressed warmly in her brand new soft cotton babygro, settled against me as I leaned against the pillows.

"Do you want me to hold her while you call James?" Hazel asked.

No. I didn't want that. I wanted to sit, quite still and content, with my beautiful baby in my arms. I didn't even want to think about James. However, I knew I had to.

"OK," I said, and couldn't help but soften a little at the smile which lit up Hazel's face.

She took Abigail so carefully, but still my little girl's fists and legs jumped momentarily into the air, though she didn't wake. Hazel sat down slowly, and gazed at her granddaughter as I stood up to get my bag. It was a strange sensation, like something was missing. Suddenly I was without that weight I'd got used to carrying before me for all of those months.

I walked tenderly to my bag, retrieved my phone, and found James' number. I dialled and he answered within two rings.

"Sarah?"

"Yep," I said, feeling slightly surreal.

"Are you... is everything OK?"

"Yes," I said slowly, "We're all fine. Hazel says hello."

"And have you had hi… the baby?"

"Yes!" I said, realising that holding out on him was making me no better than a cheap game show host, "I've had her. Her. Our little girl. Abigail."

Silence.

"James? Are you still there?"

I could hear something at the end of the line, and it dawned on me that it was the sound of James crying. My eyes filled too.

"She's fine, James. A big girl – 8lb 1oz. She's beautiful."

"Can I… shall I… come and see you?"

"Yes, you flipping idiot. Of course. What are you waiting for?"

"I'm coming, now."

The phone line went dead and I wiped my tears away before Hazel could see them.

"James is coming in now," I said.

"Of course, I'll get out of your hair. I'll just have one more moment though, please… if I may?"

That was a first, Hazel asking permission for something.

"Yes of course you may. You'll have plenty of other moments too though, you know that don't you?"

"I do, thank you Sarah. And well done. You were brilliant. So strong. I wish James had been here to see you."

"Yes well it's all over now, isn't it? He missed it. But you didn't. Thank you for being here."

I meant it. For all her irritating ways, I was glad she'd been there. There was no doubt it should have been James, but it had actually been quite an experience to see Hazel in that situation, the emotional side of her opening up and she unable to stop it. I didn't suppose I would see it again.

True to form, once she'd handed Abigail back to me, with a little kiss on her forehead and then mine, Hazel got her bag and looked in the little mirror she carried everywhere with her. She tutted then began touching up her make up.

Claire, coming in with tea and toast, grinned at me above Hazel's head. "I'd say you feel like a nice shower soon, Sarah?"

"I would love one, please."

"Well get this into you and then I'll get you wheeled over to the showers. They're just across the hall but I don't think you want to be walking that far just yet. Take the chance for a bit of laziness while you can anyway. You won't get many more."

"I'll make sure she does," Hazel smiled at me, "I know what hard work it is being a mum."

I smiled back and Hazel stood to go. She came over and gave me an almighty hug, squeezing me as tightly as she dared without squashing Abigail.

"I love you, Sarah," she said.

I was gobsmacked.

Abigail remained resolutely asleep so I placed her in the little see-through cot which Claire had placed next to the bed and Claire wheeled me across to the showers, leaving the door open in case Abigail awoke, and promising to go back in and watch her while I showered.

"Take your time," she said, "and press that red button if you feel a bit weird. Otherwise, enjoy it. You deserve to. There are loads of towels so use as many as you need. It can all get a bit messy after having a baby."

What a feeling that shower was! I was a bit wobbly, still trying to re-find my non-pregnant balance but the warm water was heavenly and I stood under it for I don't know how long. Eventually though, I had to get out, desperate to see my daughter again.

My daughter. How strange those words sounded and yet how wonderful. I felt like singing. I wanted to tell everybody I knew. I was a mum and I had a daughter. Me.

I dried myself off and put on the clean pyjamas I'd brought with me then I unlocked the door and peered into the corridor. I could see my delivery room door was open, just across the way, so I walked over, gingerly. Inside, Abigail lay, tiny and soft, inside her cot, still fast asleep. Claire had stripped away all the sheets and I noticed a trolley had been loaded with my bags.

"That better?" asked Claire, smiling.

"Just a bit."

"Isn't it weird, the first time you walk into a room and see your baby there waiting for you? That's it now Sarah, she's all yours! I'm afraid I have to get you gone though – somebody else needs this room. We'll whip you away to the ward and you can have some breakfast soon, it's nearly that time already."

"What about James?" I asked, "He's on his way."

"We'll tell him where to go," Claire laughed, "I don't mean it like that."

"OK. Well thank you so much, you were brilliant. I don't think I'll ever forget you!"

"A pleasure, Sarah, you just take care now, of yourself and Abigail."

I looked at my daughter and a sharp, fierce feeling of love stabbed me.

"I will," I said. "You can be sure of that."

Chapter Thirty Five

The new ward was a mirror image of the one I'd been on before having Abigail. It was slightly disconcerting, in my sleep-deprived and labour-worn state. As it was still early morning, many of the beds had their blue pleated curtains drawn around them. When I was deposited into my own space, and after I'd been told where to find everything on the ward, I pulled Abigail's cot close to the bedside then drew my own curtains. At last I was alone with my daughter.

Across the room, a baby cried but I barely noticed it. I picked my sleeping girl up and held her to me. I suppressed the urge to wake her. I was desperate to see those huge, questioning dark blue eyes again but I let her sleep.

I leaned back very slowly against the pillows on the bed and just listened to her breathing. Deep, relaxed, surprisingly noisy for such a tiny person. I examined her wrinkled hands, poking out from the folds of her blanket. Her exquisitely small fingernails slightly long and scratchy and skin dry yet so soft.

I was scared of falling asleep with her on me. I'd heard horror stories of people falling asleep with their babies, but despite my exhaustion, I was still riding high on the wave of euphoria.

I wondered where James was but reasoned he would be there soon. Until then, it was just me and Abigail. I didn't mind at all.

Behind those curtains I could hear the ward beginning to come to life. Voices – adult voices – could be heard, and the sound of footsteps coming and going. More babies seemed to be crying now, and I could hear the voices of the midwives as they handed over to the next shift.

I felt glad to be behind the curtains, just for a little longer, but all of a sudden they were rudely whisked open and a hatchet-faced midwife was bearing down on me.

"You must be Sarah. Can't sit behind those curtains all day, Sarah. It's not good for any of us. Now this must be Abigail. How's she feeding? Have you had any wet nappies?"

I glanced at my watch. It was 6.38. Barely more than three hours since I'd given birth.

"I... I... I..." struggling for an answer, I pulled myself up straighter on the bed, and laid Abigail gently in her cot. "I fed her when she'd just come out, and she's been asleep ever since. She's probably tired out. Like I am."

"Right, well I'll be back shortly, just get this lot going too." One-by-one, the woman went round the room and brusquely pulled back the curtains to reveal, first, an annoyed-looking Carole, then a timid-looking Amy, and finally a young black woman who I had not seen before.

I grinned at Carole and Amy, delighted to be in the same room as them. Carole made a rude gesture towards the midwife's back and I had to stop myself from laughing.

"What did you have?" she asked me.

"A girl! She's called Abigail."

Carole wandered over to have a nose at her. "I had a boy," she said, "Jonathan. After the most excruciating labour to date. Flippin' heck. Still, he's out now. Been crying all night though, little bugger."

"What about you, Amy?"

"I had a girl too," she spoke shyly, and I noted there was no trace of a stammer. "Angel."

"That's a lovely name," I said and smiled at the other new mum on the ward. "Hi, I'm Sarah. What's your name?"

"I'm Jasmine, nice to meet you."

"Nurse Nancy seems to think Jasmine's fresh off the banana boat," Carole said disparagingly. "You should hear the way she talks to her, shouldn't she Jasmine?"

"Oh, it's OK, she doesn't know any better." I noticed a slight lilt of an accent to Jasmine's voice.

"Well she bloody should know better. God, I could swing for that woman!"

"Does she do that every morning? The curtains thing I mean?"

"Yes," Amy and Jasmine said together.

"I only got in here yesterday lunchtime so I don't know," Carole said. "Luckily for me – and her – she was swapping shifts not long after I got in. Hopefully I'm going home this morning, otherwise there could be some drama on this ward!"

As she said that, the midwife came marching back in. Jasmine, who had picked up her baby to feed, had dropped a baby's blanket on the floor as she'd done so. The woman marched over to the bed, tutted and picked up the blanket.

"You take this, need to keep baby warm-warm," she said in what I presume she thought was a Caribbean accent.

I looked at Carole. I had to stifle another laugh. Jasmine, on the other hand, was calm and polite, taking the blanket and concentrating on getting her baby feeding. The tiny head – I didn't know yet whether she had a boy or girl – was covered in tiny tight black curls. Just watching her feeding produced a strange feeling in me and I was suddenly desperate to be feeding Abigail.

"Excuse me," I said to the midwife, "should I wake Abigail to feed her?"

"How long since her last feed?"

"Only a couple of hours. But I don't know how much she had or how long she fed for. It was the first feed after birth."

"I'll be back in an hour, and if Baby hasn't woken up, we'll wake her then. Get some breakfast first," she said, "that will help your milk supply."

After the woman had left the ward, Carole turned to me delightedly.

"See?" she said gleefully, "don't forget to keep Baby warm-warm will you, Jasmine? Sorry, it's not funny is it? It's appalling."

"Oh I've had worse," Jasmine smiled.

"How can you be so bloody calm?" Carole asked, as Amy gazed at her, perhaps wondering how somebody could have the nerve to be so forthright.

"It's OK, really," said Jasmine, "she's not being cruel. She just doesn't know how to talk to me. It's her problem."

"I'll second that," I said, thinking perhaps we should change the subject, "Now what do we do about breakfast? Where do we have to go?"

"Nowhere!" said Carole, "It's strictly breakfast in bed here, it's brilliant. Lunch and tea are in the common room thingy like in the last place."

"Is that where you all know each other from?" Jasmine asked "The pre-labour ward?"

"Yeah, that was a bit of a drag," I told her, "Did you come straight in?"

"Yeah, I started having contractions on Thursday night and Daniel – my boyfriend - brought me in here early Friday morning. Charley was out within about two hours of us getting here!"

"Wow, how did you get on, Amy?" I asked.

"I-it was OK-K. Ab-bout five hours from going into the delivery room."

"These young, fit women," Carole exclaimed, "I was going for bloody hours. Actually it all stopped for a while, I had to have that drip thing and then when it got going, it really got going. Mike's definitely getting the snip this time."

The sound of a trolley had us all looking round, and soon we were being brought tea, toast and cereal. Nothing special but I was ravenous and I could have eaten it again three times over. As I was finishing my last mouthful of toast, Abigail began to stir and I had her out of her cot immediately.

I tentatively pulled aside my pyjama top and adjusted my nursing bra then got Abigail into what I thought was the right position. She was snuffling around and beginning to latch onto my nipple when in came Nurse Nancy, as Carole had called her, who, seeing what was going on, was right next to me, suddenly taking hold of my breast and squeezing it painfully. I saw a few beads of milk spring out onto my nipple and Abigail, crying at having been snatched from me, seemed instantly alert. The woman moved Abigail's head gently but firmly back towards me and soon my crying baby was crying no longer as her mouth really took hold of me and began to suck. I watched her tiny cheek and lips moving and thought I could see the beginning of a dimple near the corner of her mouth.

"There," Nurse Nancy said triumphantly, "You shouldn't have any problems now."

"Erm, thanks," I said, trying to ignore what Carole was gesturing at the other side of the room.

"Any more problems, let me know."

"Well I don't think I was having any probl…"

She was already gone.

Chapter Thirty Six

"What did James think of Abigail?" Carole asked me.

"He hasn't seen her yet."

"He hasn't..? Wasn't he there with you?"

"No," I said, not wanting to say any more on the subject. I didn't want to make excuses for him.

"S-so y-you went through it all alone?" Amy asked.

"No, I didn't, I had... James' mum with me."

"Your mother-in-law?" asked Jasmine.

"Sort of... not quite 'in law'."

"Wow, you must get on really well."

"Erm, you'd think so wouldn't you?" I desperately wanted to change the subject as I was starting to feel annoyed that James had still not turned up at the hospital, but I didn't want anybody else to know that. "So who was with you, Amy? Was Rob there?" I was sure he wouldn't have been.

"Oh yeah, he were there. And me mum!" She looked pleased as punch.

"What – both in the same room? At the same time?"

"Yeah, and it were great. They both cried when Daisy came out, and me mum kissed Rob before she left."

"Oh wow Amy, that's great. Really great." I meant it. It wasn't her fault my boyfriend, some years older than her teenage partner, had sent his mum in his place.

I caught Carole sending me a concerned look but I pretended not to notice, instead wandering over to Abigail's cot. She was quietly awake, gazing out through the clear sides of her bed, just looking.

"Hello," I spoke softly, lifting her out of her cosy cocoon, and holding her to me.

At that moment, a midwife I didn't recognise stuck her head around the doorframe.

"Sarah?" I nodded. "Your partner's here."

About time, too. I went straight out of the room, taking Abigail with me.

I could see James through the glass door at the end of the corridor and I wandered up there, not really wanting to make eye contact with him, knowing I was feeling pretty angry. Instead I looked at Abigail, realising for the first time what a responsibility it was carrying somebody so small and fragile.

Then all of a sudden there was an alarm going off somewhere. I looked up, bemused, and before I knew it the same midwife who'd come to tell me James was there was at my side.

"You shouldn't have her here you know, the alarm's been set off."

"Alarm?" I asked, briefly glancing at James who was looking questioningly through the door.

"Yes, didn't anybody tell you?" she sighed. "Your baby's got a security tag on her ankle, and if she is carried past those sensors up there, the alarm goes off."

"I was just going up to see my boyfriend," I gestured at James.

"I know you were, not to worry. Look, you go and see him, and I'll take her back to her cot."

"But – but he hasn't met her yet."

"Really? Well I'm really sorry but she's got to go back to your room. It's visiting time in an hour or so. Go and have a word with him and tell him to go and get a coffee. You can't take her to the door and he can't come in at this time of day. I'm really sorry love, he'll just have to wait."

A small part of me thought, *Ha, that'll show him*. Really though, I was disappointed. I was desperate to see his reaction to her. If anything was going to change the way he thought about things, surely it would be his tiny newborn daughter. I already knew I was never going to be the same person again.

I handed Abigail back to the midwife, who took her carefully back down the corridor. I could hear her talking to her as I opened the door for James.

"Sarah!" he said, kissing me, "How are you? Was that Abigail?"

"Yes," I explained the situation to him and he looked disappointed.

"Oh, I really wanted to see her before I got to work."

"Work?" the word bounced off the walls of the hospital corridor. "You're not going to work? This is the start of your paternity leave. Hang around an hour or so and you'll meet your daughter!"

"I'm sorry babe, I just thought it would be better if I got a few things tied up while you were here then I can take the paternity leave with a clear conscience."

"A clear conscience?" I nearly shouted and felt my blood pressure rising as he looked down the corridor, embarrassed.

I turned and walked away. I didn't dare speak to him for fear of what I might say.

Chapter Thirty Seven

I did have a visitor that morning, though. Dad. He came alone, even though I would have been very happy to see Dawn too. Apparently she had thought it might be nice for he and I to have some father, daughter and granddaughter time together.

"Oh my God," he breathed when he leant over her cot, taking my hand as tears rolled freely down his cheeks. "Your little girl, Sarah. And she could be you, 24 years ago. I can't believe it."

He wiped his tears away, although some continued to fall, and gave me an enormous hug. Abigail was sleeping again, which had surprised me. I was under the impression that she should have been awake and crying at least half the time, wanting milk. Carole had said though that Jonathan had been the same the previous day, and she thought lots of babies slept a lot at first, themselves recovering from the ordeal of birth.

"Make the most of it; seriously," she'd said, walking a red-faced, screaming Jonathan up and down by the window.

Dad sat on the chair by the bed and I sat down, so happy and relieved to see him.

"How are you?" he asked, looking at me intently.

I looked away, never one for scrutiny anyway and especially now as I suspected he must know what a disappointment James was being. I didn't really want to talk about it.

"I'm OK," I smiled. "Tired."

"Of course."

"Overjoyed."

"Naturally."

"A mum!"

He laughed, and took my hand.

"I didn't want to say it, but I knew I would: my little girl – a mum! And the same age your mum was when she had you. Funny how history repeats itself."

"Do you remember when I was born?"

"Do I? Bloody hell Sarah, I'm not forgetting that, ever. Not if I end up feeble-minded and senile. Seeing you for the first time was probably the most memorable moment of my entire life."

I choked back a sudden sob. "Really?"

"Yes of course, oh it was like a light had been switched on. I knew what everything was about. I knew why I was here. After your mum had fed you, I was allowed to hold you and I stared at you, and you stared straight back. The midwife said I should stick my tongue out to see what you did. I did what she said, though I felt like a bit of an arse, and you copied me. I couldn't believe it. All that's not to say that I didn't feel like sticking you outside a week or so later when you wouldn't bloody sleep but God, Sarah, I promise you it was the highlight of my life."

"And now you're going to do it again."

"I am, aren't I?" Dad looked pensively at Abigail.

"It's great, Dad, really."

"It is, isn't it?" he grinned genuinely at me. "It's a bit weird though. I really thought that was it; confirmed bachelor and all that. Now look at me."

"I can't think of anything better, Dad, I just wish you were a bit closer."

"Ah yes, well that's something else I wanted to talk to you about."

"What?" I looked up from trying to unwrap a tiny yellow babygro that Dad had brought with him.

"Well, we think... we might move back to the UK, have the baby over here."

"Really? I said cautiously. "'Might'?"

"Well almost certainly. I wouldn't have said anything to you otherwise."

"Dad, that is amazing. That is brilliant. I – oh, I really hope you do. But you might change your minds. You might, I don't blame you if you do. And also, what about Dawn's mum? Won't she want you in Canada?"

Dad started laughing, "You sounded just like your mum then. She'd have those kinds of conversations with herself, answering her own questions, voicing her internal dialogue. No, Sarah, really, we are trying to work out how to do it. Dawn knows how much I miss you – she misses you too – and actually I haven't been able to live with being so far away from you, especially when you're going through this major thing. I do like Canada but really, I've been a bit of a miserable bugger deep down. And that's all down to you. Dawn's mum wants to be near her daughter and first grandchild but she's actually considering a move to the UK. Two of her cousins live in Bristol, and she says she'd like to spend more time with them. She's an old battleaxe anyway – don't tell Dawn – so whatever she decides, I'm pretty sure she'll be OK."

"Oh Dad," I sighed, "I miss you so much."

"Well, hopefully you won't have to for much longer."

Abigail chose that moment to wake up and Dad held her for a while before she got too hungry. I took lots of photos, with his camera and my phone, then he handed her to me and I began the long, slow feeding process.

Dad went off to find a coffee and phone Dawn and I sat quietly watching my daughter feeding while I let the news sink in that my dad was coming back to me.

Chapter Thirty Eight

I had a lovely couple of hours with Dad, who told me more about their possible move back to the UK. "We've had a few problems trying to rent the house out too. The tenants moved out last month, and we've not been able to get anybody else in their place. I'm finding it a bit stressful to be honest. But I don't want to just sell it and lose a base in the UK. Just the thought of it made me feel really scared, like I'd be giving up my right to be here and any chance of ever coming back."

"But it's just a house, Dad," I said, though I couldn't really feel that and I knew he couldn't either. It was not just a house, it was our family home. But that didn't mean he should hold onto it indefinitely. "To give you a cliché, Dad, you can't let the past control the future."

"You're right, and I don't think I would. But it's still a pain trying to manage it from a different country. And Dawn is actually missing England too, you know. The only thing is, while we were back in May, she seemed to fall in love with Cornwall. And she and I have both been looking at Falmouth where the arts college is, so I'm afraid that although we're hoping to come back, we might not be back in Yorkshire."

"Wow, really? That would be amazing! I'd love to have a good excuse to come down to Cornwall regularly! And Abigail can have holidays by the seaside with her grandad and step-grandmother and, erm... uncle or auntie."

"Shit that sounds weird!" Dad laughed.

"It does," I agreed, "But pretty brilliant too."

Just before lunch it was time for the visitors to leave and for us new mums to shuffle along to the common room to find what new delight awaited us beneath those shiny metal domes.

"Lisa's in that room there," Carole indicated one of the private rooms.

"Is she?" I asked, "Is she OK?"

"Yeah I think so, she had to have a caesarean though, so she won't be joining us at lunch."

As we took our trays, I heard a voice call my name. I turned to see a very pale face smiling at me. It took me a moment to recognise her.

"Liv!" I said, "I thought you'd be long gone! How are you?"

"I'm OK," she smiled weakly, "been better."

I took a seat next to her, Carole and the others joining us.

"What happened?" I asked, "Are you OK?"

"I'm getting there. It wasn't a... very good labour. Let's put it that way."

"Oh God, are you... is the baby..."

"We're both in one piece – or two pieces – a piece each. We're both here!" she laughed quietly, "But we might not have been..." Her voice broke and eyes brimmed with tears.

"Shit, do you want to talk about it?"

"Maybe, maybe not, I don't know. Not here."

"OK, I don't blame you, just let me know if you want a chat."

"I will, thank you Sarah. I'm in one of the private rooms, I might come and find you later."

"I tell you what, I'll give you my mobile number and you can send me a text, let me know what room you're in, I'll come and find you. What did you have by the way?"

"A boy. Joshua."

"Lovely name," I said, and Carole agreed then took the chance to try and change the subject, for Liv's sake I think.

"Liv, have you met Nurse Nancy?"

Liv frowned and looked puzzled.

"Older midwife. Lady Di haircut, circa 1983. Immensely patronising."

Liv grinned then. It was good to see.

"Ah yes, I think I know who you mean."

"She talks to Jasmine like she's just left the jungle, doesn't she Jas?"

I looked at Jasmine to see whether she minded Carole talking in this way but she was laughing.

"She's not that bad!" she said.

"Like hell she's not. Now eat up girls, while your dinner's still warm-warm."

Soon we were all laughing. It was a good feeling. We'd all been through it in this place, in one way or another and now we were out, safely on the other side.

Chapter Thirty Nine

As promised, Liv sent me a text a little later and I went to find her. "Nice room," I said, admiring her en suite bathroom and view over the fields.

I looked at Joshua in her arms and longed for Abigail. It was very hard leaving her, even for a few minutes, but Carole had said she would keep an eye on her and give me a call if she woke up. I checked my phone was not on silent. I couldn't bear the thought of my little girl needing me and my not being there.

"He's gorgeous," I said to Liv, as she proceeded to unlatch her nursing top and move him towards her. His tiny fists were clenched tight.

"That's meant to be a sign of hunger," she said. "Nurse Nancy told me that. She's right as well – the more he feeds, the less tightly curled they become. He normally falls asleep feeding and by that time they're just relaxed."

"So what happened?" I asked, "If you don't mind me asking. You don't have to talk about it."

Her face fell, and I could see she was trying not to cry.

"It was awful," she said with some effort, "I don't know what happened really. The whole thing just took ages. The contractions grew further apart, till it felt like nothing was happening. I was getting some pains but they didn't get worse and they didn't get closer together. If anything, the opposite. So they upped the dosage on the drip thingy and still it took ages then all of a sudden, after about twelve hours, it began. And I couldn't bear it. I had to have an epidural and then the worst thing happened."

I waited quietly, not wanting to push her, holding back my own tears.

"The midwife got the doctor in and told me I was losing a lot of blood. Then the room was full of people and I knew it was bad. They got Joshua out, with forceps, I think they had to cut me quite badly, and then they gave me some drugs, I was sick, and I – I don't know. I definitely passed out for a while. Poor Simon, he couldn't do anything, but I think they gave him Josh to hold. I had a blood transfusion and got put in a high dependency room, they moved me here the next day. Shit, I can't believe it. I can't believe it happened like it did."

I looked at Josh's tiny head, covered in the softest dark hair, then up to Liv's pale face, her eyes ringed darkly. I didn't know what to say. Clichés and useless platitudes sprang to mind, unbidden, but I knew all about clichés and platitudes. *Well, you're both here now. You've got to get on with life. What doesn't kill us makes us stronger.* They would not do.

Feeling quite emotional myself after my really quite straightforward birth, I could only begin to imagine how Liv felt. I just sat with her quietly until she felt like talking again.

"My parents came in and they were shattered by it. I could see it on their faces. I didn't want it to be like that. It was meant to be a happy occasion. Their first grandchild."

"I bet it was a shock for them."

"Oh my God, it was. I know I nearly died, and Josh too. I didn't really want them to know that, because we didn't, did we? And I have this beautiful little boy."

Liv was suddenly crying convulsively and I took her now sleeping boy from her, and laid him in his little crib. I sat on the bed next to Liv and let her cry onto my shoulder for as long as she needed to. It was probably easier for her to do that with me than with Simon or her parents. I don't suppose she worried about hurting me, or worrying me, like she would them.

Eventually her tears subsided and she apologised.

"Don't be daft!" I said, "You've got nothing to be sorry for. I just wish you'd had a better time of it. Will they – would you go for counselling or something?"

"They said there's some kind of 'talkback' thing here, where I can come back after six weeks and talk through what happened. God, it was terrifying. They were writing it all up on a whiteboard as there wasn't time for them to be making all those notes in the green book. And there was a paediatrician in a flowery shirt. And an anaesthetist. And some consultant. And about eight other people, I have no idea who they were. My legs were up in stirrups and I just lost all sense of myself. Certainly lost any sense of dignity!"

"Well I think that at least can be said for all of us!" I smiled and my phone began to ring. "Oh it's Carole, I think that probably means Abigail's awake. I'll have to go. Do you want to come down with me?"

"No, I think I'll just stay here for a bit – thanks though, Sarah. And thanks for coming to see me. I just feel exhausted by it all and I don't really feel very sociable. It's been good to see you, though. Sorry for the tears."

"No more apologies please, I'll see you at tea time."

I walked at a pace back to my room. I didn't want Abigail waiting any longer than she had to. When I got back, there she was, red-faced and crying. I picked her straight up and soothed her. For a moment it worked but then she began crying again.

Carole laughed, "I think that might be the end of the Long Sleep!"

I looked over and Jasmine's bed was empty, her bags gone.

"Has Jasmine gone home?"

"Yeah, she got discharged about ten minutes ago. She said to say bye."

"I wonder who we'll have next," I said and settled down to feed Abigail.

My phone began to ring again and I glanced over to see that James was trying to get hold of me. I let it ring. For one thing, feeding a baby and holding a phone at the same time seemed a physical impossibility.

Instead I sat and thought of Liv and how different her experience had been to mine – and how scary. I wondered about Simon and how he had felt. He'd watched his wife and child nearly die, then sat holding his newborn son while they pumped a stranger's blood into his wife's arm.

From the good-natured excitement and nervousness he'd displayed on that other ward, to who knew what. I hoped that Liv and Josh could go home to him soon and they could start to get used to the new normality of life as a family.

Chapter Forty

In the afternoon there was a flurry of visitors and finally, with just over an hour of visiting time to spare, James was with us. It was not how I'd pictured the moment. For one thing, I was mid-feed, so it was all a bit awkward.

"Hi beautiful," he said as he made his appearance through the blue curtains. It was a bit daft but I'd drawn them to feed Abigail because Mike was visiting Carole, along with their eldest daughter, and Amy's mum and Rob were visiting her - together. I felt quite self-conscious breastfeeding in front of them and, to be honest, I also wanted a bit of space.

They were lovely, all of them, making sure they included me in some of their conversations and asking if they could get me anything. They were all so happy, though, and so... together. Even Amy's mum and Rob, who were meant to hate each other, seemed to have become united. I sensed that they felt sorry for me, with no visitors. Of course that was probably more me than them but either way, I just wanted a bit of solitude, and a chance to think.

Simon, Liv's husband, had come in to see me on his way to see Liv and Josh.

"I just wanted to say thanks, Sarah. Liv told me you went and sat with her for a while and it really made her feel better. She needs to be in that room to rest but to be honest I think she's feeling isolated too. You made her feel normal, she said."

"It was a pleasure," I smiled, "I'm just sorry you all had such a rough time of it."

For a moment I thought he was going to cry, and I immediately regretted mentioning anything about the birth. However, he straightened himself up and swallowed.

"It was awful," he said, "but I'm so glad I was there for it. I know that sounds strange but imagine if I hadn't been. My dad said men didn't really go in for that kind of thing in his day. They just stayed at home, or paced up and down, waiting to be told their baby was there, all wrapped up clean and cosy in a blanket. I can't bear to think of Liv going through what she did on her own though, even though I know I was no use."

"I don't imagine anybody could be of any actual practical use, Simon," I said, "but just knowing you were there must have really helped. You must be shattered too, you need to look after yourself before your wife and child come home!"

"Don't worry, my dad's been round with a load of meals for the freezer. He's a great cook, and Mum keeps on telling me to get some rest. I wish I wasn't using up my paternity leave while they're in hospital, though. I want to spend it all with them."

"Then you'd better get to them!" I said. "Thanks for coming to see me, though."

"I'm thanking you, remember!" he laughed, and looked around, "Where's your bloke, by the way?"

"Oh, he'll be here soon."

I couldn't get enough of watching Abigail feed. It was an incredible thing, and such a privilege. It did tend to make me feel a bit sleepy though and I was sitting, holding her and gazing at her, through no doubt glazed eyes, when James made his appearance.

"How are you both?" he said, and his eyes fell on Abigail. He stopped, his hand poised with a bunch of flowers. I don't think he had been really prepared for that moment. Somehow I am not sure that he had ever really realised just what fatherhood meant or probably even imagined how he might feel when he encountered his baby daughter for the first time.

I just looked at him, and the expression on his face made my hostility drop away.

"She's beautiful, isn't she?" I said. "I mean, I don't suppose you can see much of her. Just the back of her head. Come here, sit next to me and watch her feed. She might fall asleep but you can hold her when she's finished feeding."

I spoke gently, and not just for Abigail's sake but for James'. I felt sorry for him all of a sudden; he had missed his daughter's birth, he'd never get those precious first moments with her, and now here he was looking vulnerable and even self-conscious. I got the impression he felt he might be intruding and I didn't want that. She was his little girl too and he had to know that.

He came round to the side of the bed, kissed me on my mouth and Abigail, ever so gently, on the top of her head. She didn't even notice, her eyes were already half closed.

"How was work?" I asked quietly and he responded equally softly.

"It's OK," he said, "but it pales into insignificance now. Paternity leave starts tomorrow. I mean, I will have to keep an eye on emails and everything...."

"Of course."

"... but I'm going to take care of you, both of you. I'm sorry I wasn't there for you last night, Sarah. This morning. When Abigail was born. I should have been."

I let the silence stand. I couldn't deny it, but I wasn't interested in making him feel bad. What would that achieve?

"It was... an experience. And it was lovely of Hazel to be there."

"It should have been me."

"James," I said gently, "There's no point saying that. I can't disagree with you, but there's no changing what happened, is there? You need to be thinking of now, not then, and this little girl will need you to be strong and positive. I've spent the last few years of my life looking to the past and wishing things had been different. I don't want to do that anymore. Mum should have been here to see her granddaughter but she isn't and wishing that she was will only make things sad when this is a happy occasion."

I wasn't sure where this speech was coming from but apparently there was more. "So let's just take things as they are, right now, shall we? Make the best of it and make this girl happy as much as we are able to."

"OK," James agreed, looking relieved. "You are amazing, Sarah, do you know that?"

"I'm not, I'm really not."

As I'd thought she might, Abigail did fall asleep whilst feeding. I knew I was meant to try and get her to feed from the other side too but I really wanted James to have his first contact with her. Very carefully, I slid her away from me, and for a moment her little mouth sucked the air, trying to get back to the source of comfort and nourishment, but as I handed her to James, she gave a little sigh and he looked at me, his eyes shining with tears.

I said nothing, just let him hold her and look at her, and I couldn't help but cry myself as I looked at them both.

"I can't wait for you both to be home with me," he said, looking at me.

I said nothing, just nodded, and cried a bit harder. I knew that we wouldn't be coming home to him.

EPILOGUE

I am sitting on the grass with Abigail, who is doing her best to crawl and getting frustrated when she finds herself moving backwards once again. I pull her onto my lap and she reaches a pudgy hand up to grab at my hair, then pulls it hard.

"Hey!" I say, gently removing her fat fist and kissing it then holding her to me, feeling her skin's warmth through the thin cotton of my top.

"Stop pulling Mummy's hair!" says Grandma, emerging from behind the cherry blossom tree.

Abigail exclaims delightedly at the sight of her great-grandma, and wobbles excitedly on my lap. I sit her down on the grass again and she immediately grabs a handful of the pink blossom, which the tree has sprinkled over the garden, moving it up to her mouth.

"Hey!" I say again and she laughs at me, refusing to let go of the pink petals, now squashed and sweaty in her grasp.

The black cat which has taken to meowing outside our back door appears, curving itself around the base of the tree. Abigail cries out with joy and moves as if to crawl towards it but lands with her chubby cheeks on the grass. I wait a moment. She laughs. The cat lies in the sunshine, rolling luxuriously on its back and squinting its green eyes against the bright light.

Grandma places a tray on a nearby table and pulls a chair over to us. I get up and move the table, taking Abigail's pot of fruit purée and plastic spoon. I know it's going to get messy, feeding her out here, unconstrained by a high chair, but I can't bring myself to take her in and miss this glorious sunshine.

Grandma sits and turns her face up to the sun.

"Who'd have thought it? Sunbathing in April!"

"I know," I laugh as Abigail opens her mouth for another spoonful, "I don't think they'll be doing this in Yorkshire!"

"No, I don't suppose they will."

"Are you missing it?" I ask her.

"What? No, not me," she says, "I mean, I miss my friends, but I already love it here. I really do. And being with you two... well, how could I possibly miss anything when I've got all this?"

She sweeps her arm in a gesture encompassing not only Abigail and I but the garden, the neighbouring houses and the vast blue sky suspended above the unseen sea. We don't have a sea view, but we can hear it here from our garden, and our flat, and all we have to do is walk down our street a little way, turn the corner, and there it is. Sometimes grey and surly, sometimes almost black with anger, and often – like today – a breathtaking, awe-inspiring turquoise which makes me want to drop everything I am doing and run down through the town, onto the beach, and headlong into the waves.

In the mornings sometimes Grandma will watch Abi for me so I can go for a swim. The beaches are usually quiet and I may only go in for a few minutes at most if I'm feeling particularly cold but I cannot think of a better way to start the day.

"Hazel was on good form today wasn't she?" Grandma says.

"She was," I say, thinking of my almost-mother-in-law's visit.

Grandma, Abigail and I have lived down here for three months now and already Hazel has been here twice. I don't mind though, I don't mind at all. I feel that my splitting from James has given her a new-found respect for me and I can't possibly ignore the way she feels about Abigail. She has revealed a softer side than I could have ever imagined and Abigail loves her to bits.

Since Gordon left his wife for her, Hazel has softened anyway. He didn't come down this time but I heard her on the phone to him.

"I know.... I miss you too..." she went quiet, listening, then giggled, "Oh Gordon, don't... you shouldn't... Alright, well I love you too, babe." I nearly spat out my coffee. 'Babe'? I never would have imagined her talking like that.

James has been down only once so far, and wouldn't stay in our spare room, even though I told him he was very welcome to.

"No, no, that might be a bit... weird."

That made me feel sad. I don't want it to be weird. I do feel bad about taking Abigail so far away from him but in the first six months of her life he was barely around, so often away on work-related trips and regularly cancelling times we'd agreed to spend together.

I knew he loved her, I didn't doubt that for a minute, but somehow she was not a priority for him the way that work was. I wondered if it would have been different had we lived with him, together as a family, but – although I'll never know for sure – I doubt it.

When Grandma suggested the move down here, I initially thought I couldn't do it, that it wouldn't be fair on James. Abigail and I had moved in to Grandma's house when we'd left hospital. There had been a heartbreaking scene when I told James what I was doing. However, going back to the cottage would only have made things harder.

Since then, Grandma and I had been to visit Dad and Dawn every few weeks. One day, Grandma had just said that she thought it was time for a change. She didn't want to travel so much, and she wanted her family close together. I couldn't believe what I was hearing and I held Abigail close to me, our two hearts beating rapidly next to each other. Could I really do it, though? Would it be fair on James – and Hazel?

Grandma pointed out gently that I needed to think of myself and Abigail, that James seemed to think more of his career than his daughter.

It was a hard thing to hear but I knew Grandma was right. Nevertheless, I do feel bad, and I wonder if he is more bothered than he appears to be. Whether it's a pride thing because I left him. Or maybe because he has never lived with his daughter, they haven't properly bonded.

Still, I spoke to him about this move, many times, trying to gauge his thoughts and opinions, but he just told me to do what I wanted to do.

"You will anyway."

I took that. Even though I felt it vastly unfair, especially given that the years leading up to that point had been very much based on what he – and Hazel – wanted.

"Well I'm not going to take her away from you if you don't want me to, James…"

"Of course I don't want you to."

"But, that being the case, I am going to pass up on an opportunity here to do something I really want to, which I think will be great for Abigail as well as me. I will do that though, if you can promise me you're going to take more of an active role in Abigail's life."

"Active role?!" he practically spat the words at me. "How the hell am I supposed to do that? I'm working 60-hour weeks, travelling up and down the country. I've got to do it, Sarah, I've got to keep at the top of my game."

"OK," I said slowly, feeling vindicated in my actions by his words, "I can see that. You love your work. You want to be the best at it. And I know you're brilliant at it. But we can't just sit about up here waiting for you to pay a visit when you have a spare moment. If you could promise me you would see her at least once a week – and I mean do something with her, not just pop in on your way home – then I would stay. But if it's going to continue like this, I think I've got to take this opportunity. I've got to go to Cornwall."

"So you can all play happy families down there. Fine. But what about Mum? What do you think this will do to her?"

Truth be told, I felt worse about Hazel than I did about James. I was sure it would break her heart to think about her only grandchild so far away. I made James promise not to tell her and resolved to go round that evening. I wouldn't take Abigail, I didn't want her involved in the upset. I asked James if he would look after her but he said he was working (surprise!) so Grandma looked after Abigail for me.

Gordon had answered the door to my slightly nervous knock.

"Hello love!" he said, greeting me with a kiss, "No baby?"

"Not tonight Gordon," I smiled, "she's snoring soundly away in her cot."

"I'll just let Hazel know you're here."

"Thank you," I smiled.

He was a nice man. A bit younger than Hazel but well able to stand up to her and also to talk her out of her stubbornness. I didn't want him there when I told her what I'd come to say, though. Luckily he was in the middle of cooking dinner. He disappeared, wine glass in hand.

"Are you OK, Sarah?" Hazel asked, forthright as ever. "You look nervous."

"I," I cleared my throat. "I am a bit, sorry Hazel. I – oh I'm just going to tell you. I'm thinking of moving to Cornwall."

Hazel's wine glass paused halfway up to her lips.

"To..?"

"Cornwall," I confirmed. I began to babble, "I really wanted to tell you straight away. I… well it's a great opportunity for me. I've found a job at a school. Part-time learning support assistant so I can see if I like it. And Grandma wants to go, and what with Dad and Dawn being in Falmouth…"

"It's OK, it's OK Sarah," Hazel said, almost softly, "You don't have to justify it. You want to be near your family. I can understand that. And you love it down there. And James… well, I'm so sorry to say that James isn't being much of a support to you and Abigail. I can't tell you how disappointed I am."

"It's his work…" I began to make an excuse for him.

"Yes, it is his work," she said despondently, "And it's my fault, isn't it? I made him like he is. I wanted him to do well. Now he's bloody obsessed, like I was."

"Well…" I say, but I don't quite know where to go after that.

"Exactly," she laughed, "Well. There's not much more to say than that, is there? He has apparently got his priorities all wrong and the only person I can think of to blame for it is me. I've been in his position and yours, Sarah, and believe you me, if I had a chance to do it again, I wouldn't have put work above my family. I know I provided the boys with everything materially but I wasn't there for them. Not properly. Why do you think I hardly see the other three? It's only because James has moved back in that I see anything much of him."

I move over and sit next to her. I've never seen her like this.

"Hazel, I can't tell you how bad I feel about moving Abigail away from you. I know how much you love her – and how much she loves you. You've been great and a real support for me since she came along. You are welcome to come and visit whenever you like. I mean it. And I will bring her back up here to see you, too."

"You're a good girl, Sarah. I'll miss you too, you know."

Then Hazel hugged me. A full-on, genuine hug which almost

made me jump, it was so unexpected and out of the ordinary, but ended up with us both in tears.

So here we are. Grandma, Abigail and me. Dad, Dawn and Toby are just 30 minutes' drive away. Dad has taken a place at Falmouth College of Arts and Dawn sometimes works there or at a secondary school and sixth form college. I look after Toby – who is my half-brother and my daughter's half-uncle even though he is six months younger than her (I try not to think about all that too much) – for a couple of hours each week, to give Dawn a bit of a break, and Dawn comes with Toby to look after Abi twice a week while I am at school. Grandma fills in the odd hour of childcare here and there but I don't expect her to do too much. Babies are a handful and besides, she is busy making a life for herself here. She's joined a group of elderly artists and goes to loads of social events. She has really thrown herself into this move and making life down here work.

In another week or so, Liv, Simon and Joshua are coming to visit, and I can't wait to see them. Liv and I kept in touch after we'd left the hospital and used to get together every week before I moved; usually more than once. It was nice having somebody to get used to motherhood with. Because it was a shock, that was for sure. Rashes, temperatures, teething, weaning, sleepless nights, projectile vomiting. It was good to have somebody else learning alongside me. We quickly formed a strong bond and it's possible I miss her more than anybody else from my 'old life', as I now think of it.

So is this a happy ending? All those loose ends tied up? It looks very much like it but I know, maybe more than anyone, that there is really no such thing as a happy ending. Once upon a time, Dad asked Mum to marry him and they thought they had their happy ending sorted. The problem is that life still goes on. Disasters occur, tragedies reveal themselves, such that you could never have imagined. Good things happen too, I know that, but I don't take anything for granted.

So I don't think in terms of happy endings. For all that I have learned about looking at, not past, things - recognising warning signs, and acting upon them - I understand that it is impossible to know the future, so I try to think only of now. And now, I am happy. That's enough for me.

Acknowledgements

I have loved writing this book, and become very fond of (most of) the characters. Hazel ended up far more sympathetic than I'd originally intended!

Thanks are owed to my friends and 'beta readers': Beverley Knowles-Howard, Jane Gill, Nancy Perks and Catherine Clarke. Feedback, encouragement and typo-spotting all very much appreciated!

I also owe a huge amount of thanks to Catherine for her beautiful cover work, once again. Who knew there was so much talent in a little Shropshire town?

To my Dad, thank you for putting in the hours to meet my deadline, even though the original email never turned up. And Mum, just thank you. I know how lucky I am to have you both.

For my own in-laws, Kaye and Barry - just in case you're wondering, Hazel is NOT a reflection on you!

And for my brilliant family: Chris, Laura and Edward, thank you for letting me get on with all of this, and inspiring me to write about the things I do.

If you have enjoyed this book, we would be very grateful if you would take the time to review it on the Amazon website. A positive review is invaluable and will be greatly appreciated by the author.

Please also visit the Heddon Publishing website to find out about our other titles: www.heddonpublishing.com

Heddon Publishing was established in 2012 and is a publishing house with a difference. We work with independent authors to get their work out into the real world, by-passing the traditional slog through 'slush piles'.

Please contact us by email in the first instance to find out more:

enquiries@heddonpublishing.com

Like us on Facebook and receive all our news at:

www.facebook.com/heddonpublishing

Join our mailing list by emailing:

mailinglist@heddonpublishing.com

Follow us on Twitter: @PublishHeddon

Printed in Great Britain
by Amazon